Danos:
Surviving the Orphanage

Danos:
Surviving the Orphanage

a novel

Inspired by A.D. Knight's Twenty-Two-Page Memoir, dated March 21, 1929

John J. Uskert

Danos: Surviving the Orphanage

Inspired by A.D. Knight's Twenty-Two-Page Memoir, dated March 21, 1929

Printed in the United States of America.

Cover art by Toni Noël Brown (toninoelb@gmail.com)
Cover design by Toni Noël Brown (toninoelb@gmail.com)
Formatting services by Word-2-Kindle.com

This novel is based upon the twenty-two-page memoir of Andrew Danos Knight set forth in *italics* at the end of most chapters. The narrative of this novel is a creation of fiction by the author. Any names used or resemblance of names of characters are fictious, coincidental or, in some cases, actual names.

ISBN: 979-8-218-04618-7

Imprint: Independently published.

Dedicated to

Mom and Dad

Contents

About the Author........ ix
Author's Note........ xi

Chapter 1........1
Chapter 2........6
Chapter 3........14
Chapter 4........26
Chapter 5........31
Chapter 6........37
Chapter 7........46
Chapter 8........50
Chapter 9........58
Chapter 10........68
Chapter 11........74
Chapter 12........80
Chapter 13........93
Chapter 14........98
Chapter 15........103
Chapter 16........110
Chapter 17........119
Chapter 18........130
Chapter 19........139
Chapter 20........146
Chapter 21........159
Chapter 22........173
Chapter 23........183
Chapter 24........193

Chapter 25 206
Chapter 26 222
Chapter 27 227
Chapter 28 235
Chapter 29 238
Chapter 30 242
Chapter 31 250
Chapter 32 252

Appendix – A: Book Club Proposed Discussion Questions 261

About the Author

John J. Uskert is a USAF veteran having served 1968-1972 with overseas assignments in Okinawa and the Republic of South Korea. Uskert earned his B.S. in Pharmacy in 1976 and his J.D. in 1990, both from Samford University (and Cumberland School of Law) in Birmingham, Alabama. He practiced retail pharmacy (FL, AL, IN) until his retirement in December 2014. Simultaneously he engaged in the private practice of law (FL and IN) from 1990 until his retirement in June 2018. Uskert was a contract writer for James Publishing (legal publishers) writing family law newsletter articles from 2019 until 2021. Uskert makes his home, with his wife Peggy, in the Indianapolis area.

Author's Note

My former next-door neighbor is the experienced and talented entrepreneur, Steve Lambert. For several years, we lived in a small, sociable subdivision situated in a popular northwest Florida beach community. Our relationship grew based on the eternal, as two Christian brothers having much in common. Over time, this relationship deepened fraternally and developed into an informal partnership resulting in this book idea, and now this novel.

The subject character, a Spanish boy, born in Cuba as Jauan Fernandez, also casually known as Jim Roberts for roughly ten years, changed his legal name to Andrew Danos Knight. Steve Lambert is the maternal grandson of the principal character in this novel, A.D. Knight.

In the month of June, 2021, while Steve and I were in the backyard enjoying the brilliance and warmth of the Florida sun and a lazy tropical afternoon breeze, we found ourselves engaged in a new topic of conversation. As we savored the relaxation and our choice of premium cigars, a heavy maduro for Steve, and for me, a mild, brown wrapped Honduran, Steve shared the original twenty-two-page memorandum hand-written by his grandfather, A.D. Knight, dated March 21, 1929. The memorandum was faded, largely due to the mild acidity of the paper on which it was written ninety-two years ago, much of which was illegible with only scattered, disjointed sections which could be deciphered. Steve explained it was a journal concerning a portion of Danos' life beginning in 1894 when he was three or four years old, soon to be orphaned.

Steve hired a forensic document restorer to enhance the writing to legibility. After I read the twenty-two-page enhanced version, Steve inquired if I would consider writing a novel about his grandfather based on the restored document. As a retired attorney, I had much experience drafting legal documents and pleadings, writing briefs, legal memoranda, persuasive appellate briefs and scores, hundreds or thousands of legal communications and correspondence over nearly thirty years of law practice, as well as trial preparation, court hearings and litigation experience. This would be a venture into a less than familiar writing style. I had never before written a novel. Having read the twenty-two pages numerous times thereafter, I agreed to write this book.

The *italicized text* at or near the end of most chapters is the actual text of A.D. Knight's memorandum transcribed from the professionally enhanced original document. The body of this historic novel, much of which is fiction and poetic license, closely follows Knight's twenty-two-pages and draws logical inferences and reasonable conclusions, contains rational suppositions and historic facts. This novel, **Danos: Surviving the Orphanage**, is based on the personal account of A.D. Knight, written as historical fiction, but it is Danos' story.

Reading this novel, hopefully, will be informative and stimulating, evoking emotion. Above all, reading this novel is intended to be pleasurable entertainment. It is offered as historical fiction in a simplistic style, easy to read for your enjoyment. If the reader is entertained and enjoys this venture in reading Danos' journey of words, the author has succeeded. So, light up your favorite cigar, pour a cup of coffee, or your favorite beverage, and begin Chapter 1. Please enjoy. Happy reading.

Steve Lambert's mother, Violet Lambert, is the daughter of Andrew Danos Knight. Violet passed away in 2009 in Kentucky at the age of 91. A.D. Knight, born in 1891 in Cuba, died in Kentucky in 1953. Steve Lambert had a close relationship with his mother and recalls stories about his grandfather in Cuba and life in the southern United States. His knowledge and infatuation with A.D. Knight's life and genealogy gave rise to his interest in Cuba. With anticipation, Steve visited Havana in 2008 to personally experience the Cuban culture and cuisine. Steve is a principal in the business known as Danos Cigar Lounge, LLC in Owensboro, Kentucky. Danos Cigar Lounge, LLC was established in 2021 and is owned and operated by Steve's daughter, Stevi, the great granddaughter of Andrew Danos Knight.

Thank you for purchasing our novel.

John J. Uskert

You may contact the author through his website:
johnuskert.com
johnuskert.org

Chapter 1

As it began, Jauan Fernandez heard the shrieks and cries in the recesses of his mind. The Spanish soldiers, wounded and dying on the plantation battleground, were defeated. Spanish garrisons writhed in pain and agony pleading for help and mercy as their spilled blood seeped into the foreign Cuban soil. They cried out to God in anguish as their lives were ending in torment. With machetes, sickles and clubs, the Cuban revolutionaries maimed and killed the Spanish defenders. As he ran for safety toward the owners' mansion, a fallen garrison grabbed Jauan by his right foot restraining him, imploring his assistance. Jauan could not break free of the soldier's grip. The garrison, with bloody face, neck and torso, was unable to move. Near death, the wounded soldier pleaded that this seven-year-old boy plunge the bayonet directly into his heart, mercifully ending his life. Jauan heard rifle shots, cannon fire and explosives detonated as the Fernandez sugar cane plantation was overrun by native Cuban revolutionaries. He visualized his parents, dead, in the flower garden near the mansion as they left him orphaned. Multiple incidents of trauma and horror experienced in the distant past flashed in explosive view as night terrors. As if still a child and young adult, A.D. Knight was fraught with terror as he recalled scenes of his past. Starving, searching for edible scraps in the garbage heaps. Homeless, but also relegated to an orphanage. Abandoned, inexplicable disappearances and deaths of family members. Terrified, living in fear on his own as an orphan. Panic-stricken, facing death as a stowaway. Demoralized, in throes of numerous destructive relationships. Incarcerated, through no fault of his own. Standing, appearing before a caring judge meting out justice.

He was faced with the task of recording this, his personal history.

He awakened before daybreak, drenched with sweat, bed sheets wringing with perspiration, drained from a night of sporadic, restless sleep with sights and sounds randomly passing into view in a twilight dimension. Were these scenes imagined or prompted by reality of his past? He dreaded the dawning of this day and the event he had scheduled for this afternoon.

His task today will devolve into a chronicle of darkness.

* * *

He designed his manicured backyard retreat creating an environment of diversion, tempering the anxiety of everyday events and problems, past and present. Whites, reds, pinks and yellows exploded in visual sensuality this spring day. His mature azaleas, daffodils, gladiolas and peonies burst in full bloom unusually early this year in San Antonio. As the sun reached its apex, it intensified the botanic contrast with his thick Bermuda lawn, enhancing the array of colors. A choice, aromatic cigar, the Partagas brand with woody tones of leather and cocoa, complimented on occasion with a glass of blackberry brandy, enriched the splendor of his horticultural achievements. Seated with feet and legs propped on a white wicker foot stool, relaxation and reduced stress were his objectives as he frequently enjoyed Mozart's *Eine Kleine Nachtmusik* played atop the Victrola on his outdoor veranda.

However, today was quite the exception to this routine. As he pondered his planned event scheduled for later today, there would likely be no time available or taken for retreat to the sanctuary of this botanical splendor. A formidable, dreadful task was at hand. Commencing such project would be most onerous. He had considered the undertaking repeatedly, only to delay the inevitable. He was not a procrastinator, but he had postponed this mission for over five years for good reason. This daunting task would reinforce the dread, the anguish he preferred to avoid. With unease, his gut wrenched at the mere thought of the promise made to his wife in years gone by. This venture into the past will be detrimental, he feared, yet he is compelled by the magnitude and significance of the undertaking. Facing anticipated adversity, he must take a cautious approach in this endeavor. Now a married man, he prioritized the routine of work, family and obligations. Fragments of incidents of the past escaped his lips on occasion, providing only passing injustice to the actual ordeal and horrendous events which transpired years prior. The erratic recounting of these occurrences caused him great anguish, but his wife found his experiences extraordinary. To put his tragedy in written form may be useful to him, in some sense, but also beneficial to those having the opportunity to read his recorded personal account. There may be a lesson to be learned, but at inordinate detriment to the author.

The lower level of his home was a favorite place during the stifling months in southern Texas. Consistent coolness of his cellar provided a respite from the unrelenting heat and humidity of the Texas spring and summer. As he maintained his balance gripping the left handrail, he treaded up the wooden staircase one step at a time. He carried an ominous black leather satchel, worn and battered, with his dominant hand. The satchel endured for the last three decades. The contents of this black case were not foreign to him, for it was he who assembled the memorabilia. He will expose the relics of his unforgettable past and bring them into reality on this eventful day. Preserved by several wrappings of waxed paper, each of the artifacts was effectively sealed to prohibit moisture from damaging the contents. The eventual unwrapping would not only be anticipated but would reveal tangible explanations concerning the person of Andrew Danos Knight.

* * *

He had chosen an upstairs room designated the library, even though the library contained a mere total of eight books, which included one King James Version of the Holy Bible. The wall shelving was virtually empty yet prepared to accommodate A.D. and Martha's eventual personal collection. This room was austere and formal, but comfortable, furnished with two brown leather, high-back chairs and a writing desk. The Bible, bound in a black soft-leather binding with "Holy Bible" inlaid of gold leaf script, positioned open on its reading stand, a prominent place, was easily accessible and read by A.D. and Martha Knight. The truth be told, it was Martha's regular use of the Bible which caused the pages to be worn and the binding to be well patterned. While A.D. was not entirely irreligious, his past found cause to believe, if there is a God, that God had little concern for this man He had created. A.D.'s past was not complimentary of a Supreme Being, as he was so convinced. While Martha encouraged A.D. to read and absorb Holy Scripture regarding eternity, A.D. was unable to assume the requisite religious candor to develop such habit. Perhaps one day he may recognize such a need.

The library was naturally illuminated while the sun tilted just beyond direct overhead until it sank beyond the San Antonio River. The brightness of the room maintained a conducive environment to temper the unpleasant thoughts of past events. His proper frame of mind was mandatory. A library desk of heavy oak wood, well used over the years, was paired to an oak chair with a padded black leather seat riveted to the wooden bottom. Comfort, he thought, was necessary. The time was upon him. With a sense of dread, A.D.'s throat became parched. He leaned his weight against an available corner wall. He sipped from a glass of cool water taking a shallow swallow, licking his lips with a thick tongue. A.D. looked across the room at the desk, chair, black satchel and the blank tablet. Will he have the patience and fortitude to anchor himself to the desk, grasp his monogramed black ink pen and complete this undertaking? His mind was staggered and jumbled with violent, unspeakable memories. Mental impressions which caused him torment over decades came to the forefront in full exposure of the task he was to undertake. A.D. Knight's story must be told.

A.D.'s knees weakened. He didn't know if his legs could continue to support his body weight as he stood at the corner of the library and reflected. Whether he would make it across the wooden floor was uncertain. He could collapse in an instant as he faced the reality of putting pen to paper. Summoning the courage of a battle-tested soldier, A.D. put one foot ahead of the next and came to stop at the place where past and present would converge. Reality is now as he embarks on this journey of words. He was sweating to the point of discomfort. His eyes were peeled, his face donned an inquisitive expression not knowing if he could see this project through. A.D.'s long sleeve white shirt, once cleaned and pressed on the early morning of this momentous day, is now wrinkled, worn and soaked with perspiration. His desk abuts the window overlooking the garden. This view may provide some solace throughout his difficult project. He pulls the chair out from the desk and makes his way to the seat. The experience of sitting at this desk to commence a writing of significance is the promise A.D. made to his wife. He will record the events on these blank sheets to the best of his recollection. He will not reveal the writing to anyone, including his wife, until his task has been completed. His past experiences, together with inner thoughts, feelings and fears are quite private. The completed work will eventually be shared. He commenced his chronicle as dark memories from the past came into focus. He concentrated his effort. With pen in hand, he commenced his journal.

Chapter 2

Don and Carlita Fernandez, seasoned cruise passengers, sailed from Old Spain on a steamer ship launched from the Port of Barcelona in early 1888. Their three-week, one-way voyage set sail for Havana Harbor for a one-night stop and continued on to their destination, the Port of Matanzas, Cuba, fifty miles to the east. As an agent and agricultural manager of the Spanish government, Don Fernandez accepted the challenge and position as operations manager over the Spanish-controlled 1,400-acre sugar cane and tobacco plantation near Matanzas. Don Pedro received formal education at *Universidad de Barcelona* where he studied agriculture science and mechanics. Upon graduation, *magna cum laude,* he concentrated in foreign, large operation agriculture, focusing on the sugar cane industry in the Caribbean. A bright and promising executive, experienced in Spanish agriculture, he was particularly suited for managing sugar and tobacco plantations throughout the island of Cuba. Pay for experienced management was handsome. Tropical life in the Caribbean was rich and unsurpassed in comfort.

Philosophically opposed to slavery, his acceptance of the management position was timely. Don Pedro Fernandez understood his responsibility to operate the plantation efficiently, maximizing production of sugar, molasses and tobacco, and profit. The labor component for efficient operation of the plantation had traditionally been established over three centuries by utilizing an unlimited supply of African slaves supplemented by other labor types. While Fernandez grappled with the morality of the slavery concept, in all practicality, he determined slavery was a necessary evil required to maintain profitability in the production of sugar, molasses and tobacco.

Captured by profiteering entrepreneurs and trade dealers, the Black Africans were abducted from their homelands, ripped from their villages, from their children, from parents and families and sold into bondage for physical labor in Cuba and other Caribbean islands. Spanish plantation owners and managers relied on the abundance of this slave labor to produce the large, commercial quantities of sugar, molasses and tobacco demanded for export and domestic use.

Although these African slaves had been declared freed by practical proclamation in 1880, many of the slaves continued incarcerated as indentured servants for an additional eight years and longer, serving as "contract labor." Slavery in Cuba was legally abolished in 1886. However, the indentured servants continued to provide required labor on many of the Spanish-run plantations. The new-found freedom realized by the Black African slaves came at a great price paid over three centuries of tragedy.

Survival of the captives on voyages from Africa to Cuba was uncertain as the slaves, restricted and shackled to immovable bulkheads, were subjected to inhumane atrocities: continual whippings, intentional starvation, lack of nutrition, exposure to the elements, untreatable disease, attempted escape. Slave labor was essential. Field work, harvesting and cutting sugar cane and tobacco leaves, and working in the mechanized mills producing sugar and molasses, were subhuman, grueling: slaves labored eighteen and more hours per day. Once healthy and strong, the Africans found themselves captured, confined and weakened in bondage, unable to escape. They perished routinely from exhaustion, dehydration, exposure and overwork. Unannounced, half-starved and dehydrated, slaves routinely keeled over, falling at the spot where they toiled, giving no notice of impending death. The fallen slaves, clothed in rags, scarred from beatings, emaciated by lack of nutrition, were removed to a common grave to avoid the stench of decomposition. The dead were replaced by the regular arrival of "fresh" slaves sold at auction by the experienced, profit-driven slave-traders and entrepreneurs replacing attrition of the weak, infirm and dead. When the Black Africans were freed, much of the necessary manual labor was supplied and augmented by the involuntary influx of white Chinese workers forced into servitude as contract labor, also for eight-year periods and longer. Such contractual arrangement with the white Chinese laborers marked no improvement over the status and conditions suffered by the Africans. Long days engaged as forced labor under insufferable conditions, were accompanied by disease, dehydration and defeat, frequently ending in death. Entry of the machine age enhanced the efficiency of mechanical production of sugar cane into "white gold," crystalline sugar. The Matanzas territory became the epicenter of sugar cane processing, sugar and molasses production in 1894.

Jauan Fernandez was born to Don and Carlita Fernandez near Matanzas, Cuba on May 15, 1891, so he was told. Jauan was a most fortunate child in the Matanzas nobility. He wanted for nothing and was lavished with every material advantage and comfort. Spanish and international supply vessels serviced the Port of Matanzas regularly providing the Fernandez family the newest and most advanced equipment and furnishings. Don Fernandez was accorded every modern convenience enhancing the family's opulent lifestyle. Life for management on the Fernandez plantation was abundant and rich having every benefit of an elite class. The two Fernandez siblings, Jauan, and Maria, two years his junior, were comfortable in their environment, innocence and naivety . Near the Fernandez plantation, a Spanish Catholic mission was built and staffed as part of Pope Alexander VI's edict centuries ago that the Church establish missions throughout Cuba with the purpose of converting the natives to Catholicism. The mission's Catholic priest conferred the Sacrament of Baptism on Jauan Fernandez at the age of two weeks old. Maria, likewise, was baptized at two weeks.

Jauan, dressed in finest quality traditional Spanish sandals, shorts and shirt, strolled in an easterly direction, up the gradual rise toward the owners' mansion from his designated safe area on the plantation grounds. The pale-yellow plaster exterior of the Fernandez mansion reflected the intensity of the mid-afternoon sun. This tropical, light-colored exterior contrasted with the deep brown, solid wood double doors forming the entryway. As Jauan approached the wrap-around porch surrounding the mansion's front, he savored the sweet fragrance of his mother's eight potted, flowering red and orange hibiscus plants, Carlita's favorites. Six small trees in oak planters, in full white bloom, were randomly situated on the expansive porch near the entryway. Outdoor kerosene "Luz Brillante," bright light lanterns served to illuminate the porch and front exterior after dark and served as repellants to annoying flying insects and pests. Several white wooden chairs, padded with round, matching yellow cushions accented by embroidered floral patterns, were positioned on the porch further from the entryway, but distanced to afford accessibility. Male guests often joined Don Fernandez on the open-air porch after dinner to enjoy a quality Cuban smoke and brandy, compliments of the gracious host.

Before he ascended the three steps to porch level, Jauan counted the eight large, framed windows, four on each floor, matching the wooden entryway doors. Jauan recalled storms during which driving rain pelted the eight windows and beat down on the flat roof of wood and tin. Substantial metal sheets, coated with a black tarry, water-repellant substance covered the wood and remained unseen from ground level. Unseen, perhaps, but audibly identified with ferocity when a tropical storm assaulted the mansion.

Jauan grabbed the black iron handles and strained to open the heavy front doors. He walked through the entryway and strode across a rectangular, pictorial throw rug of a bright green and eye-catching yellow feathered Cuban parrot, perched on a lower branch of a scrub oak tree. Gray-green Spanish moss hanging from the tree's branches added natural flavor to the pictorial scene. A lighted cigar was embroidered into the rug's left margin and identified as the sponsored Partagas brand.

To the right of the entryway, an elegant, large, cherry wood table centered in the dining room was prepared for the evening meal. Four polished brass holders supported twelve white, tapered, unlit candles, as though twelve guests were expected for a formal evening. This room was reserved for special occasions with Spanish, Cuban and American dignitaries. An elaborate kitchen and pantry were adjacent to the dining area. Carlita personally selected her maid servants and cooks, talented and trained chefs, who specialized in authentic Spanish and Cuban cuisine. The mansion's maids and male servants were chosen for their unique skills, ability to follow detailed instructions and temperament. Only the best and most capable servants would find assignment in the owners' mansion, serving as indentured cooks, housekeepers and gardeners. The aroma of ground coffee and vanilla beans filled the pantry, along with hints of saffron, paprika and cinnamon. The scent of these spices comforted Jauan, adding to the permanence and stability of childhood.

Jauan's bedroom was located on the second floor directly above the formal dining room. From his window, Jauan observed the expanse of the plantation, focusing his attention to his designated and authorized safe area. The remainder of the second floor was designed as sleeping quarters. The lower level consisted of communal living areas for the family with significant accommodations dedicated to comfort and entertaining. The owners' mansion had twelve rooms, each with a specified purpose.

Their 1,400 acres, planted in sugar cane and tobacco, featured flat lands and gradual, rolling hills for cultivation and growing crops. Don Fernandez dedicated smaller areas to relaxation and recreation. Equipment, machinery, tobacco leaves, bags of sugar and containers of bulk molasses were routinely shipped on the Fernandez private railway spur into the Port of Matanzas. Shipping product from the plantation directly to the port was efficient and convenient using the spur which terminated at the shipping docks in Port Matanzas.

* * *

Decades earlier, native Cuban descendants, known as the Taino, and the mixed-race Cubans with African, Chinese, Spanish, known as mulattos, grew weary of three centuries of Spanish control. Rebel groups formed and fought for freedom against the well-armed, well-trained Spanish garrisons. Cuba was colonized as a Spanish territory at the expense of the natives and ravaged for the resources discovered throughout the island. Spain, unconcerned about the Taino, mulattos and slaves, cared only about the profit which it could generate from this Caribbean Island discovered centuries ago by one of their own, Christopher Columbus. Great investment was made, and risk undertaken to dominate and colonize such a wealth of real estate. Much had been reaped, more was expected.

After countless battles and wars between Cuban rebels and the Spanish colonizers in the 1800s, rebellion neared its climax. By 1894, rebellious uprisings became more than sporadic. Cuba's disdain for the Spanish escalated to overt hatred. The rebels were poorly armed but occasionally effective, driven by their determination to be free of Spanish control. In defense of its sugar cane and tobacco operations, Spain assigned General Valeriano Weyler to quell the rebellious uprisings. Weyler, highly decorated as an experienced combatant, soon gained the reputation as a ruthless leader. He was a career officer known as "The Butcher" intent on crushing these rebels in furtherance of Spanish domination. The heavily armed Spanish soldiers defended principal Cuban cities, ports and plantations. Factions were drawn and prepared for ultimate armed conflict. The Spanish ruled as they had for over three hundred years; entrenched to protect their interests for continued colonization and profiteering. The native rebels focused their attacks on the economic empire of the Spanish plantations. By burning sugar cane, tobacco fields and barns, the rebels effectively disrupted the profits and economy of these industries. To counter the destruction, Spain increased its military levels from 80,000 to 300,000 troops in the late 1890s. The Spanish army, with its military might, protected its sugar cane, tobacco fields and production mills from the freedom fighting rebels.

Spanish garrisons, dressed in full military-battle uniforms, equipped and trained for war, functioned as seasoned security patrolling perimeters of the Spanish plantations, keeping the Cuban rebels at bay outside and the management and contract laborers safely protected inside. The Cuban rebels sought to eliminate the Spanish plantation managers and overseers, along with the Spanish defenders. What better way to halt sugar and tobacco production than by eliminating the management? Demolition causing irreparable destruction to the plantations was the objective of the rebels. The strength of the Spanish garrisons stationed near Matanzas was legendary. Militarily and vastly successful in times past, the plantation owners and managers had little reason to fear these disorganized, sporadic uprisings and attacks by untrained rebels. The Spanish government previously banned possession of firearms by the native Cubans two decades earlier during the Ten Years War (1868-1878). Thus, the rebels were militarily disadvantaged. Virtually unarmed, untrained, unorganized. This grand plantation and the Don Fernandez family were protected and impervious to rebel attack. Fernandez was confident in the ability of the Spanish defenders.

A.D. commenced his journey of words on this twenty-first day of March, 1929 with the historical setting in which he was born and lived for nearly eight years. A foreboding start to his life required some detail, but was penned as sketchy…

A. D. Knight
828 N. Newbrunfels Ave.
San Antonio Texas
3-21-1929

ORPHAN

I am no story writer or much of a conversationalist

But my wife says I have a story that might help someone.

So here goes,

I am an orphan, do not know the love of a mother, brothers, sisters. All I know of my father and mother is what a soldier conceal told me is what a woman is.

Supposedly my sister could tell history during the Spanish American War what little a four-year-old can remember.

So am giving a sketchy outline of my parents and early life.

My father, Don Pedro Fernandez and his wife, Carlita, came from Old Spain and settled on a sugar plantation in Cuba.

Where I, Jauan, was born near Matanzas, just about the time the war began between Cuba, China, Spain and other national wanting possession of Cuba.

Chapter 3

Jauan Fernandez, of insufficient age and intelligence, was unable to comprehend the need for protection provided by the Spanish garrisons. Not quite seven years old, Jauan was unable to understand the risk the Don Pedro Fernandez family had assumed by accepting the position of operations manager of this Cuban plantation. Platoons of veteran Spanish soldiers and mercenaries, spitting, cursing and intimidating their foes, marched on patrol in thunderous pulse assuming strategic positions along the plantation's boundaries as an impregnable defense. Lines of defenders positioned two deep, often three deep, kept vigil and made ready for any attack, no matter how insignificant. Spanish soldiers, equipped with daggers, swords, rifles and bayonets, strapped with multiple cartridge belts, were primed to suppress the smallest disturbance or crush a full attack. The multitude of Spanish soldiers defending the perimeter of the Fernandez plantation would only strike fear in the minds of those rebels considering an offensive attack. Spanish fire power had been confirmed as without equal. Displaying his Spanish allegiance, armed with a shortened willow stick tucked into the left side of his brown leather waist belt and a longer, heavier stripped oak branch perched over his right shoulder, feigning sword and rifle, Jauan marched in subdued cadence alongside the Spanish units as a volunteer in the mercenary and regular forces. Jauan utilized a safe and designated portion of the plantation to conduct his military drills. This authorized area was lush grassland bordering on a portion of woods.

Dense forest demarcated by a shallow stream near the boundary of the plantation permitted Jauan to run free in the grassland. Jauan's abandon and independence were innate and on full display. Freedom to roam the designated area permitted Jauan to develop his own defensive military strategy, learning survival skills, if ever needed. He was an uninvited member of the Spanish patrols prepared to thwart the Cuban rebel attacks, assisting the platoon leader as if regular army. Jauan's familiarity and faith in the defensive abilities of the Spanish defenders concluded these soldiers were invincible. His faith in their defense was, however, misplaced.

* * *

The Cuban War of Independence was declared in February, 1895. Attacks by rebels throughout central and western Cuba, including the Matanzas territory, became more frequent and intense. Earlier infrequent attacks launched by the rebels were considered marginally successful, as covert attacks resulted in effective damage, often under cover of night or inclement weather. Most recently, clandestine political sympathizers provided foreign armament into the hands of the Cuban rebels, causing greater damage to the plantations; the Spanish defenders suffered mightily. General Weyler, proud of several scars he wore as battle ribbons, along with other Spanish leadership, could not ignore, nor accept, these disastrous results. The rebels employed stealth tactics killing Spanish garrisons, murdering plantation managers, demolishing sugar mills, tobacco and sugar cane fields and sacking plantation operations. For the next several years, the United States monitored the military and political climate of Cuba, as many U.S. companies and investors held stakes in Cuban sugar and tobacco.

Unrealistically, as a privileged youth thriving on the Fernandez plantation, Jauan remained naïve, unafraid and unconcerned about possible rebel attacks. He had previously witnessed skirmishes, generally brief in duration, between the Spanish platoons and pockets of rebels from afar. Jauan observed for periods of minutes and longer as Cuban rebels advanced and were beaten back, advanced again and pushed back further. The rebels were resolute in their fight for freedom but largely unsuccessful. From Jauan's perspective, the Fernandez plantation was ably protected by the Spanish contingent; it remained his sanctuary.

Jauan's younger sister, Maria, often joined him on excursions to various locations in the designated area. The siblings raced over the gradual rise which sloped away from the owners' mansion and down to their favorite observation point in the underbrush serving as camouflage within the tree line. From their vantage point, they could see a portion of the mansion's roofline and remained within earshot of their mother. Carlita had faith in the security provided by the garrisons protecting the designated areas. Jauan and Maria were able to monitor the Spanish garrisons marching, positioning and maintaining defense of the boundaries surrounding the perimeter of the plantation. The two children remained concealed and undetected. Assigned in multiples, two columns of Spanish soldiers marched to their positions. Marching steps, in unison, caused the ground to reverberate as each boot was driven into the soil. Dust flew as the columns of defenders marched toward their assignment, relieving the previously positioned platoon. The siblings could also see and hear the Black African and white Chinese laborers harvesting sugar cane in the fields, loading produce onto wagons and hauling loads into the mill for processing. On most days when labor was at full measure, the intent observer could hear the laborers at a distance break into metrical chanting, accompanied by rhythmic melody beaten on simple percussion instruments, encouraging efficiency in labor with minimal effort, as sugar cane plants were chopped and felled by machetes in tempo. The mulattos and white Chinese blended voices with the Black Africans chanting rhythmically, producing harmony in sound and productivity.

As attacks became more frequent, but launched sporadically, the Cuban rebels gained experience with each new offensive, growing more organized and deliberate. The plantation workers, the Spanish nationals, and others uninvolved in the freedom skirmishes raced for cover during attacks. Workers, able to run, ran. The wary hid themselves inside buildings, behind and between machinery and wagons, under tarps and other places offering concealment and protection. The two siblings continued their surveillance and remained undaunted despite the skirmishes. Jauan and Maria were oblivious to the risk of danger.

* * *

By 1898, Cuba was on the brink of military and economic collapse. The *U.S.S. Maine*, categorized in a class of heavy battleship, was anchored in the Port of Havana, fifty miles west of Matanzas. The massive armored vessel cruised to its assigned position and anchored on January 25, 1898. While not the largest warship in the U.S. inventory, the *Maine* dwarfed the firepower of the other ships in the Port of Havana. This display of U.S. force was meant to deter the ongoing chaos of the fighting between Cuban rebels and the Spanish garrisons. The *Maine* was manned by a crew of 353 Navy personnel and armed with four ten-inch guns, as well as numerous smaller sized guns, prepared to quell the fighting between the natives and the Spanish. Its two black exhaust stacks extended high above the top deck of the ship. The perimeter of the highest deck was lined with over 300 uniformed seamen, strategically positioned to intimidate, as the ship sailed to its point of anchor. The ten-inch guns, angled forward, were directed toward the city of Havana. The battleship was capable of destroying a great portion of the Havana territory, including the destruction of homes and businesses, wiping out the entirety of the port and surrounding areas, taking many lives in short order. The thick plates of armor, blue-brown metallic, affixed to the sides of this warship, signaled a defensive caveat to its enemies that the ship could withstand many rounds of enemy fire under heavy attack. Built at a cost of over two million dollars, it weighed in excess of 6,000 tons and was capable of a speed of seventeen knots. Anchored in place, this massive battleship cast its foreboding shadow against the east docks of Port Havana as the sun sank to the horizon. In the following days, on February 15, 1898, the anchored *U.S.S. Maine* was heavily damaged when a gaping hole was ripped in its side at the waterline under surprise attack. The *Maine* sank into Havana Harbor in a matter of minutes. Caused by the explosion of a submerged enemy mine, the battleship sank before it could fire its first cannon blast. The destruction of the ship cost the lives of more than two-hundred sixty U.S. sailors. Presumed to be a Spanish detonation, there was also speculation the explosion was caused by a combustible fire in the coal room. No matter, the sinking of this U.S. asset precipitated the declaration of war by the United States against Spain.

* * *

On the gray morning of March 21, 1898, Jauan and Maria sneaked to their favorite station on the sloped side of the rise within the tree line and surrounding brush. They concealed themselves covering with leaves and branches, serving as natural camouflage avoiding detection. Platoons of Spanish soldiers marched confidently along the Fernandez perimeters fortifying their strategic defensive positions. Platoon members began to disappear inconspicuously, drawing no attention. As Jauan and Maria observed from their position in the trees, the sound of repetitive rifle fire erupted. Continuous shots rang out sounding from all directions. Jauan pushed Maria's head and body to the ground in a protective position, covering her tiny body with his. With his face pressed into the ground cover, Jauan tasted dirt, roots, weeds and observed spiders and insects crawling about their normal daily lives, unconcerned about the raging battle. Jauan and Maria listened as canon blasts and multiple explosions of all varieties of ordinances accentuated the rifle fire. The low hanging smoke and haze caused by every type of weaponry grew dense and darkened the skies. Distinct odor of discharged gun powder from the Spanish rifles infused the humid air. The Fernandez plantation quivered and rumbled with every canon blast and explosion, as if tremors during an earthquake.

Fires ignited throughout the 1,400 acres. Sugar cane fields were burning. Tobacco barns were burning. The mill was in flames. The roofline of the owners' mansion was ablaze. The skies darkened from detonations and smoke of the fires. Jauan and Maria recognized the sounds of hammers beating against the mechanical equipment and metal vessels used for cooking stalks and cane juices. The native rebels demolished and destroyed the machinery and cookware beyond use and repair, thus destroying the means of sugar production. Explosives were detonated inside the mill destroying the equipment. Everything was burning.

Maria, still pressed to the ground and camouflaged, squirmed and wrestled free from Jauan's protective grip. Unaware of the risk, Maria bolted and raced up the hill toward the owners' mansion, partially hidden by the tall grasses, but identified and distinguished in her red play dress and brown leather sandals. No doubt she sought the protection and comfort of her mother. Jauan peered up the slope from the underbrush hoping to see Maria's long dark hair flying as she raced up the hill. He could no longer see her as she disappeared over the rise. Inhaling gun powder from rifle shot, canon fire and explosions left a strange tangy and bitter taste in his mouth. His lungs were inflamed from the smoke-filled air causing Jauan's labored breathing. The once fresh country air was displaced by thick, choking odor of explosions, spent gun powder and burning grass fields and crops. The sounds of the fighting indicated this battle was more than a small skirmish. Casualties were likely. Although heavily armed, the experienced Spanish platoons were unable to hold the west perimeter. The freedom fighting Cuban rebels successfully took control of the Fernandez sugar plantation. Guerillas exerted constant fire power verifying their intent to destroy the economy and thwart Spanish colonization and their immoral greed of profiteering. Armament of machetes, swords, knives and clubs were adequate and effective this day. However, the native rebels augmented their inferior weaponry with foreign gun powder, handguns, rifles and explosives which delivered ultimate destruction, giving them a decisive victory in this battle to destroy the Fernandez sugar and tobacco operations.

Jauan, not quite seven years old, continued to ply the ground under thick cover within the trees. Agonizing screams of Spanish defenders pierced the air as they were maimed by machete, clubs and detonations. Pleas for medical assistance echoed throughout the sugar cane fields of the Spanish-owned Fernandez plantation, now a battlefield. Distressing cries for aid accentuated the chaos in vain, helpless and unheeded. Much Spanish blood had already been spilled in the defense of three centuries of colonization and the raping of Cuban resources. Shrieks of indescribable agony and suffering indicated death drew near. Jauan covered his ears to muffle the cries for help, gun fire and the sound of explosions. Yet, the cries of the Spanish defenders were unyielding and would not be silenced. Pleas of unrelenting torment would ring in Jauan's ears long after this battle had ended. Constant pounding and tremors felt in the ground under his body, resonated up his feet and legs, through his abdominal cavity, into his rib cage, reverberating against his diaphragm. Jauan's heart raced in fear that these explosions would befall him in the next instant. The vibrations and tremors caused by each deafening explosion eliminated any hope of safety to which Jauan had been accustomed. He resisted his urge to run wild and free. If the fighting were to ever end, the aftermath would be horrific. Jauan hoped Maria found the safety and security of their mother.

As gun fire continued to erupt, Jauan saw no one running or crossing in his vicinity, nor in his line of sight up the slope and toward the owners' mansion. He thought about his father, Don Pedro Fernandez. Jauan reflected on his father's absences, extended during his lengthy workdays. Although Don Fernandez provided the material needs of his family, he was lacking from an emotional sense. Jauan's anticipation of growing and maturing under the supervision and tutelage of his father was, however, comforting. The desire for a masculine, authority figure instructing this child in the ways of the world and navigating chronologically was considered of utmost importance to Jauan. Through his own personal observations and assessment, Jauan did consider the relationship he had with his father to be constructive and positive. Don Pedro was invincible, full of strength and life, a rock of a foundation. Perhaps, one day in the future, Don Pedro would become a legitimate role model whom Jauan could emulate. Yet the mind of Don Pedro Fernandez was presently occupied with many things worthy of his attention, least of which was his son, seven-year-old Jauan Fernandez. Jauan considered his father's safety as the plantation was overrun with Cuban rebels during this attack. Don Pedro and Carlita Fernandez would remain safe; Jauan was certain.

From his camouflaged bunker, Jauan also considered his mother, Carlita. She was Spiritual and gentle, giving freely of herself, but also a strong woman who cared for her children. It was her daily effort, joined by the domestic servants who cleaned the mansion, cooked meals, washed clothes and tended to many other domestic duties, that was evident to Jauan. Routinely, Carlita read story books and led bedtime prayers each night with Jauan and Maria. She also administered correction and discipline to the children when required. As supervisor of the owners' mansion, his mother merely assigned specific tasks to the servants. Carlita did love her son, for she told him so. What more was needed to convince a seven-year-old child of his mother's love? She would be protected by her husband as they sought refuge at another plantation until this rebel attack could be suppressed by the Spanish garrisons.

The rebels continued their attack on the Fernandez plantation. Jauan could now see from his vantage point the motionless bodies of wounded and slain Spanish soldiers. Injured platoon members continued to cry out. Shrieks of the soldiers would remain with Jauan, repeating their refrain in life ending agony. Memories of this attack would evoke horrific emotion and impart sensory reminders of the atrocities witnessed and experienced this March 21, 1898.

With nightfall near, the rebel attack subsided and appeared to be ending. Jauan must determine the fate of his parents and sister. As he moved from his observation post in the tree line, he slithered up the rise toward the mansion, maintaining a low profile below the knee-high grasses avoiding detection. Jauan remained concealed. Unexpectedly, his right foot was caught by the bloody hand of a fallen soldier. Jauan could not move. The Spanish garrison lie in pain praying and pleading that death would take him. His 1893 Mauser bayonet tip was vertically positioned to puncture his breast and be driven into his heart, ending his life. This would be the humane way to die. Swiftly, not languishing and writhing in unconscionable pain and requiring the assistance of compatriots. Burning fields, canon fire and explosions lighted the skies in hues of orange and red set against the backdrop of night. The Spanish soldier, in full field-battle uniform, lacked the strength to complete the mortal deed himself. He begged Jauan to plunge the sharply-honed bayonet into his chest. Jauan observed the bloody mess; the soldier's face was unrecognizable as human form. Jauan felt sorrow for this person he did not know. He grabbed the soldier's left hand in an unsuccessful attempt to comfort him, or at least to impart sympathy. He did, however, understand the request. Empathy caused the seven-year-old to end the soldier's suffering as he pressed his body weight on top of the bayonet. The steel-cold metal pierced the dying soldier's uniform, easily slid through his chest cavity and sheared the heart muscle with the precision of a surgeon's scalpel. The soldier verbalized no appreciation as he became motionless and at rest. His heart functioned no longer. Jauan watched as his defensive compatriot, fully prepared for battle, died in noble duty to his oath of service as a Spanish garrison. Jauan then realized, there are circumstances most worthy of death. Accommodating this soldier's final request on the battlefield was unquestionably merciful.

Crawling up the rise, his home came into view. Jauan, depressed, yet fortified by the fatal, merciful aid rendered to the Spanish soldier, was overcome by grief as he witnessed his burning mansion and its destruction. Nearly all of the once stately two-story home, with only a partial wall still ablaze, was smoldering ash. Little was left of the structure. Jauan's few personal items were completely destroyed as he determined the location of his razed bedroom. He anticipated his parents sought refuge and safety at a neighboring plantation. Jauan inspected the grounds and sifted through the burning remnants for salvage. He looked for items which he could use in the days to come. Jauan anticipated the Spanish defenders would soon regain control and restore order.

One could not anticipate the anguish that young Jauan was about to experience. While searching the outlying garden area, Jauan found two bodies lying face up on the ground mere paces from the smoldering mansion, next to Carlita's flowers. A single bullet shot tore through the forehead of his mother and his father. Bloody bruising on Don Pedro's face was prominent. His shirt was ripped by obvious flogging of a whip. Blood oozed from the pale skull and dried across his forehead. Blood seeped through his hair into his ears and down his neck. It was difficult to positively identify mother and father so brutally murdered. Their clothing confirmed their identities. They did not attempt escape. Rather, they had been executed. He was certain death to each was instant. Jauan's initial reaction was to run, but he could not. Gripped with fear, he was overwhelmed. The seven-year-old, trembling, lips quivering uncontrollably, scenes racing through his mind, was unable to process the moment and began to vomit. With weak knees he fell to the ground and cried spontaneously, heaving unnaturally. His parents paid the ultimate toll of this war. What love he experienced from his parents was artificial or imagined from a prior time. He was sick and ached physically, emotionally. The image of Don Pedro and Carlita executed in the garden was indelible, inescapably seared into his memory for all time. Jauan's presumption that his parents made it safely to another plantation was a mere hope, an expectation. The love his parents had for Jauan, together with the love he had for them, if such existed, was short lived. Jauan had little opportunity in his brief life to learn and develop a capacity for love, to love or be loved. So it would be.

As he sat in the dark of night, next to his executed parents, dimly illuminated by the partial mansion wall still ablaze, Jauan pondered the fate of his sister, Maria. The gold chain necklace and heart shaped locket worn daily by Maria, given to her by her father, was clutched in her mother's left hand. Maria was nowhere to be found; her whereabouts and fate unknown. Jauan, in a state of shock, was unable to fully comprehend his predicament. His parents are dead. They were unable to protect themselves. The owners' mansion has burned to the ground. The faithful maids and servants assigned to mansion duties were nowhere to be found. Jauan had no knowledge of the precision or extent of the rebel attack, nor the current status of the Fernandez plantation. His thoughts were muddled; he was unable to devise a strategy. He shifted to a kneeling position next to his dead parents, sobbing, and eventually fell asleep holding his mother's cold, dead left hand, Maria's necklace intertwined. He wrapped his right arm around her shoulders and held her tightly.

As the skies brightened the following morning, Jauan remained kneeling at his parents' side, still in shock of his reality. Jauan had not seen her in a number of months, but readily recognized his older married sister, Isabella, as she approached. Out of a sense of obligation, she looked for relatives at the owners' mansion, finding Jauan, the only survivor.

"I found mother and father here last night. Dead, shot in the forehead. Executed."

"I'm sick. I can't understand any of this," Jauan wept.

"Our property was overrun by the Cuban revolutionaries last night, but we were spared for some reason," Isabella stated. "They were looking to destroy the plantations, the sugar and tobacco crops and mills and left us alone." Isabella knelt beside Jauan grasping her mother's left hand clasped around Jauan's grip. Jauan and Isabella cried together, shaking uncontrollably. Isabella, considerably older than Jauan, must take the lead. The sight of her dead parents was incomprehensible, yet the rebels continued their onslaught of the Spanish soldiers. The Spanish garrisons renewed their feeble defense of the sugar cane plantations, yet chaos continued. Remaining on the Fernandez plantation was not an option. It was unsafe for the Fernandez family.

Other family relatives were discovered executed on the plantation grounds in similar fashion. Isabella grabbed Jauan by the hand. The boy resisted. He would not leave his parents. Jauan insisted on maintaining this vigil for his parents as he would eventually accept their deaths if he could only remain there for a while longer. Isabella attempted to force Jauan to leave. He would not. His loyalty remained with Don and Carlita. Isabella finally convinced Jauan he could do nothing further for his dead parents. Jauan kissed his mother on the cheek, squeezed his father's hand and departed. He followed Isabella's lead and accompanied her away from the Fernandez mansion.

These most traumatic and devastating days of his life were described by A.D. Knight in unusual brevity as follows…

My first remembrance was of soldiers marching and fighting. And people hiding trying to find a place to rest for a while.

My father, mother and some of my older brothers and sisters had already paid the toll of war with their lives.

Chapter 4

With management and supervision executed, with escape of the slaves and laborers, operation of the Don Pedro Fernandez sugar and tobacco plantation ceased. Sugar cane and tobacco fields continued to burn and smolder for days. The stench of burnt and decaying bodies intermingled with the lingering odor of spent gun powder and burning tobacco was heightened by the foul odor of burning sugar cane plants. Indentured servants, Black Africans, the mulattos and white Chinese, banded together in a coordinated effort escaping to the rural areas in the hills experiencing freedom. The whippings, poor living conditions, hard labor and exposure became incidents of the past. Not forgotten, but now avoided. In this sense, forced labor in the plantation fields had finally ended.

Jauan's living condition with his sister's family was less than satisfactory, even though likely an improvement over how life might be envisioned at the smoldering plantation. General Weyler's Spanish defenders, enraged by the defeat in battle for the Fernandez plantation, conducted unannounced raids and ransacked Cuban and Spanish homes and farms, buildings and businesses, including Isabella's home and grounds, searching for Cuban rebels in hiding. The Spanish authorities were determined to quash all resistance. Jauan's sister and her husband were unable to adequately care for all of their children. Adding Jauan to their responsibility for food and protection compromised their ability to function as a family. Isabella's home was chaotic just as the Fernandez plantation had been, except now, the penalty for aiding or hiding rebels or the discovery of revolutionaries on their grounds was death by immediate execution. Persistent Cuban loyalists, resolute in their mission, continued their attacks not only on the Spanish garrisons, but on all Spaniards, killing, eliminating as many as possible. With little food and continual raids and inspections, survival in Isabella's home was uncertain. Jauan determined it was unsafe to live with this family as death at the hands of the Cuban rebels or Spanish soldiers appeared imminent.

Jauan's instinct in this madness was to run free. He took a little girl with him, his niece, whose name he believed was Angelina, but was unsure. Angelina insisted on accompanying her older companion. Perhaps Angelina couldn't resist the family's innate trait to run free as well. They escaped from Isabella's home undetected just after dusk; they wouldn't be missed until the following day. Extent of property destruction, disorganization and chaos in the Matanzas territory were beyond comprehension. Jauan and Angelina escaped as companion runaways to the port area of Matanzas the next day traveling little known trails to avoid Spanish soldiers and Cuban rebels. It was unlikely they would've been detained by either had they been noticed, but they were not. Jauan and Angelina had unknowingly become members of the street class, an unorganized assemblage of homeless child-orphans fending for themselves. Eradication and separation of intact families were the byproducts of war, during life and at death. Unfortunate, dependent children were transformed into orphans overnight with little or no warning, and certainly no explanation. Within days, countless children, some dressed only in rags, most without shoes or sandals, roaming the streets of Matanzas and the port area, became common sights. Drinkable water was difficult to obtain; food was scarce, unavailable. Tenacious rummaging, begging and thievery were the means to existence for this seven-year-old and his niece. Forced to scavenge for food in garbage heaps, the two fought with dogs, rats and other vermin for anything edible in order to satisfy their hunger.

As the sun set the following evening, Jauan defended the pair beating away aggressive rats with a length of board used as a club. Angelina successfully dove for a loaf of stale bread pitched onto the trash heap. Starvation, constant hunger pangs and stomach cramping had soon become natural motivation in their search for food. Orphans of varying age and physical size competed with Jauan and Angelina in the garbage rummaging and fighting for anything that could be considered food. The two ate of the loaf of bread that evening, saving one-half the loaf for the following day. They took shelter for the night near the garbage heap, curled on the ground under a discarded scrap of brown tarpaulin and a wooden plank. They secured the remaining half loaf of bread tucked between them. Protected by the tarp and wood shelter at twilight, Jauan sensed the presence of nocturnal rodents. The occasional flickering light from a nearby shed exposed gray rats, thin and malnourished, beady eyes darting in every direction, attentive antennae-like ears, yellow teeth grinding, greasy matted fur, bent, half-torn whiskers and repulsive hairless tails, continued foraging throughout the night, directed by their keen sense of sight and smell. Jauan listened to the rats fighting among themselves, screeching in mortal combat for possession of a scrap of food. He also focused on the sounds of distant battle, gun fire and detonations. He relived the screams of maimed rebels and soldiers about to meet their Maker. The sound of hammers destroying the machinery assembly used in processing sugar cane was distinct. Jauan recalled the image of his dead parents permanently fixed in his mind. Don and Carlita suffered a merciless fate and were no longer able to offer Jauan protection. They were unable to protect themselves at the moment of their deaths. Tragic. The love they may have had for their seven-year-old son could not be fully validated by Jauan, nor could Jauan possibly learn to love as a depraved child. He focused on survival and existence under new rules brought about by the greed and hatred of his fellow man. Jauan would learn survival on his own; his goal was to be free. He would not be dissuaded from his independence.

As dawn broke and daytime activity around the port increased, Jauan shook Angelina. She didn't move. Their half loaf of bread was missing. Their food for the day had been thieved by child-orphan competitors or eaten by the rats. Jauan shook Angelina more aggressively. Still, she remained motionless. Overnight, this little girl, appropriately named Angelina, gave up her spirit and died from unknown causes. Her spirit had gone to live with the angels; her desire to run free had been granted, so Jauan believed. She was at liberty, free from the noise of battle, free from the sounds of gun fire and explosions, free from the terror of fighting, free from starvation and free from the challenge of surviving in this chaotic hell in Matanzas. Jauan felt relieved of his responsibility for Angelina. Whether he believed he failed to protect Angelina overnight will not be known. He left Angelina's body lying under the brown tarpaulin. But the person and mind of Jauan Fernandez were now occupied with many things worthy of his attention, most importantly, his own survival.

Reflecting on Angelina's death in a heap of trash and garbage, overrun by rats and other vermin, was a despicable end to her short life on earth. She's in a better place free of war and chaos. A.D. recalled and entered his memories on a blank page…

The children scattered the largest ones to take care of the smaller ones. A married sister was trying to take care of me along with her own.

I finally had to take one of her little ones, a girl. I kept the little girl with me always searching junk heaps for food in the day time and curled up under door steps or on the ground with her in my arms at night. I was six or seven years old at the time. One night we had rummaged a piece of a loaf of bread and ate of it then curled upon the ground and went to sleep with the remainder of the bread between us.

When I woke up in the morning our bread was gone and also the little girls spirit had gone to live with the angels away from the noise and terror of fighting and hunger.

Chapter 5

With the responsibility for Angelina taken from him suddenly and mysteriously, Jauan obsessed on his own survival. Searching independently for food, without concern for another mouth, was simplified for one, rather than two. While living in the owners' mansion, Jauan never had concern of a next meal. Such is the recurring theme today, and the next. Discerning between the palatable and the poisonous was Jauan's common denominator with wild animals. Foraging for food placed the young boy at scavenger's level with vermin and vultures. Jauan joined the ranks of the street orphans running in packs. No shelter. Clothing turning to rags. Unbathed. Subject to starvation and dehydration. For weeks Jauan roamed Matanzas competing with displaced orphans and the rats scurrying about in the filth, muck and grime of the port area. In any other circumstance, the Port of Matanzas would be teaming with foreign mariners sailing under national flags of all description, engaged in commerce. Sailors assisting the homeless and orphans around the port with small plates of food and a few coins was once virtuous. But no more. The substantial wooden bulkheads at the Matanzas docks had been bombarded, destroyed and reduced to spears of splintered wood; on- and off-loading of commercial ships was impossible. Cuba was a war zone; ships registered under foreign flags stayed clear. There were no sailors serving as benefactors.

The following morning, Isabella's husband, Marco, worn, weakened and pale, found Jauan groveling for food through trash on the edge of the port area. Justifying his proposition as an act of brotherly love, Marco commissioned Jauan into the rural brush of the near hills. He requested that Jauan look after the six horses he managed to conceal from the rebels and Spanish cavalry. Marco lifted Jauan up into the wagon as they made their way to the hills, pulled by a single gray mule.

"We looked for family survivors of the rebel attack, but found none, except you. We expected you would stay with our family at our farm until this fighting has resolved."

"Why'd you leave our farm?" Marco inquired.

"The Spanish soldiers were looking for Cuban rebels, intent on killing them and anyone who assisted. The rebels were looking to kill any Spaniard they found. I couldn't assume the risk of being found on your farm. I escaped with Angelina… for our own safety."

"Marco, Angelina died overnight. She was frail and hungry. I don't know how or why she died."

"Yes, I'm aware. I found Angelina on the other side of the trash heap under a brown tarp. There's much death and destruction in Matanzas. I'm unable to deal with the loss of my little girl, with our family." Marco sobbed in grief losing control to his emotions. Marco's hands began to shake unnaturally as he tried to direct and control the mule's gait and pace. He continued to sob, grasping for air to control his runaway heartbeat. Marco looked into space in all directions as if there was an answer to this chaos, an answer to the death of Angelina, somewhere out there in the distance. There was no acceptable explanation, only the consequences of war and destruction. Marco weakened further into his grief. But he was determined to go on, as he had the responsibility for Isabella and his other children. This reality of life in Matanzas is so very fragile. Marco wailed.

"Angelina was innocent. She did nothing to deserve death. All I know is that this war has affected us all. Whether it concludes, I don't know. Our farm is searched constantly by the Spanish soldiers looking for Cuban rebels. They barge in unannounced, breaking our furniture, defacing and destroying our home, enforcing their ruthless authority. Should a native rebel be found on our farm, we'll all be shot as traitors."

"My five-year-old son, Christopher, was playing and hiding in my work shed just the day before I found Angelina. While conducting their search, the Spanish soldiers detected movement to the right of the shed door. Believing such movement to be a native rebel in hiding, they all opened fire randomly shooting directly into the shed. The movement ceased. I found my Christopher, bloody, on the floor of the shed, dead from many gunshot wounds. The garrisons retreated from my property after murdering my son, unapologetic and unconcerned they killed an innocent Spanish child. I'm unable to deal with this madness."

* * *

After he took several long moments for introspection in silence, to regain a semblance of control, Marco said, "Jauan, I have my six remaining horses hidden in the rural hill country. I need you to care for them for a few weeks until I can re-fence my pasture and repair the barn. It won't take long, hopefully. There's a basket of Cuban bread we can eat on our ride to the horses. I have a blanket and a tarp in the back of the wagon, along with a sickle and a bag of dried beef jerky for food. I'll return in less than three weeks for you and to retrieve the horses. I know you are capable."

Jauan could say little. The six horses were fenced in the hills in a crudely constructed corral of rope, yet adequate to contain them during Marco's absence. They did not see any Cuban rebels or Spanish soldiers on their way into the hills. Hopefully the horses were sufficiently concealed by Marco's design and will not be discovered.

The responsibility of the daily routine caring for and feeding six horses was overwhelming for this seven-year-old, especially since Jauan's chief concern was his own existence. The gray blanket Marco left with Jauan was thin and torn. The brown tarpaulin was old and peeling apart, ripping into shreds from aging while exposed to the elements and prior usage. It would not protect from rain if needed. The bag of jerky left for Jauan consisted of four pieces of dried, salty beef which lasted a single day. For the remaining days, Jauan subsisted on berries and wild fruit. He continued to exist alone in a primitive, desolate environment. No food. No shelter. Exposed to the natural elements of the wild tending to Marco's six horses. How long would this responsibility last?

Compounded by carelessness and inexperience, an unfortunate accident cutting grass for the horses with a semi-circular sickle caused a gash to Jauan's left hand. As Jauan grasped a bundle of grass with his left hand and prepared to chop at root level, the sickle twisted in his right hand and sliced near the tip of his left index finger. The sickle came down with such force exerted by his dominant hand, it continued to rip down the length of the left finger and lacerated the meaty part of his left palm area severing a deep gash. The cut bled for hours. Jauan applied pressure to the laceration, wrapping his hand with several thick pieces of blanket and forcefully pressed his hand against his left leg and shorts. Using his injured hand was impossible. The hemorrhaging eventually stopped with the constant pressure Jauan applied. Over time, the cut healed but resulted in permanent disfigurement, scarring his left hand.

In less than a week in the rural bush, fourteen members of the Spanish cavalry appeared at the rope corral displaying drawn swords, rifles and bayonets at the ready. They appeared from behind a large rock and tree formation and announced their authoritative presence. Jauan feared his safety was in jeopardy. The soldiers intended to harm the boy verbally threatening assault, intimidating by aggression as they sat mounted on high, looking down at this inferior boy-child. The situation was dire; seven-year-old Jauan was struck with fear. Encountering these dramatic circumstances in the hillside caused Jauan to recall the Bible story of David and Goliath as read to him by his mother. The smallish boy, David, grabbed a smooth stone and slew the giant Goliath with one accurately aimed sling to the giant's forehead, summarily knocking him to the ground. Jauan reflectively assumed a defensive posture standing in the breach directly between Marcos' six corralled horses and the fourteen soldiers. The boy, left hand sore and tightly wrapped in pieces of the tattered blanket, grabbed his sickle with his dominant hand. He brazenly shook the sickle at the Spanish garrisons, taunting them, preparing his defense of the six horses. The soldiers bellowed in laughter at the boy's feeble gesture. In an abrupt, continuous motion, the soldiers dismounted, pushed Jauan aside and continued shoving him in the back distancing him from the corral. With his left hand somewhat protected, tightly wrapped in the blanket, the soldiers knocked Jauan sprawling face down into the sand. They kicked him repeatedly with impassioned force, bruising his back, legs and arms, until the soldiers retreated to take possession of the corralled horses. Jauan, hand throbbing in pain, was helpless as he cocked his head upwards out of the sand and watched the soldiers commandeer Marco's horses. The soldiers roped each horse and tethered them together. The six horses were trailed off to presumably join the Spanish calvary. Jauan, hand injured, swollen and still bleeding slightly, his back, arms and legs severely bruised, was informally discharged by the Spanish cavalry of the responsibility assigned by his brother-in-law. Jauan posed no real opposition. He was left fending for himself again. He returned to the port area of Matanzas where his search for food, begging and thievery were more promising than gathering berries in the hills.

Reflecting on his life alone in the rural countryside and the streets, subject to abuse from many sources, potential disaster at every turn, A.D. made this entry recounting his personal experience into his journal…

I was alone, this had it's advantages as I could beg and hunt for food for one better than two. I came across one of my brotherin-laws, he sent me in to the hills to take care of his horses he had hiding in the brush.

I had to cut grass and carry to them and while doing this I slit one of my fingers open from my hand to the end of my finger which has left a scar that will be with me when I am in my grave.

I had to live on berrys and wild fruit, finaly the soldiers found and taken the horses freeing me from my care but myself once more.

Chapter 6

Jauan found life in the streets of Matanzas treacherous and deadly at his young age. He was a mere child with limited survival skills. Jauan did learn some lessons and techniques on his own fending for himself based on few previous real-world experiences. He developed usable skills over the last two months. However, Jauan was experienced mostly in the finer things of life in the owners' mansion: daily changes of under clothes, rugged shorts, pants, shirts, leather sandals and shoes made of the highest quality Spanish materials, clothes regularly laundered and clean, his own room and bed, regular meals, bathing and cleanliness and specific times to be tutored and read entertaining and educational books. Older and stronger street kids developed proficiency at thievery and intimidation. Engaging in stealth to secure garbage was Jauan's first concern for finding his next meal. Fighting off street bullies continued. Jauan soon learned the benefit of being a successful loner, avoiding the bands of orphans while roaming about the port area. Not joining them but distancing from them. Bands of homeless orphans, thugs really, attempted to steal what few morsels Jauan could scrounge for himself. He learned there was no respect for life on the street, only survival of those who were the toughest competitors. Hiding from the Cuban rebels, from the bands of street kids and fighting off the vermin at the trash heap continued. Sleep deprived and malnourished, Jauan found this competition one sided. His reality was an empty stomach as he crawled through filth and garbage seeking crumbs and scraps. His clothing was becoming rags of filth, encrusted with layers of dirt, dried mud, garbage and raw sewage. A fortunate turn of events occurred when the priest and nuns from the Catholic mission established an orphanage in Matanzas not far from the destroyed and abandoned Fernandez plantation. Jauan believed his young life may be at a turning point as Divine Providence had materialized.

Filthy and hungry, Jauan reeked with the smell of rotting garbage as his stomach growled while he combed the edge of the trash dump searching. He looked up the pathway opposite the garbage pile. At a distance, he spotted a mule with one braided red ribbon attached to the right side of its halter and a white ribbon attached to the left side. He later learned red signified mercy and forgiveness, white signified salvation. However, mercy, forgiveness and salvation were not apparent, nor available this day. The young, strong mule pulled a large wagon led by a nun dressed in her black and gray habit, rosary hanging loosely at the side. The hem of the nun's habit dragged the ground absorbing filth, as its length trailed through trash and garbage along the paths and streets of Matanzas. A second nun walked alongside the wagon carrying a basket containing rolls of fresh Cuban and Spanish bread and dried meat, calling for the orphans to gather. She was enticing the street kids, as many as would come, with bread and meat inviting them to accept residence in the orphanage at the Catholic mission they had established. Food, clothing, bathing would be available to all who cared to join. The older orphans were skeptical and fearful of the nuns' pretense, not knowing if this was entrapment or an attempt at religious conversion; they ran for the underbrush. Jauan was not suspicious, but trusted the nuns, at least for the time being. He consented, agreeing to go to the orphanage. The nun carrying the food basket gave Jauan a piece of roll and broke off pieces of the dried meat. Jauan devoured the first meal he had not scrounged in months. She put the basket into the wagon and hoisted Jauan onto the wooden floorboard he shared with six other orphans sitting atop three blankets fixed as pallets. The nuns continued their rounds in the port area and solicited three or four other young children, just as filthy and hungry as Jauan.

Although Jauan was baptized at the Catholic mission seven years ago, he did not know the priest who founded the orphanage, nor did he know any of the three nuns operating the orphanage. Their identities did not matter so long as they provided food, clothing and safety. Sleeping quarters for the orphans were simple and tolerable. The wooden, one-story dormitory building was long and narrow with rooms on either side of a center aisle. The individual sleeping rooms equated to prison cells: smooth, hard floors and bare walls, with only basics for the children. Each of the dozens of rooms were furnished with two or three small cot-like beds, sufficient to support the weight of a small child, with a thin blanket as padding or covering. In addition to being sleep deprived, Jauan was malnourished and exhausted; sleep came easily. He had little strength when he first arrived. After several weeks or a month of regular meals, Jauan regained his vigor. Despite daily interaction with the orphans, Jauan chose to deflect commonality with the others. His spirit clamored to be free again, willing to accept the risk of encountering skirmishes between Cuban rebels and the Spanish garrisons on his own.

The courtyard adjacent to the sleeping quarters was a grass field spotted with blank dirt areas which turned to mud during rainstorms. The exercise area was walled-in by a black wrought iron fence with pointed rod pickets. The orphans spent their days in the large yard equipped with three baseballs and two bats for community exercise. The bats were old and cracked but reinforced with black tar and tape. The orphans knew the history of baseball in Cuba and the results of the first game played in Matanzas twenty years ago on December 27, 1874. A ball team from Havana defeated the Matanzas team 51-9. Baseball became popular in Cuba over the prior two decades as its national sport. It was their favorite game but was also exercise for the orphans, boys and girls. Under normal circumstances, every young boy in Cuba played and trained to excel at baseball. This desire for baseball excellence lost its luster as the orphans, including Jauan, sought only to survive.

Looking across the dirt and grass field, Jauan suspected the fenced rods were substantial and narrowly spaced; escape by squeezing between the rods was impossible. The tall fence rods precluded the orphans from simply climbing over as an escape route. Yet, the wrought iron fence was not considered to be protection for the orphans, as the Cuban rebels could enter the courtyard scaling the fence unimpeded. Although he was fed and clothed and accompanied by dozens of orphans in similar circumstance, Jauan dwelled in the solitude of his own mind. His somber face projected the loneliness he experienced despite the social network of parentless children. Jauan's few conversations with the others were short and simple. There was no reason to develop any significant relationships with these kids as Jauan's escape was planned and scheduled. He expected little from the orphans, little from the priest and nuns and received less. Jauan suffered in silence in his solitaire world without parents, without his sister, Maria, without his niece, Angelina, and with no possessions. He often wondered about Marco and Isabella and their family and whether they found safety or disaster. He may never learn of their fate. His intent was to escape to freedom.

Jauan remained underdeveloped emotionally and socially. He refused to acquaint himself with the other orphans, as they were his competitors. He loved no one. Those he was suspected to have loved were brutally taken from him. At such a tender year he could love no one, for there was no one left to love. His role models were nonexistent. Don and Carlita were lovers to a point sufficient to procreate a family, but they demonstrated no outward affection for one another. Jauan never observed his parents hold hands. He never saw them kiss. He never saw them embrace. To this young observer, the marriage between his parents and the life they shared was loveless. Observing this life-style as a seven-year-old became fixed in his memory. Jauan determined such was the normal way of life, a normal marriage.

Scavenging for food as a novice was fashioned on instinct. He learned the art, if such was an art, of thieving food from any conceivable source. Jauan learned by doing and was inclined to do so again if he could free himself from this prison, professed to be an orphanage. Meals were repetitive and unsatisfactory.

Life outside the courtyard would be challenging but may also be rewarding. A successful breakout would determine future results. Jauan must escape this orphan's sentence which he initially found acceptable, but he now deemed immoral.

A fenced area in the yard designated off-limits to the orphans was located at the far end of the grassy portion of the courtyard, approximately sixty feet directly north of the dormitory door. Jauan roamed freely and came near the off-limits area. He determined the area to be a small cemetery. There were three child-sized graves with no distinguishing markings. The identities of the deceased children buried there were unknown and would remain undisclosed. What could have caused the deaths of these children was mere speculation. The three nuns patrolled the courtyard carrying walking sticks but used them primarily as swift-acting batons. Any orphan choosing to rebel against the commands given by the nuns was pummeled by striking on the back, legs and head. These beatings occurred on rare occasions only, as the orphans came to understand the penalty for defying their directives. Meting out punishment in full view of the captive children served as a warning for the observers. Using the walking stick as a weapon, the nuns demonstrated their authority and power. Any child could be beaten to the point of unconsciousness, or death. Jauan deduced these three graves were occupied by orphans who succumbed to disease or were beaten beyond survival.

Equally disturbing, it appeared the nuns took turns disappearing from the courtyard engaging in sexual gratification with the older orphan boys. Quite ironic, as the nuns required the orphans' attendance at the priest's daily Mass and at vespers led by the nuns each evening. During times of yard play, one of the nuns would secret to the dormitory with an older boy for a twenty- or thirty-minute rendezvous, while the remaining two nuns patrolled the grounds keeping the other children disciplined and confined to the courtyard. Jauan observed this frequent behavior by the nuns. He feared the day when he might become the fancy of one of the sisters. On more than one occasion, Jauan scrutinized the youngest of the three nuns, Sister Philomena, designated "Sister Meany" by the orphans, returning to the courtyard from the barracks with one of the older orphans, a fourteen-year-old boy, after an absence of over thirty minutes. As she returned, Sister Meany adjusted her black and gray habit into proper position, tucking and concealing her dark brown hair underneath her head piece, straightening her black rosary beads to properly hang down the right side of her habit, exuding faithful religiosity. The orphan boy tucked his shirt in at the waist and re-fastened his pants as he reentered the courtyard. Simultaneous absence of these two, Sister Meany and the older boy, was more than coincidental and suspicious. Jauan deemed this conduct immoral. But no sense in raising this issue to the attention of the other two sisters, as they engaged in similar escapades with their favorite boys as well. Approaching the priest with such an issue might likewise complicate matters. Jauan considered escape from this prison his only option.

While the three nuns conversed among themselves, relatively unconcerned about the little orphans expending pent up energy about the courtyard, Jauan recognized an opportunity which had fatefully arisen late one afternoon. As the three sisters sat together, they whiled away their time in philosophical discussions about the morality of the Cuban rebels murdering the Spanish to escape the abuses of colonization. The nuns continued, subconsciously or unconsciously, inaudibly reciting the rosary, touching each small, black bead, connected one to the next, winding their way independently and spiritually through each decade of the rosary. As the priest drew the attention of the nuns with an announcement of sorts, Jauan found his opportunity for escape.

"Tomorrow's evening meal will be served thirty minutes earlier than usual so the staff can meet with a clerical visitor from Havana," announced the priest.

As the nuns collectively turned their heads and attention to the priest, Jauan bolted for the nearby fountain, inoperative for the past two weeks and void of water. He crawled into and under the inner rim of the fountain wall nearest the children. He was undetectable by any cursory glance from the supervising nuns. His official prison escape was in progress. Jauan dozed off and fell asleep in the confines of the twelve-inch-deep fountain, unseen.

As darkness fell, Jauan awoke from his sleep. The sun had set. The courtyard was dark. Jauan was momentarily unsure of his whereabouts. He touched the inside wall of the cold stone fountain as he regained his orientation. He realized the three nuns were gone and the rest of the children were presumably inside the barracks preparing for sleep. Jauan had neither been counted, nor missed. He could not hear or see any activity in the dormitory. Were the children still there? Were the nuns still supervising? Had the Spanish soldiers taken the priest? The nuns? The children to a safer place? Had the native rebels executed all the children and the nuns? There were any number of possibilities, but no evidence for conclusions. The stillness of the night, interrupted by rifle and canon fire in a distant battle, would assist Jauan in his escape.

Jauan's eyes had grown accustomed to the dark. A soft light from a window at the far end of the barracks imparted just enough lighting to see across the compound, yet enough darkness to conceal his run for the fence. A portion of wrought iron targeted by Jauan was purposely chosen. The iron rods were of uneven height. Four or five consecutively placed rods had no pointed spears and were half the height of the remaining fence. Jauan scaled this area of fence with ease and without fear. Launching himself over to the other side, he fell safely to freedom and sprinted into darkness.

His companion, unrelenting hunger, came along for the escape. His belly was rumbling for fill, but no food would be found this night. Jauan must increase his distance running from the orphanage. He must not be discovered or caught near the Catholic mission, or he would be sent back. His desire to be free proved nourishing as he reflected on the daily meals he had at the owners' mansion. All of this could be restored. Not soon, but with difficulty and persistence. Tonight's direction after escape was to head for the port area. There may be older street kids roaming who had secured quantities of food for redistribution; there may be an opportunity to break into a closed bakery or meat shop under the cover of night. After an hour of walking and running, Jauan became disoriented and lost his way. He took to the ground where he fell asleep for the night, covering himself with a large piece of discarded rag, anticipating the light of early dawn would help him find his way.

* * *

A.D. paused his writing momentarily as he reflected. Examining the scar ingrained in the palm and index finger of his left hand, he recalled the velocity of the sickle blade as it struck downward and split through his flesh ripping skin wide open. Blood gushed from his left-hand splattering over his shirt and down his legs. He deemed survival of this incident fate and good fortune. Putting down the pen, he stretched his right hand relieving the stiffness developed from the unchanged position of his pen grip. He shook his writing hand from the wrist to fingers four or five times increasing the circulation. Instantly, loneliness consumed him and became his reality, just as he experienced in Matanzas. A.D. opened the black leather satchel. Respectfully, he unwrapped the first item. It was Maria's gold chain necklace and heart-shaped locket. He found the locket preserved just as it was clutched in his dead mother's left hand thirty years ago. He lowered his head and eyes overcome with grief and sorrow. A.D. considered the hopelessness of his loss. Still an orphan, no parents. Not knowing his sister's fate was incomprehensible as he was consumed with the emptiness from decades ago. He coped with the execution of his parents for the last thirty years, as he knew their fate. Maria's status remained unknown, a mystery. Despite his reluctance, A.D. forced himself to continue in his task of recording the past as he intended. However, readers of this writing will discover the atrocities of this war and experience the pain suffered by this young orphan. A.D. would remain faithful to the project undertaken and the promise made to his wife. He continued on his journey of words…

About that time, the Priest and sisters of the church began to gather the little children. I was hearded with the rest and placed in an Orphans home. We were put in long cell like rooms with dozens of little beds at night and in the daytime were allowed to play in a walled in courtyard.

The wall had a fence of iron rods making points at the top so the children could not climb over. I did not know anything but to run wild and being confined behind that fence did not suit me. I soon began to try and get out, and fate or luck seemed to help me.

I crawled to a dry fountain one day while the other children were playing I went to sleep and when the sisters marched the other children in that evening they did not miss me.

When I awoke it was dark, I could not think where I was until I touched the stone of the fountain then I remembered but couldn't understand what had happened. The soldiers might have come and killed all those other little waife but all was still except for the noise of battle in the distance.

I did not risk being found there and I left any longer. I made for the fence and found a place I could climb over and I was free and wild again. But I was hungry still could not risk being seen close around there.

Chapter 7

The Cuban War of Independence merged into the Spanish-American War in 1898. As hostilities between Spain and the United States escalated, the chaos created by the rebels fighting the Spanish sent Cuba into military and economic mayhem.

Six weeks after the *U.S.S. Maine* was sunk by enemy detonation, the United States issued its ultimatum to Spain that all Spanish troops immediately withdraw from Cuba. Spain rejected the demand. By 28 April 1898, war was declared and mutually acknowledged between Spain and the United States, now recognized as the Spanish-American War. Cuban rebels, revolutionaries as they became known, fought fiercely to regain their independence. With equal vigor, the Spanish Army fought to maintain and protect the rights acquired over centuries of colonizing and dominating Cuba, claiming the resources of this bountiful Caribbean Island. Only after intense political debate in Washington did the United States commit to intervene. American businessmen and corporations held investments and interests in Cuban sugar, tobacco and other industries. America had specific interests to defend. The native Cubans, protecting their natural resources, fought the Spanish seeking to end the colonization of Cuba. They were locked in a catastrophic, military and economic quagmire. Overwhelming damage was inflicted on this small island which possessed seemingly endless resources and potential.

* * *

As the first light of dawn broke at the horizon, Jauan became oriented to the locale. With eyes barely opened, Jauan focused on the gnarled roots of a familiar scrub oak which projected into the sandy soil just twelve feet from his resting spot. Thick strands of Spanish moss draped as natural accents over the rugged branches of the oak tree. Jauan had routinely climbed this tree during his youth and was familiar with the area in which he slept overnight. Near the Port of Matanzas, Jauan considered rummaging the garbage heap for food as he had previously done, hoping to be productive.

Closer to the port, orphaned street kids and unfortunate adults clamored and squeezed for space along the perimeter of a drainage ditch. This crowd of suffering humanity lined the edge of the ditch, shoulder to shoulder. Unappetizing and foul smelling, the ditch appeared to be a food source which Jauan must consider. The ditch was adjacent to and drained down from an elevated wooden slaughter pen where cattle, sheep and hogs were killed and butchered. One side of the pen was a solid wooden, eight-foot-tall wall. The faded, red painted wall overlooked the ditch. Bloody scraps of slaughtered livestock, fat, bone, protein and gristle were pitched into the watery ditch for later burial in a remote garbage trench. Butchered pieces, raw and bloody, were of little culinary or hygienic concern to the weak and malnourished. This mass of homelessness must fend off dehydration and starvation consuming all form of nourishment. The adults and orphans possessed tin cups and other vessels, fighting and competing with each other, with the rats, dogs and other vermin to secure a scrap of bone, intestine, meat or liquid fatty waste. Attacks by hordes of menacing flies, gnats and disease carrying insects were unbearable, flying into eye, ear, nose and other orifice. Dense swarms of insects hovering above the ditch were maddening, but those seeking drink must accept the onslaught to secure a position at the edge of the pool. The maggot-filled, murky water in the ditch, unclean and likely contaminated by every type of parasite and bacterium, proved liquid enough for hydration. The water, a red-colored semi-solid waste, flowed slowly down the hill from the slaughter pen into the ditch. Spanish butchers, smoking cigars, chewing and spitting tobacco, slaughtered and dressed various cuts of meat from cattle, sheep and hogs and the occasional brood of chickens. Jauan bullied his way to the edge of the ditch, dipping his cup into the red liquid to satisfy his thirst, gulped in the red slime. The semi-solid was foul and rancid. Yet, without hydration, liquid or slime, the human body would cease to function. Jauan squirmed his way closer up the ditch nearer to the slaughter pen, his source of food. He reminisced as he conjured the aroma of a hog roasting over a firepit on a Sunday evening as the Fernandez family ate its fill of ham and pork. Today was vaguely reminiscent in an odd way, but the food supplied was disgusting, even though it may have nourished those drinking at the ditch.

On reflection over the years, Jauan understood the red semi-solid slime obtained its tint from the blood spilled of butchered animals. However, he could not help but consider that Cuban revolutionaries and run-away slaves were routinely executed behind the slaughter pen against the red wall by firing squad or the executioner's blade. The dead bodies of the executed were dumped into the waste ditch along with chunks and pieces of the butchered animals. Could a portion of Jauan's drink from the ditch be human blood? This caused Jauan distress as he became nauseated with such prospect.

A.D. memorialized this most unfortunate recollection on the following blank page of his tablet. He wrote…

I made my way to an old slaughter pen as there was a crowd with old tin cups and cans catching and drinking blood as it ran out a ditch for the purpose of carrying waste away from the building.

As they were all doing it, it did not seem so bad to me then but to me know it nauseates me. As I think it might have been the blood of humans I was drinking. As I seen them stand round of natives up along the wall and shoot them letting them fall into the ditch.

Chapter 8

Austin, Texas 20 May 1898

It appeared to be a completely disorganized effort. Hundreds of soldiers had assembled after days of travel from all parts of Texas, arriving in Austin on foot, horseback, wagon and rail. Tents, gray, soiled and weathered, some with prominent black numbers displayed and centered on the roofs, dotted the expansive grass field next to the rail tracks. All billeting and mess tents were ordered taken down, disassembled and stowed, per military regulation, in preparation for the next encampment. A private, John D. Knight, arrived by horse and buggy with three compatriots from Corpus Christi. They were part of the 1st Texas Volunteer Infantry, First Regiment. Company E consisted of three officers, six sergeants, eight corporals and sixty-seven privates. Eighty-four men in all led by Capt. Grant R. Bennett. Men were assigned to break camp and to load supplies onto preassigned rail cars. Others labored corralling infantry horses and pack mules for loading on designated cars heading to Mobile, Alabama. Capt. Bennett, six feet tall, forty-four years old, married with two teen-aged children and an experienced, decorated war veteran, was unconvinced of his volunteers' ability as a fighting force. Most were green and untested in battle. Bennett, however, had his orders. His destination had been disclosed, but the orders would not be revealed to Company E until the following month or later, depending on progress consistent with the itinerary of the assignment. Despite weeks and months of training, Bennett was concerned about his troops' battle-readiness. He could only prepare his men through repetitive drills, simulated exercises and memorizing and understanding battle plans and strategy. Their current rail journey may permit additional time for needed advanced training under adverse conditions. However, all strategy could change once the landscape of the battlefield is identified and assessed. Ensuring all equipment was in proper working order, including the arsenal of pistols, rifles, and cannons, was the objective. Ammunition, gun powder and other explosives were to be kept dry and stored securely. Machetes, swords and bayonets were sharpened with jagged edges to inflict maximum casualty and death during hand combat.

The last of the tents were down, packed and stowed. The camp site, cleared by an assigned delegation of volunteers, was left pristine, void of litter and debris from soldiers and service animals to the satisfaction of the officer in charge. Complying with muster protocol required mandatory accounting for each soldier. Troops were allowed to select which rail car each desired. The four privates from Corpus Christi found available seating on the car directly behind the engine and coal car. Animals were loaded on designated livestock cars without difficulty, save for one stubborn mule which decided it would rather remain in Austin. So, it did. No time would be wasted on one uncooperative service animal.

In the early morning hours of 20 May 1898, the soldiers departed. As the engineer pulled forward, the 1st Texas Volunteer Infantry announced its departure to family, friends and well-wishers by a long blast of the engine's shrill whistle. The four soldiers stowed duffels and unloaded playing cards, hand-rolled Cuban cigars, chewing tobacco, a harmonica and one pocket Bible. One of the four, a superficially errant soul, concealed two bottles of choice Kentucky bourbon whiskey; Private Knight would be unaware. He knew John Knight would not be pleased, nor tolerate such provisions. These two bottles will be kept discreetly from Private Knight's discovery. Whiling away time on board would have benefits. Traveling by rail was a sophisticated luxury compared to foot, horseback or wagon. Time and travel on the train were relatively carefree and comfortable compared to any other mode of travel.

As the sun began to set, the troop train headed east making progress through southern Texas toward Louisiana. Location of the train at any given moment could not be determined in the dark or in an unchanging rural countryside. Their destination was Mobile, Alabama, as far as the enlisted troops knew. Although many of the soldiers suspected foreign duty, none could be sure. Speculation rumored that armed service in Cuba should be anticipated. Such presupposed orders were logical. The details of the 1st Texas Volunteer Infantry assignment would be disclosed at the appropriate time. In the meanwhile, Company E maintained readiness, tended to the livestock on board and whiled away their time playing poker, smoking cigars, chewing tobacco, discreetly sipping whiskey and resting.

Private John D. Knight kept his Bible in the buttoned, left breast pocket of his uniform. The Bible fit perfectly in this pocket just over his left chest, nearest his heart. Knight believed this to be God's repository for His Holy Word. While the boys enjoyed a Cuban cigar, played poker and chewed tobacco, Knight read the Psalms usually in silence. However, a meaningful or prophetic verse would be shared aloud with the others. Words of comfort before battle. Words of wisdom spoken to the faithful, and the not so faithful. Words spoken of acts of kindness toward his fellow man, despite the likelihood of engaging an enemy on a bloody battlefield. Knight's allegiance to Texas was superseded only by his devotion to God Almighty. God giveth, God taketh away. Knight's military service, toting a rifle equipped with bayonet for the taking of human life while battling an enemy, served a greater good he believed. Such would be demonstrated in the months to come, yet Knight was unaware of what would eventually be required. He was ready to serve his Lord and Savior, and the state of Texas.

On the very early morning hours of 22 May 1898, the troop train came to rest in a field just to the east of Mobile, Alabama. The 1st Texas Volunteer Infantry set up camp next to the tracks as they had done in Austin before their departure. How long they would camp near Mobile was undetermined, but the 1st Texas Infantry was happy to disembark from the train. Green pasture was available for the livestock, as was a plentiful water supply from the nearby river. Soldiers were able to bathe, wash clothes and relax in the slow flowing waters.

Company E remained in Mobile, Alabama for one month from 22 May 1898 until 22 Jun 1898. Time was spent feeding, grooming and exercising the livestock. Company E engaged in defensive skirmishes and developed aggressive techniques attacking an imaginary entrenched enemy. Rumors continued to circulate that Cuba was their destination and combat their mission. Private Knight and his compatriots were satisfied with the mission assigned to the 1st Texas Volunteer Infantry. Despite his youthful age of eighteen years, Knight had the knowledge and ability of a seasoned minister accompanied by the proper Spiritual temperament. His words were comforting to his three buddies. Do unto others as you would have them do unto you. Words of wisdom began to sink into the three despite late nights engaged in poker playing, smoking cigars and inconspicuous short snorts of whiskey, all such activities of questionable morality in the eyes of Private Knight.

On 21 Jun 1898, 1st Texas broke camp and readied the train for early departure the next morning. This train would travel at high-speed heading for Miami, stopping only for coal and water to supply high-pressured steam to power the locomotive's engine. No reason was given for the train's higher speed except that arrival the next day was imperative. As the train headed east through the panhandle of northwest Florida and down Florida's western coast, the first passenger car, occupied by the quartet of privates, was spared the coal smoke from the engine's high rising stack; heat of the steam belching from the locomotive rose above their passenger car. Unfortunately, the incessant, irritable sounds of the engine working under full power, at maximum speed, was disturbing. Rail noises at the highest speed made restful sleep impossible. Heading south indicated disembarking from Miami was probable, thence heading to Cuba.

One of the Corpus Christi four, Timothy Anderson, a professed eighteen-year-old, actually under the age of seventeen, verbalized to Private Knight his fear of battle and hand combat in Cuba.

"I fear our continued track along the Florida west coast heading toward Miami," he stated to Knight.

"We'll be in Miami in just over a day. Then on a ship to Cuba. Then battling an enemy in hand combat to the death. I'm sick with fear that I've volunteered for this duty. I'm just over sixteen years old and lied about my age to qualify for military service. I got what I asked for; now I'm scared."

"How can you justify our mission and remain calm before certain death on a battlefield?" he asked Knight.

Knight found this query to be an uncontrived opportunity to explain his Spiritual view on the evils of mankind contrasted with the Providence of God Almighty. A simple, fundamental response is required to allay the fears of Private Anderson. Knight was chronologically eighteen, but Spiritually he was middle-aged. Knight knew Tim and the Anderson family lacked spiritual direction. He was thankful for the opportunity to preach a little to his younger compatriot.

"Timothy, you must first understand that mankind has a depraved heart seeking to profit from the ways of the world, sacrificing nearly all for profit, fame and power. This is precisely what's happening in Cuba. The Spanish control the people and economy of the island. They reap profit and proclaim the fame for its three centuries of Spanish colonization and domination. Their continued dominance over the Cuban natives has destroyed the island. The 1st Texas Volunteer Infantry has its mission as a fighting force to free the Cuban natives of three centuries of domination."

"So, our mission is a noble one. How can I remain calm? Very simple. As a Christian, I have given my life Spiritually to Our Lord, God Almighty. He is in control. As long as I do as Father God directs, I have no fear of death. So I remain calm realizing that death of the human body is a mere transition to life everlasting in the eternal presence of our Maker."

Timothy Anderson was satisfied with Knight's response for the time being, yet he desired to carry on this conversation in deeper detail. So it would be.

Arrival in Miami on 23 Jun 1898 was planned and militarily precise. A tent city was organized and set up efficiently as done in the past. The 1st Texas Volunteer Infantry would remain in the swelter and humidity of south Florida until 8 Aug 1898. During this period of encampment, the infantry engaged in hand-to-hand combat scrimmages daily in the oppressive heat with the company divided into opposing forces. Over six weeks would be spent in the scorching heat and draining humidity of the south Florida summer preparing for the predictable assignment to Cuba. This lengthy layover was required to acclimate the soldiers to an environment similar to what would be experienced in Cuba. Heat. Swelter. Humidity. On 7 Aug 1898, the soldiers were ordered to break camp, anticipating heading to the Florida coast south of Miami for transport by ship to Cuba.

On the morning of 8 Aug 1898, just prior to their departure, Col. Charles Riche, commander of the 1st Texas Volunteer Infantry, gave the command to each of the company officers to disclose the particulars of the orders to Cuba. Capt. Bennett assembled his troops of Company E and spoke to them as men, even though most were 18 years of age, or younger, and untested. The fear anticipated in the minds of the young infantry became reality. On this morning, the troop train would be loaded as before, heading to Jacksonville, Florida for one last stop. This was contrary to the speculation and expectation of the troops. Why go north if we have been ordered to Cuba?

The 1st Texas arrived in Jacksonville, Florida at *Camp Cuba Libre* (Free Cuba) the following day, 9 Aug 1898. The troops engaged in realistic sword and bayonet drills, tested rifles, handguns and canons and other equipment for efficient, proper operation, as well as accuracy of gun sites. They also spent time studying battle strategy and decisive plans preparing to assist the native Cuban revolutionaries wresting control of Cuba from Spanish forces.

Company E prepared to ship out from the Port of Jacksonville in route to Havana. Captain Bennett informed the troops of the sinking of the *USS Maine* battleship in February and made them aware war had been declared against Spain two months later. Within one week of their arrival at Jacksonville's *Camp Cuba Libre,* an armistice was declared between Spain and the United States, thus avoiding Company E's anticipated battle with the Spanish and possibly with native revolutionaries and emancipated slaves. The 1st Texas Volunteer Infantry remained at Jacksonville's *Camp Cuba Libre* when it received further and amended orders. The troops, expecting orders for their return home to Texas, were disappointed when ordered to travel on to Savannah, Georgia. The soldiers broke camp and loaded the train for their departure.

From 23 Oct 1898, the infantry remained camped in Savannah but ceased training for battle. The troops received detailed training instructions to provide humanitarian aid to the Cuban natives, revolutionaries and Americans living and working in Cuba. Instructions included introduction to the Spanish language, medical and first aid classes, which were taught as indispensable tools in rendering humanitarian aid. For two months, the troops organized U.S. medical supplies, food in the form of wheat and flour and lumber to load on the transport. Cuba's Port Havana and Port Matanzas were heavily damaged by the United States' bombardment which partially led to the armistice. 1st Texas Volunteer Infantry's humanitarian effort will be concentrated in the ports of Havana and Matanzas. Of particular importance will be the repair of all piers and docks to accommodate sailing vessels transporting personnel, trade, commerce and needed supplies from the United States and elsewhere. Company E had been assigned to reconstruct the heavily damaged Port of Matanzas fifty miles east of Havana. Private Tim Anderson expressed his relief to Private Knight that the fighting mission has changed to providing humanitarian aid to the Cubans. He would live to see his eighteenth birthday. By Christmas Eve, 1898 at Port Savannah, the transport ship, *MOBILE,* was fully loaded with medical supplies, food and other humanitarian provisions, together with building materials for the repair of both ports. Eight hundred soldiers, with tents, armament, bedding and clothing, boarded the *MOBILE* as it prepared to weigh anchor for Port Havana, Cuba. On 27 Dec 1898, the *MOBILE* dropped anchor at Port Havana. Offloading of personnel and supplies commenced immediately. A portion of supplies and construction materials remained on board the *MOBILE* for delivery to Port Matanzas with Company E and B. The humanitarian aid to Cuba commenced. The Spanish-American War ended almost as quickly as it began. This entire declared Spanish-American war lasted less than four months, 21 Apr 1898 to 13 Aug 1898.

Chapter 9

Having escaped undetected from the Catholic orphanage, Jauan ran free, responsible for no one but himself. His independence relieved him of any possible obligation. No family. No loved ones. No one to love. No consolation. No support. His loneliness, his depression was replaced by his need and will to survive. Jauan's older married sister, Isabella, her husband, Marco, and their children had not been seen for months. Missing, perhaps dead, killed by the Spanish execution squads during their search for Cuban rebels, Jauan speculated. They may have been murdered by the Cuban revolutionaries who abhorred the Spanish for its centuries-long occupation of their Caribbean island. Jauan's sister, Maria, missing. Angelina, deceased…her spirit gone to the angels. Jauan, however, retained the memories of his family. Horrific memories. Memories which will dwell in the depths of his soul, psyche and character for decades.

For the last ten months, excluding his brief residence at the Catholic orphanage, Jauan remained in the port area of Matanzas thieving, begging, scrounging for daily sustenance. He fought with the marauding gangs, many older and stronger than the seven-year-old orphan, and with wild animals in competition for a limited food supply. Scavenging and thievery were Jauan's life as he focused on survival. Acts of desperation, breaking into bakeries and butcher shops at night to sustain life were challenging and necessary. Certainly, worth the risk. However, Jauan remained hungry, filthy and unkempt. He lacked any measure of personal hygiene as he lived among feral animals, sifting through mounds of trash, homeless and a beggar. His living conditions found no improvement, that is, until the new soldiers arrived in Matanzas.

At the end of December, 1898, Jauan encountered a new, foreign military unit. Company E of the 1st Texas Volunteer Infantry arrived just after Christmas Day at the Port of Matanzas, not that Jauan would have particularized a seasonal calendar. Just as the Spanish garrisons, this infantry unit was in full military dress, heavily armed for conflict, but now engaged in reconstructing the demolished piers and docks of the port. In addition to the construction repairs, Company E spent apportioned time throughout the day conducting drills, marching in cadence and engaging in physical training, but generally displaying a jovial and relaxed temperament. Jauan's curiosity piqued on the unique language spoken by the soldiers, sounding unfamiliar and quite strange to the boy. Jauan appeared out of nowhere, approaching this group of peculiar-looking, foreign-speaking soldiers, maintaining a safe distance, yet prepared to bolt should caution or danger dictate. Jauan's introduction to the new military unit was odd and cumbersome. He was limited to hand gestures as the logical mode of communication, leaving mastery of their foreign language for another time.

Rebuilding the Port of Matanzas piers and docks occupied a substantial part of their workday as Jauan observed from a distance. Approaching too closely would assume unnecessary risk. In time, Jauan ventured nearer. Soon he could physically differentiate one soldier from another with detailed distinction. Each soldier took on unique familiarity the longer Jauan studied each of the men. During the workday, the soldiers appeared content with repair and construction of the docks, singing and laughing spontaneously. Jauan especially remained close during meal times and realized these new soldiers had much to eat, a seemingly endless supply of food. Jauan did, however, continue to scavenge the trash heaps and garbage dumps. This need for scavenging, however, abated over time. Within the next days, Jauan observed the company cook tending to large open fires roasting butchered hogs. A palatable aroma emanated from the fire pits as the chef rotated the butchered pieces of meat on large spits. Jauan assumed additional risk despite his passing familiarity. He drew closer to the cook's position with caution. A roasted cut of pork, or simply bread crumbs, could sustain Jauan and relieve the hollows of hunger. His risk, although high, was calculated and taken. From the activity Jauan observed, these soldiers were genteel and benevolent, revealing genuine concern and sincerity for the native Cubans, and, hopefully, one Spanish orphan. How much more harm could come to the seven-year-old requesting a bite of food, or a small plate, from his new military benefactors? Jauan mimed to the cook, motioning to his mouth with his right hand and his stomach with his left that he was famished. The cook understood the boy's request. He obliged.

Jauan, thin, skinny, with a gaunt face and malnourished, had brown eyes and thick locks of black hair, matted and stringy, falling below the boy's shoulders. He had not bathed or washed in months. His foul smell, a putrefying, unclean odor preceded the boy and announced his presence. Jauan was pitiful as he advanced toward the soldiers. Hoping not to startle or scare the boy, the soldiers tossed scraps of muffins, bread and roasted pork to this wild, animal-like creature named Jauan Fernandez. He instinctively dove to the ground for the pitched pieces of bread and meat as they landed near his feet, as if Jauan was competing with the rats for a few edible morsels in the garbage. His fear was eventually allayed. Jauan soon became comfortable, perhaps complacent, near and around the soldiers, especially during mealtimes. The lively singing and industrious activity of Company E impressed Jauan as he recalled the harmonious, metrical chanting of the Africans, mulattos and Chinese. As the soldiers repaired the docks, cutting lumber, bracing and supporting wooden walkways extending over the deep waters of the port, the soldiers kept a watchful eye on Jauan. This child became a customary fixture with Company E at Port Matanzas. He appeared and ventured near the worksite frequently throughout the day. But he always presented at mealtime for the unfamiliar, but satisfying food, generously provided by the troops of Company E.

Relying on his polished parade skills, honed with the Spanish platoon, Jauan did not miss a beat, nor an opportunity, to march alongside the soldiers of Company E. With a belly full of meat and muffins, Jauan fashioned a branch as a rifle flung over his right shoulder and his sword of a stick at his left side. He marched in unison alongside the soldiers each morning and at sunset, impressing the enlisted men, as well as Capt. Bennett, with his natural rhythm and precision. For a seven-year-old, Jauan's military bearing was learned and rehearsed. It demonstrated an instinctive ability to follow the intricacies of this military unit's defined cadence. Jauan's rapport with Company E developed and grew despite the lack of any significant or meaningful verbal communication. The boy's abhorrent physical appearance and odor demanded that Jauan's personal hygiene be addressed. Company E would find its opportunity.

After completing their Saturday morning eight-mile march, actually a platoon run through the hills and wooded areas, accompanied by the homeless boy, Company E approached the river's edge. They stripped off their packs, their sweat-soaked uniforms and mud caked boots, diving into the wide, meandering river. It pooled at the river's bend providing a natural bathing area at a shallow depth of less than three feet. Private John Knight, who had been intrigued by this seven-year-old's plight from a distance, believed it was time to show Jauan a portion of God's providential, brotherly love. Jauan's clothes, worn daily for months, were little more than rags. His shirt and shorts, made of the finest quality Spanish materials, had been reduced to bits of cloth scraps. Soiled from rummaging, Jauan's "clothes" were stained by his own bodily fluids and waste, ripped to shreds fending against the dogs, rats and other bully types. His Spanish sandals had worn thin from constant use and abuse. He reeked with the putrid smell of rotting garbage and raw sewage. Although this was offensive to those around him, it somehow made the boy attractive as a dependent child in dire need of hygiene and assistance. Private Knight took on the role of mentor, a father-figure to Jauan. Company E spent the greater portion of this mid-morning bathing, lathering, shaving and cleaning to be a presentable military unit. The soldiers also laundered soiled uniforms and cleaned their black boots on this Saturday morning.

Jauan was captivated by the sense of frivolity and fraternity as he observed the soldiers cleansing in the river. Jauan sat on the river bank exposed in his nakedness, but for the few shreds of cloth which remained intact. Private Knight, a young-looking lad matching his chronological age, could have been Jauan's brother ensuring the child's well-being. Knight, speaking softly to Jauan so as to comfort the boy, invited him into the shallow water by a hand gesture which Jauan readily interpreted. Jauan's clothing literally melted away as he entered the river and stirred the water. Knight possessed a cleansing product that amazed young Jauan. This product was created and known as bar soap by two entrepreneurs, William Procter and James Gamble. They purchased the rights to a new soap and developed it, introducing it in 1879 as Ivory Soap, a pure bathing soap. The U.S. military purchased massive quantities of this bar soap for its troops. Jauan relaxed in the river bathing himself from head to foot. Knight's attention focused on the boy's filthy hair. He cleaned grease, dirt and picked parasites out of the boy's scalp to the extent possible. Jauan was thoroughly cleansed after an hour of bathing; he did not resist, nor did he express any reluctance to this adventure in cleanliness. He didn't want the bathing session to end as he continued scrubbing his entire body with the fascinating cleansing bar. Jauan was clean indeed as he exited the river and was towel dried by his "brother," Private Knight. After this bathing experience, Jauan emitted the unaccustomed fragrance of wholesome cleanliness. The smell of his body reminded Jauan of his mother's pink flowers in the mansion's garden. Jauan, standing alone on the bank a distance from the soldiers, watched as the troops busied themselves unpacking and dressing in fresh, dry uniforms. Jauan was adequately clean, yet exposed in his nakedness. He was set apart from the other cleansed bodies by the gold chain necklace and heart-shaped locket hanging about his neck, last worn by his sister and a reminder of his dead mother and father. An artifact of life once experienced as personal and civilized. Private Knight presented Jauan with a set of shorts and a shirt he had hand sewn and fashioned out of used and surplus Company E infantry uniforms. Jauan's new wardrobe simulated nothing less than the finest military clothing nearly identical to the uniforms worn by his friends of Company E. He could only show his gratitude to Private John Knight by bowing and weeping in thanksgiving and gratitude for such an act of brotherly love. His relationship with a "friend" commenced at this basic, fundamental level. It was clear that Private John D. Knight was the benefactor this Saturday morning, giving greatly to this needy recipient. But it was John Knight who received God's blessing for furnishing Jauan's morning bath, punctuated by his military attire as he extended his portion of brotherly love.

Standing erect, fitted with his new "uniform," Jauan's ease with Private Knight and the soldiers of Company E had risen to an extraordinary level. His initial fear of these strange men had been misplaced, thankfully. Trust in one's fellow man can often be assessed in brief encounters. Such was the case at the river's edge near Matanzas on this significant day.

Private John D. Knight positioned a wooden stool next to Jauan on which he was motioned to sit. Knight grabbed Jauan's right hand exposing the tips of his stained fingernails. He employed a set of Army-issue clippers trimming the nails of Jauan's right hand and then the left. Knight scrubbed Jauan's hands and fingernails with a soft brush, removing the debris and stains embedded under his nails. Private Knight then similarly trimmed and scrubbed Jauan's toenails using this technique.

Jauan was given a military issue toothbrush with flavored dental paste. Knight demonstrated the proper use of such toothbrush on his own teeth, instructing Jauan. Brushing Jauan's teeth was most gratifying as the boy appreciated the freshness of the peppermint flavored paste combined with the slight cleansing abrasion of soda. Jauan's body was clean, his teeth clean, nails trimmed and clean. Jauan was revitalized in his new uniform.

With Jauan's thick black hair nearly dried, Knight displayed his skill with the use of his hair-cutting scissors, as he customarily obliged throughout Company E and beyond. He began to trim at first, then made wholesale cuts to the boy's locks. Knight fashioned short hair for Jauan which would be much easier to scrub and keep clean. This first bath and haircut courtesy of Private Knight and Company E would not be Jauan's last. Regular bathing and hair trimming will be the standing order. Jauan was overcome with delight that he had acquired this new friend in John Knight. As the haircut neared completion, the harmonica melody of "The Yellow Rose of Texas," played by Knight's Corpus Christi compatriot, Tim Anderson, echoed throughout the bathing area. The company joined in unison, belting out the lyrics of their Texas favorite:

There's a yellow rose in Texas
That I am gonna back to see
Nobody else could miss her
Not half as much as me
She cried so when I left her
It like to broke my heart
And if I ever find her
We never more will part

The dinner bell clanged and reverberated, announcing meal-time. The soldiers assembled accompanied by their new and invited friend, Jauan Fernandez.

* * *

Company B of the 1st Texas Volunteer Infantry had also been assigned duties in the Matanzas area. Company B's orders were primarily to furnish practical humanitarian aid to the Cuban natives. Bags of wheat and corn flour had been offloaded at Port Matanzas from the hold of the transport ship *MOBILE*. Company B made food products from the corn flour and wheat, principally loaves of bread, easily stacked, distributed and ready for distribution to the Cuban natives. It was learned that one volunteer in Company B, a private by the name of W.J. Roberts, Jr., spoke fluent Spanish. His family from San Antonio were all conversant in Spanish. Private W.J. Roberts, Jr. learned Spanish at an early age and was frequently requested to interpret conversations between John Knight and young Jauan. Such translating by Roberts served two purposes: not only could they understand and effectively communicate with one another, but, also, Jauan easily and quickly learned to speak the English language. The relationship between Knight and Jauan Fernandez soared to great heights and loyalty with the breakthrough in effective communication.

From this point forward, Roberts was happy to avail himself to serve as Jauan's translator. John Knight and Roberts were ecstatic when able to determine Jauan's needs and desires. Although this was pleasing, Jauan was unable to adequately express himself with descriptions of his status as an orphan, nor able to fully articulate what he had recently witnessed and experienced at the Fernandez plantation, and the months following. The events of Jauan's short life were inexpressible and would remain repressed within the seven-year-old as his experiences continued to evolve and unfold. Despite this emotional trapping, Jauan progressed by developing and cultivating his relationship with Private John Knight in every circumstance. Foremost, Knight ensured Jauan had enough to eat and other needs met. Haircuts and bathing in the river occurred weekly. Jauan received additional uniforms as often as Knight could find time during the coming days and weeks to serve as Jauan's personal tailor and attendant. With Roberts translating, Jauan expressed appreciation to Private Knight for his attention to a little orphan boy whose life has been shattered by tragedy. Jauan evoked emotion rarely and to little degree. With few life experiences on which to draw, emotion may have just been underplayed or unfelt by Jauan. He understood his family vanished from this earth due to epic battles between the revolutionaries and the Spanish army, while he repressed emotion. The Spanish garrisons have been replaced by a fraternity of cheerful, noble men from another country. If these soldiers accurately represent life as it is in their country of origin, young Jauan decided he wanted such an experience. That day may come. His prior life in Cuba, as Jauan had grown to know and in which he was familiar and comfortable, had been destroyed beyond comprehension. The brutal execution of his parents and other relatives, the shock of the physical damage and destruction to his plantation, the fires and the economic ruin realized, together with the scarcity of food and basic necessities of life have damaged this child physically and psychologically. What life would be like in Matanzas in the immediate future, or in times to come, could not be known. Today, Jauan is thankful his belly is full, hair trimmed, nails clipped, teeth brushed and bathes regularly. He wears a uniform of sorts and blends with Company E. He is a part of the unit; he mimics and emulates the soldiers. Jauan's life had turned in a positive direction. There is reason for Jauan's optimism as he is experiencing and benefitting from the many developing social relationships. His physical needs are met and the bleak past has been replaced by a grand adventure. Jauan was currently satisfied despite the family tragedy in the months of recent past. The days ahead can only brighten for Jauan Fernandez, as he considered, optimistically.

Deep reflection on his introduction to the 1st Texas Volunteer Infantry, although requiring detailed journalism, A.D. Knight wrote only briefly…

About this time, I noticed some soldiers in a different uniform and speaking a different language that I could not understand. The most interesting thing of all they seemed to have plenty to eat.

I followed them, they would throw me scraps and crumbs as if I were a dog at first but when they marched I marched right with them.

They soon began to notice me and try to get me to come up closer to them. I was naked they made some clothes out of worn out uniforms.

After I seen they would not hurt me and would give me something to eat even though it was strange food it satisfied my hunger. I was not afraid of them and would stay close to them all the time.

Chapter 10

As the calendar page of February turned to March, 1899, the 1st Texas Volunteer Infantry received orders returning both battalions home to the state of Texas. The men of Company E were elated with the good news. Capt. Grant Bennett, a quarter century older than the average enlisted man, addressed the troops as family. He thanked each of them for their expertise and efficiency in rebuilding the piers and docks of Port Matanzas. He also expressed gratitude that the company was transformed from a fighting unit into a humanitarian component rendering aid and assistance to the natives of Port of Matanzas. He thanked Almighty God that Company E was freed from fighting, although they were so prepared, and thanked God many lives had been spared, friend and foe alike. He announced the orders to the men. The steam transport *MICHIGAN* would arrive in Havana Harbor on 20 Mar 1899. Both battalions of troops working in Havana were ordered to load all materials, supplies, personnel and equipment onto the transport. Most horses and pack mules were to be left with the regular U.S. Army continuing the humanitarian efforts in Cuba. The transport *MICHIGAN* (later renamed the U.S.A.T. Kilpatrick) was scheduled to shove off from Port Havana on 23 Mar 1899, docking at Port Matanzas at 1100 hours that same morning. Similar loading instructions were to be carried out by both Companies E and B, with only four hours allotted to complete the Matanzas loading. Transport *MICHIGAN* was ordered to leave port setting sail on the afternoon of 23 Mar 1899 for its destination, Galveston, Texas.

The orders were given and understood by the men. The troops commenced implementation immediately.

Attired in his custom-tailored uniform, looking every bit the military soldier, Jauan stood with the assembled troops as Capt. Bennett continued with his announcement. Cheers went up. Troops became raucous. Uncontrolled and elated. Jauan, not understanding a word, joined in the exuberance but was unable to comprehend the significance of what the commanding officer just announced. Private John D. Knight, standing next to Jauan, must explain the celebration. In the large crowd of huddled men, all indistinguishable in uniform, it was nearly impossible to find a particular soldier, much less draw his attention in all the commotion. John Knight required the translation services of W.J. Roberts, Jr. from Company B. The call went out. In time, Roberts was located and made his way to Private Knight. John Knight, happy to be returning home to Texas, was distraught that his friend, Jauan Fernandez, was not a military member, nor officially affected by the orders just read by Capt. Bennett. Knight was unsure how to break the news to the seven-year-old orphan-child. Roberts was most direct in his approach.

"Let's take the boy with us. No harm in that if we can get Captain Bennett to go along with it." Private Knight was conflicted. He was unsure if Jauan desired to leave Cuba, his homeland. Roberts and Knight agreed that permission from Capt. Bennett must be secured before such news could be shared with Jauan. Company E had three weeks to prepare for the loading of materials, equipment and personnel onto the transport on 23 March. There was sufficient time to discuss Jauan's future with Capt. Bennett. Private Knight would do so at his earliest opportunity. As activity in the port area increased, Jauan recognized that something of significance had taken place. The reasons and details would eventually be explained.

Private Knight managed to get Capt. Bennett's attention after dinner the following evening. Bennett re-lit his half-smoked cigar and puffed, assuming a relaxed position in the officer's leather-backed chair. As the orange sun dropped in the background, a cloud in the curious silhouette shape of an angel positioned into a portion of the sun's periphery, perhaps a good omen. Private Knight, fearing Capt. Bennett's rejection of such an idea as preposterous, said a quiet prayer to the Lord for His favor.

"Capt. Bennett, sir, Company E has its orders to return back to Texas in a few weeks," Knight began.

"I understand the assignment. I'm the officer who just announced the order," he retorted as he chomped on the cigar butt and took a sip of cold black coffee.

"Yes sir. We have a company member with a unique status, sir, who deserves consideration," Knight continued, hands fidgeting as he delayed, attempting to gather confidence in formulating his request.

"Company E has adopted a mascot, as you are aware, sir. Jauan Fernandez is an orphan. The Cuban revolutionaries executed his parents and family. He has no one left in Cuba, has no home in Cuba and has little chance for survival in Cuba on his own. Sir, we'd like him to return to Texas with us where he will have an opportunity for a better life," Knight said convincingly.

Although he had not fully thought through a plan for Jauan's future in Texas, Knight felt strongly that Texas would be a happier place for a young child to grow, become educated and find employment as he embarks on adulthood. Private Knight, however, was simultaneously formulating his argument to challenge Capt. Bennett's rejection and denial.

"Private Knight, are you fully aware of what you are requesting?"

"Yes, sir," Knight said squarely, assuring Capt. Bennett of his position.

"Fine. I'd already been considering how to respond when asked about taking the boy with us back to Texas. Jauan Fernandez will be permitted to board the *MICHIGAN* on 23 March. This will be your sole responsibility, Private. The boy will be kept concealed as a stowaway. I want no trouble or problems. When we arrive in Galveston, he is no longer a mascot, and he is your sole responsibility. Understood?"

"Yes, sir." The angelic cloud formation was indeed prophetic of the favorable response from Capt. Bennett. Private Knight must notify Jauan of the news that Company E is leaving in just days and that Jauan has the opportunity to accompany the troops to Texas.

Roberts joined Knight and they summoned the boy. Jauan had become familiar with W.J. Roberts, Jr., as they met and conversed often. Jauan could understand Roberts in his native language lending comfort to the meetings. Knight made comments to Roberts, then Roberts translated into Spanish for Jauan's consideration. Private Knight watched Jauan's demeanor and body language as Jauan began to comprehend the circumstances and the news. In reflexive action, Jauan glanced briefly towards Knight's eyes and began running in place, taking one fast step up after the next which became uncontrolled jumping up and down. Jauan twirled on his tiptoes. The boy could not contain himself. He ran to Private Knight, hugged his legs and wept. Although he did verbalize consent to Roberts in Spanish, this act of a physical hug was the confirmation hoped for by Private Knight. Jauan would be the company mascot, boarding and sailing on the transport *MICHIGAN* commencing a new life in the United States.

The transport *MICHIGAN* docked at Port Matanzas precisely as anticipated at 1100 hours on 23 Mar 1899. Company E and B methodically and efficiently loaded their supplies, equipment and personnel aboard in one hour less than the time allotted. All building materials and foodstuff were ordered left for the use of the occupation forces of the regular U.S. Army with specific orders for distribution to the Cuban nationals. The *MICHIGAN* set sail that day in early afternoon, destination Galveston, Texas, United States of America. A blast of the steam horn and the loaded ship would be ocean bound.

A heavily used transport, *MICHIGAN,* could accommodate two battalions of the 1st Texas Volunteer Infantry. It was capable of transporting forty officers, eight hundred men and eight hundred horses sailing at eleven knots. The livestock on board were few on this voyage, Cuba to Galveston, as most U.S. horses and mules remained on the island making for a much lighter load. With a lesser cargo, the ship could make top speed easily with arrival in the Port of Galveston anticipated on the twenty-eighth or twenty-ninth day of March.

Jauan stood with Company E on the dock prepared to embark on his voyage. The *MICHIGAN* was a massive spectacle as viewed through the eyes of this nearly eight-year-old child. Its length of 370 feet and beam of forty-four feet, testified to its ability to navigate and command the seas of the Gulf of Mexico, providing smooth sailing to Galveston, despite the gulf's reputation for rough seas. Jauan stared in awe of this colossal sailing vessel. The troops of Company E were commanded to occupy the top deck in the forward section of the ship for weight and balance purposes. Such was done as ordered.

The top deck was clear and empty but for many uniformly spaced deck shackles to be used as tie downs. Encountering rough seas could be perilous, perhaps fatal. Everything must be secured in its place and tied down to avoid loss and injury. Private Knight fashioned a pallet near a coil of large diameter rope, apparently unused and not needed due to the limited livestock on board. As the troops of Company E secured themselves, they fashioned sleeping quarters on the open deck, their cots and pallets securely attached to tie-downs spaced and anchored to the wooden deck, prepared for a rough sailing. Time at sea was anticipated to be a maximum of six days. In the vicinity of Knight's pallet was a large, heavy burlap sack of undisclosed contents. Knight and his cohorts secured the sack within the confines of the rope coil. Once secured, and appropriately camouflaged, Jauan Fernandez pulled the burlap to his side, peered over the bow of the ship, and was prepared to set sail for the United States of America.

A.D. described this episode of his young life with the following entry…

When they were sent home, they kept me as a mascot of their company. On the ship coming to the U.S.A., I was so sick they cared for me all the way.

Chapter 11

Once into the open waters of the Gulf of Mexico, the transport *MICHIGAN* rolled, pitched and yawed at the mercy of random rogue swells. The 1st Texas Volunteer Infantry, although having previously sailed to Cuba from Savanah, were not considered sailors in any sense. Their usual environment of sound footing on solid ground was left back at the Port of Matanzas. They were unaccustomed to the repetitive, stomach-churning cycle of the open gulf, bearing only a hope of developing sea legs at some exacting price. Soldiers yearning for home, many still in their teen years, sought the minimal comfort of a stable platform on this ship to smooth the voyage. Seeking to escape the constant motion as tossed about on this mammoth vessel, they sought stability on the top deck, or on any deck, for relief. Flattening the roll, slowing the motion and reducing the swells were impossible. Those affected with the seasickness recalled their similar experiences during the voyage from Savannah to Havana, Cuba. However, nearly four months on dry land while in Matanzas distorted the reality of their previous encounter with the open sea. This voyage was equally as challenging, perhaps more so. Ocean bound and longing for return to their families, the troops wondered if this ship would ever reach land in Galveston. This was the prayer of these young soldiers. *MICHIGAN*, heavy in weight, built for strength and cargo, headed against torrential wind, butted the strong current and pounded against persistent waves. Nighttime sailing exacerbated the nausea as the horizon, which lent a degree of stability, was hidden in black. Eating was no longer a priority, much less a necessity to many of Company E. Vomiting, diarrhea and malaise validated those adversely affected.

Jauan Fernandez, hidden in coils of ropes, fared well during his first three days of this historic passage from the Caribbean to the United States. In the early evening of the third day at sea, just before sunset, the *MICHIGAN* appeared to be less massive than Jauan initially considered. With his head peering over the top of the burlap sack and coiled rope, he looked forward at the expansive open sea. Jauan was struck by the reality that the massive swells were manhandling this vessel. First to a portside roll, then to the starboard side in a vicious right bank. The ship's bow, lower deck and railing dove deep, plunging into the Gulf of Mexico taking on massive amounts of seawater. The weight of the heavy sea was tossed atop the Company E troops securely shackled to the top deck. The stern dropped precipitously into a hollow of vacated sea causing the bow to rise above the still lighted horizon erasing any point of reference. The ship would soon crash forward again for another refrain. This cargo vessel seemed a mere cork in an immense gulf, bandied about as if stuck in the opening of a discarded wine bottle. Jauan began sweating profusely, personal hygiene was no longer considered as the boy became nauseous and began a loose, runny stool. The boy's diarrhea continued as the mammoth ship rolled at will, controlled not by a rudder but by the rhythmic, blue-green and white surges of the gulf. Jauan began to vomit and continued until he expelled all matter of stomach contents, after which the boy continued with the dry heaves. Private John D. Knight recalled Capt. Bennett's words that he wanted no trouble, no problems.....and that the boy is Knight's responsibility. Knight continued this duty with brotherly love, tending to the immediate needs of his "responsibility," the company mascot. Knight had previously tailored additional uniforms of shirts and shorts for little Jauan. Hanging on lest he be washed overboard, John Knight removed the boy from the camouflaged pallet consisting of ropes and burlap. Knight held tightly onto the boy's arm with the assistance of Knight's Corpus Christi compadres. Jauan's privy bucket was emptied and cleaned. As vomit and body waste were removed, the putrid smell began to abate. Jauan was cleansed as best could be done on the rolling transport. The ship continued its roll and pitch unabated. A new pallet lining consisting of a thick, gray blanket emblazoned with "U.S. Army" was fashioned, and a clean bucket replaced the soiled privy bucket. Knight, fearing Jauan's dehydration, continued to force-feed sips of cool water to replace the loss of body fluids and to help stop the churn in Jauan's stomach. Jauan was washed down with sea water to remove the filth caked on his front, backside and legs. Dried down to the extent possible, Jauan was fitted into a clean uniform. Knight prepared a cool compress for the boy's forehead and held him by the arm to steady him against the ship's motion, violent at nearly all times. Jauan, unable to audibly express gratitude, looked in Knight's eyes with a mere glance of appreciation, thanking him for his concern and care as Jauan attempted to settle onto the pallet.

Jauan regained a degree of composure as he laid in the ropes. He was lightheaded and weak. Knight regularly removed and cleaned the privy bucket, brought drinking water and bathed Jauan. With little nutrition and hydration, Jauan occasionally experienced dreams and visions concerning his current passage. Was he imagining this voyage? Was this reality? Who was his traveling company? Were they his friends? His acquaintances? Or had Jauan been forcibly removed from his mansion and homeland after his family had been brutally beaten and executed? Has he been taken as prisoner to be thrown overboard in the middle of the sea? Jauan felt his chest tighten as the reality of concern of these questions surfaced. Jauan rested uncomfortably as he considered his fate with a band of foreign soldiers prepared to dump him into the Gulf of Mexico. Such fate may be better than the motion sickness with which Jauan was dealing. Jauan sought to declutter his mind, to turn off such thoughts, but he could not. He needed reassurance these soldiers meant no harm. Jauan drifted off to a quasi-sleep, as the transport continued its uncontrolled passage. The boy woke abruptly, wrapped in a burlap sack, sitting on the edge of a wooden plank extending over the ship's edge, as he peered into the watery abyss. Stricken with terror, the boy could feel his heart beating out of his chest while he screamed in panic. He was about to be delivered to the depths of the sea, to be thrown overboard. What a fate for a mere child, he realized. A burly U.S. soldier strode toward the end of the plank where the boy was holding on, squeezing the edge of the wooden plank, as his finger nails dug into the board. At this moment, Jauan prepared to face his doom at the bottom of the gulf. As he approached, the soldier grabbed the boy by his left shoulder and touched his right arm. Jauan prepared to plunge into the sea, an act of desperation and final escape. Jauan continued to scream in horror as he awoke with Private Knight sitting next to him holding his left shoulder and touching his right arm, safely tucked in his pallet in the rope coil. Jauan's life-threatening experience was a brief, mental encounter with a nightmarish ending. He was safe. Jauan felt the love, care and concern of Company E, for he was indeed their official mascot.

It was day five of the voyage, 28 Mar 1899. Jauan's seasickness had subsided to lesser extent. The violence of the sea had diminished. His diarrhea ended as Jauan was able to consume a little water and managed to ingest a piece of familiar Cuban bread. *MICHIGAN* was finally controlled by the rudder heading on due course into Galveston. Jauan had been assured by his friend, his "brother," John Knight, that all things would be right in this new world, in Texas. Jauan was persuaded in his own language, through W.J. Roberts, Jr., that he made the correct decision. He had no other option for survival but to commence his beginning in this new land with new friends. Jauan anticipated his arrival in the Port of Galveston with excitement. He envisioned disembarking the *MICHIGAN* prepared for life in Texas, with a new identity far from chaos, destruction and death in Matanzas. Jauan, feeling relieved, escaped the Spanish orphanage with its simplistic beds, rationed food and its harsh rules imposed on the orphans incarcerated in its prison-like compound. For Jauan Fernandez was born to run free, run wild. Although the priest and nuns likely meant well, Jauan managed a short stint in this orphanage. He survived this imprisonment all the while lacking love, lacking social and meaningful relationships, lacking fulfillment of his desire to love and be loved. On this date, 28 Mar 1899, Jauan reflected on his recent past and emptiness as an orphan, alone and desperate. Jauan Fernandez believed there was cause for optimism. He would arrive in Texas with his best friend, Private John D. Knight. Unlimited opportunity with the assistance and camaraderie of Company E was his. However, Jauan would soon discover he was mistaken. Disappointment would inexplicably suck the oxygen from his lungs and drain the blood from his head. Now on this direct course, the *MICHIGAN* was mere hours from docking at Galveston, Texas.

* * *

As the Texas shoreline and the Port of Galveston came into view from the deck of the *MICHIGAN*, the troops gathered at the ship's forward rail cheering in thanksgiving they had returned safely home, having been sent to a far-off land for combat on foreign soil. Private Knight and Roberts found Jauan indicating they needed to speak. Somewhat apprehensive, Jauan assumed they were to give him instructions on disembarking from the *MICHIGAN* once securely docked. This indeed was the topic of discussion, but it was not all. His "brother," his best friend, his mentor, his father-figure, Private John D. Knight, seemed to have struck Jauan in his stomach with a ball bat to elicit his reaction. Jauan could barely breathe, he dropped to his knees as he became light headed, feeling he was about to lose consciousness. Private Knight explained he had chosen to join Company B, no longer a volunteer unit, as Knight left the 1st Texas Volunteer Infantry and transferred into the regular U.S. Army. Knight would leave for Austin, Texas as soon as disembarking the *MICHIGAN*. Knight had his duffel, rifle and a black leather bag at his side. Knight spoke. Roberts translated. Jauan listened. Jauan heard only half and believed even less of what was being translated. Jauan's life in America would be absent the father-figure with whom he had grown accustomed and learned to trust for the better part of four months. The man to whom Jauan looked up, the man who cared for the child-orphan, this man, Private John D. Knight, would vanish, no longer a fixture in Jauan's young life. As his last act of kindness to Jauan, Private Knight gave him his black leather satchel containing one uniform hand-tailored by Knight. The black satchel had two leather straps fastened to both ends of the bag, with three long leather cords securing the satchel closed. Jauan opened the satchel and peered inside; he inspected the one uniform, unworn and made ready for Jauan's use. Reaching into his left breast pocket, Private John Knight retrieved his King James version pocket Bible inscribed on the inside page simply with the name "Knight." Knight gave the Bible to Jauan and motioned it was his to have and keep. Jauan obliged tucking the pocket Bible in the black satchel together with his uniform. Such were memories of a short, but meaningful relationship that would have a long-lasting effect on this orphan, now nearly eight years of age. Jauan understood Knight's decision to join the regular army, but he could not comprehend the destruction being levied by the unforeseen, unfortunate ending of their relationship. Jauan was unable to cope with this reality; he was devastated. The optimism he previously enjoyed was ripped from his chest; his stomach churned with anxiety. Jauan was engulfed with apprehension and gripped by fear of the unknown as John D. Knight hugged Jauan Fernandez one last time. Knight turned and quickly climbed down the ladder to the lower decks, prepared to disembark. Jauan was left alone, abandoned by his "friend."

Chapter 12

A.D. Knight, cognizant of the lump in his throat, with chin and lower lip quivering, stopped writing and laid his pen next to the tablet. He instinctively removed his wire-rimmed spectacles and wiped the tears streaming from both eyes with the right sleeve of his white dress shirt. A.D. was powerless to avert this unplanned lament. Spontaneous shedding of tears turned into uncontrolled weeping; A.D. was overwhelmed with grief from three decades past. Reliving the tragic loss of his family members and the disappearance of his friend, mentor, brother and father-figure initiated this compelling reaction. No one was present to observe his display of emotion. No one was present with whom to share his misery, nor was anyone present to console and comfort him during his time of need. He absorbed the moment in solitaire, alone in spirit.

After regaining his composure, calming himself as tears dried, Knight respectfully reached into the black, leather satchel with his left hand. He retrieved the worn King James pocket Bible given to him thirty years ago, reflecting as he sat motionless in the library. With feet centered directly in front of the oak chair, Knight sat erect at reverent attention. He stroked the inside page adjacent to the cover of the Bible with his right index finger. He reflected on the name "Knight" inscribed on that first page. A.D. held his finger on "Knight" and pulled the Bible close to his heart. He felt and embraced the sense of camaraderie he had developed and shared with Private Knight. A red, cloth bookmark had been intentionally positioned in the Bible by Private Knight. The red cloth marker was permitted to remain at that precise page for the last thirty years, undisturbed at Psalm 100. It would not be moved. A.D. read in silence.

"Psalm100. Make a joyful noise unto the Lord, all ye lands.[2] Serve the Lord with gladness: come before his presence with singing.[3] Know ye that the Lord he is God: it is he that hath made us, and not we ourselves; we are his people, and the sheep of his pasture.[4] Enter into his gates with thanksgiving, and into his courts with praise: be thankful unto him, and bless his name.[5] For the Lord is good; his mercy is everlasting; and his truth endureth to all generations."

Thirty years ago, as a young boy, Jauan could not read or understand this passage from Psalms, nor did he then possess sufficient literacy of English words, as they were comprised of unrecognizable characters in a language foreign to the orphan. Whether these printed words could offer any condolence or relief to Jauan may be considered, but not then; perhaps one day, perhaps this day. Jauan only knew this pocket Bible was once owned and cherished by his "brother," John D. Knight. This Holy Bible was given to Jauan on the last day they would see each other. Private John D. Knight vanished almost as quickly as he entered Jauan's life years ago. Just as Jauan's family members had been taken from him in an instant of brutality, John D. Knight quickly disappeared from view into a disembarking crowd of indistinguishable uniforms, leaving immense void in the depths of Jauan's being. At the time, Jauan struggled to justify Knight's departure. He could not.

* * *

The *MICHIGAN* was securely tied to the dock at the Port of Galveston. Fore and aft supporting gang planks were lowered and fit into stable portside position spanning the short distance from ship to dock. Immediately, on verbal command of the officer in charge, disembarkation commenced with Company B regular army leading the way. Private John D. Knight blended with the other troops from the Company as they assembled in formation and marched three blocks to the rail station. They boarded the train starting with the passenger car coupled directly behind the idling steam locomotive. The train was due to depart Galveston in a matter of minutes heading to Austin, Texas. Knight did not, or could not, look back at the top deck of the *MICHIGAN*, nor did he make the faintest attempt to identify young Jauan Fernandez peering over the ship's forward rail, straining for his last glimpse of John Knight. Before Jauan could disembark down the forward gang plank, Private Knight was already situated in a passenger rail car and on his way to Austin. Their "goodbyes" had already been exchanged, however imperfectly. W.J. Roberts, Jr. explained to Jauan he was taking him home to San Antonio, a long journey, but he would be welcomed. As they disembarked the *MICHIGAN* down the solid wooden plank, the fore gang plank, Jauan heard three blasts of the locomotive's whistle as it announced its departure. Private John Knight was boarded, headed for Austin. The whistle blasts caught Jauan by surprise; they verified John Knight's transformation to regular army and express departure from Galveston to his Austin, Texas destination. Jauan's eyes, again, welled with tears which released spontaneously running down both cheeks, flowing into the corners of his mouth. His mentor, united in Matanzas, Cuba, was now gone from Jauan's life. Vanished. Incomprehensible.

* * *

W.J. Roberts, Jr. and Jauan waited patiently at the station, sitting on a dirty, uncomfortable, well-worn, wooden bench, prepared to board the San Antonio Express Line. The Galveston rail station waiting area had become a refuse for discarded newspapers and magazines, half-smoked and chewed cigar butts, beer and wine bottles, discarded food wrappings and other unsanitary debris, inhabited by the loitering unfortunates. Despite the central rail station's plea and policy to refrain from loitering and littering, passengers and passers-by simply didn't comply. Arrival in San Antonio would take less than a day. Although apprehensive, Jauan's ability to converse in Spanish with Roberts was reassuring. Certainly not the beginning Jauan had envisioned, but a new beginning, nonetheless. While heading to San Antonio by rail, Jauan presumed they would encounter no revolutionaries, no fighting, no detonations, no screams of terror. Mechanical rhythm of the engine, combined with repetitious noises of metal wheels riding the rails toward San Antonio became sleep-inducing. Jauan slept soundly for three hours, absent the rolling waves of the Gulf of Mexico, as the passenger car tracked the rails anchored to solid Texas soil.

Jauan woke from his sleep observing the passengers seated in his vicinity. All manner of businessmen were dressed in suits and fancy ties made of the finest materials. Their shoes were exquisite, black and shiny, elegant. Passengers, likely seasoned riders, wrote in journals, read newspapers, drank strong coffee and smoked cigars. Many conversed as old friends, neighbors or business associates and colleagues. The vagrants and loiterers present at the Galveston station were apparently not bona fide passengers. Merely destitute persons looking for a place to loiter, sleep and simultaneously litter. This train ride was peaceful and uneventful. Jauan reflected on his Cuban home and blood-soaked soil, now merely one week removed from the only home he had known. The nucleus of his family was ripped from him in barbaric fashion, yet there was nothing he could do to change the traumatic events. He thought of his parents, sister and niece, now all in a better place. Jauan was drawn to thought about commencing another life in San Antonio. He could only place his trust in W.J. Roberts, Jr. and hoped W.J. would give him insight into the life he should anticipate.

Jauan looked at his worn sandals, Spanish-made of quality, natural brown leather. They wore well and withstood a year on the run as an orphan. Jauan asked W.J. if there might be an opportunity to purchase a new pair of sandals to go with his fresh start in his new home. Indeed there would be, as W.J. had planned. At the moment, W.J. considered himself a blest man, having received a considerable sum of "muster out" pay onboard the *MICHIGAN*.

W.J. and Jauan will shop for shoes and clothes in San Antonio before their arrival at the Roberts farm.

When the two "soldiers" arrived at the central rail station in San Antonio, they looked for a diner and general store. Food and clothing were on both their minds. As they meandered down the city streets, they avoided the horse and buggy traffic. Jauan marveled at the organization and sophistication of this large, modern metropolitan city with amenities and congestion combined. After a breakfast-style meal of bacon, eggs, grits and biscuit, W.J. escorted Jauan to the general store conveniently located next to the diner. Jauan appreciated the aroma of newly-tanned leather shoes, polished, waxed and buffed for protection. The scent was exquisite; leather shoes exuding newness. Jauan tried on two pairs of replacement sandals. The second pair fit comfortably, made of soft, brown leather with substantial soles. W.J., knowing what type of farm work Jauan could anticipate, also recommended a pair of half-boots, which could be worn in the fields, barns and to school, and church if thoroughly cleaned the night before. Jauan's foot fit comfortably within the shoe, with a little room to spare for projected growth. Purchase of the sandals and boots was accompanied by underclothes, socks, two shirts and trousers. W.J. found similar clothing for himself as "civies" replacing the 1st Texas Volunteer Infantry uniforms. The boy put his purchases in his black leather satchel along with his unworn, tailored "uniform" and pocket Bible. The satchel began to accumulate significant weight for the soon-to-be eight-year-old; hopefully this pedestrian journey will terminate at their intended destination soon. He wore his sister's gold locket around his neck. As they ambled further down the street, Jauan gushed a fountain of questions partly in Spanish, partly in broken English.

"Where are we heading?"

"Where will we be living?"

"How far must we walk?"

"Do you have brothers living there?"

"Will there be plenty of food there?"

"Who lives there?"

"Does anyone else speak Spanish?"

"Will I have more clothes to fit me?"

"Will I have a place to sleep?"

"Will I be able to bathe and wash?"

W.J. Roberts, Jr. assured him that Ma and Pa Roberts would provide for Jauan, along with the ten brothers, all older than Jauan. Roberts explained he happened upon Jauan's married sister, Isabella, weeks ago. She disclosed Jauan's legal name and age and a little information concerning the boy's background. "He is a runner, runs free, runs wild," Isabella stated. After walking for some distance, W.J. flagged down a horse and buggy for hire indicating they were still quite a distance from W.J.'s home. The Roberts farm was beyond San Antonio's north edge; a considerable distance to walk from the central train station.

Mr. and Mrs. Roberts immediately accepted Jauan on Ma's insistence. They named him and began calling him "Jim Roberts." In Jauan's Spanish comprehension, he believed they were calling him *Jim Rofarts.* It was of no real consequence. A name was just a name. Jauan understood his place in the household hierarchy of ten boys, now eleven. Jauan would have his eighth birthday in a few days and believed he could adapt to any environment, especially with matronly Ma Roberts capable of running the household, assisting with chores and livestock and keeping all those boys in line. Ma displayed her softer side to Jauan. She cared for the Spanish boy as if he were one of her own. Although Jauan believed he could fend for himself, based on the independence he developed in Cuba after his parents were executed, Ma Roberts took on the role of mother and protector. She saw to it that Jauan's cot in his sleeping area under their home's main stairwell was fitted with an extra blanket each evening. During meal times, whenever the family could gather together for a communal meal, Ma Roberts included Jauan in the conversation around the dinner table. The older boys snickered, laughed, made faces and obscene gestures at Jauan when Ma was distracted or not looking. Ma saw to it that Jauan had an additional biscuit and slice of bacon at breakfast and made sure Jauan had a second helping of the main dish each suppertime. She recognized Jauan's nutrition had been compromised over some length of time, as she would later confirm. An eight-year-old required a full belly as he began to mature. Ma would do her best to see that Jauan had plenty nutritious meals.

At least three times a week, along with everything else she had to do around the farm, Ma insisted Jauan get out his black satchel. She pulled out the King James Bible and opened the Scriptures to a meaningful verse or chapter and read to Jauan aloud, helping him follow along with the word sounds, vowels and consonants, and, most importantly, the meaning of the verse or chapter. She also spoke the Spanish language and assisted Jauan in his understanding. Ma preferred conversing in English and hoped that Jauan learned to speak fluently and write English flawlessly. Ma was a warm, kind and loving individual, doting on Jauan at her every opportunity, yet with a sad expression on her face. Yet she was enamored with young Jauan as they developed a close mother-son relationship. The older boys were jealous. They piled on direct, merciless abuse of Jauan outside of Ma's presence and made snide remarks, in absolute derogation, when they were in a family setting. The siblings' verbal attacks against Jauan were pointed and intentional. He was unable to fully comprehend Ma's care and concern for him although he enjoyed it. Jauan knew Ma cared for him, perhaps loved him in a sense, yet the reason Ma displayed such love was not understood. From the outset, Jauan recognized he was an outsider; Pa made this clear by expressing contempt for bringing another mouth to feed into the family. Perhaps Jauan was incapable of understanding the meaning of love, but he did appreciate the benefits of Ma's attention to him. Once again, as if living at the owners' mansion, Jauan felt secure in this environment. Unfortunately, Ma's protection was limited and, at times, unavailable.

Despite being the youngest resident in the Roberts household, Jauan was required to work in the fields, barns and animal sheds tending crop and raising livestock. Even as an eight-year-old, Jauan's experience with Marco's livestock gave him familiarity with minimal experience. Pa Roberts was a rough man whose demeanor was inherited by the ten boys he brought into this world. Pa had little patience with the boys in completing physical tasks and had even less patience with Ma when she mentioned the necessity of formal education. The older boys had scant schooling. It would be different for Jauan, Ma decided. Pa's sons were rough mountain-type men, managing a living by back-breaking work growing crops and raising livestock. Pa was strong and would frequently demonstrate his physical dominance over the uppity older boys who believed it was time to challenge the old man for leadership. Jauan observed such battles. The young bucks stood in line to challenge Pa. They were routinely defeated as Pa held his rightful place as patriarch of the family. It was in this environment that young Jauan perfected his combative ways and skills and stood nose to nose with the older boys; he would not be intimidated. As Jauan matured, he increased in strength and masculinity. Jauan feared no one, even at his young age. This attribute, while advantageous, may not bode well in all situations. Jauan learned to fight with the older boys, using his agility and wiry strength to his advantage. He learned how to quickly disable and inflict pain on a larger, older boy, thereby subduing him decisively in short order. Continuous fighting and confronting the older boys gave Pa a sense of pride in the little Spanish kid from Cuba, although Pa was disappointed the older boys could barely hold their own against the baby of the family. On occasion, two or more of the boys would join forces to teach Jauan a lesson. The older ones attacked the younger Jauan, taking unfair advantage of their size, strength and number. Jauan suffered often but would not let the older boys know he was hurt. He willingly fought them again. An older sibling, Tom, routinely stuck up for Jauan and fought the two or more offenders as Jauan watched from a close distance. The Roberts boys were, in all respects, an unruly bunch with a notorious reputation that any outsider must take on the entire family if he intended to take on one member. As a consequence, the physical disputes which took place with the Roberts boys were routinely in-fighting among siblings. The outsiders decided they were disadvantaged when coming to challenge a Roberts boy, when in reality it was challenging the entire family.

Ma enrolled him in school with the intent Jauan would be formally educated and learn to properly communicate in the English language. A young Spanish boy from Cuba needed much to get on his feet, to become independent in a new land. Ma would see to it that Jauan had all the tools necessary.

On one routine weekday, W.J. Roberts, Jr. disappeared. With no notice, he left the Roberts farm never to be seen again. W.J. Roberts, Jr. was gone; he left within six months of their arrival. However, within those six months, he did spend time assisting Jauan and tutoring him in the English language. W.J. took no time to say goodbye… to anyone. He merely left a simple note to the family declaring, "I cannot live here any longer," and with that he vanished, just as Private Knight took to another direction. The nine remaining siblings had little tolerance for Jauan, except Tom. Unlike the others, Tom exhibited a degree of maturity and civility. He looked after Jauan in W.J.'s absence, sensing Jauan's needs and assisting Ma in her self-imposed obligation for the Spanish boy.

Ma Roberts accepted Jauan into her home graciously, warmly and with sympathy, not as one of her own, but still at a deep level, as a disadvantaged orphan detecting Jauan had been permanently damaged. Ma imagined, and eventually learned, Jauan had been tormented by all manner of atrocities in Cuba. To what Jauan had been exposed over the last year resulted in the boy's permanent scarring. His inability to comprehend the resulting demise of family within his short life was tragic. Ma Roberts learned much of Jauan's experiences during her brief discussions with the child as he studied and conversed with Ma in English. Ma Roberts appeared to be an elderly lady in her sixties due to a harsh, cruel life. The ten boys she birthed were raised to be rugged men who found farm life a bit too civilized. They looked forward to primitive living in the mountains. The youngest of the remaining Roberts boys, Daniel, was several years older than Jauan. As a smallish eight-year-old, Jauan was routinely bullied and physically abused by the older boys, experiencing their contempt and hatred. Following Private

Knight's transfer into the regular U.S. Army, Jauan's loneliness was further compounded by W.J.'s unannounced disappearance. Jauan's mentor, Private John D. Knight, was never to be seen again despite Jauan's expectation and optimism that they would eventually reunite somehow. Somewhere. Sometime.

W.J.'s disappearance was a psychological blow to Jauan's ability to socialize and fraternize with "brothers," and with others. W.J. vanished suddenly just as did John D. Knight; the marked difference was that Jauan felt the love of John D. Knight as a caring person, emoting unconditional love which gave Jauan a sense of peace. Despite John Knight's departure, Jauan kept that sense of peace deep within. W.J.'s care for Jauan seemed to be of a perfunctory nature, as if Roberts was being duly compensated for monitoring and supervising Jauan for a brief, predetermined period. Jauan concluded W.J. had completed his obligation to Private Knight and must move on. Tom took on a protective role of Jauan, standing up for Jauan against any duo of brothers intent on abusing the young boy just for the sport. Jauan was appreciative of Tom and regarded him as friend and guardian. On a chilly winter morning, Tom was found lying dead in an outlying pasture up the side of a mountain from exposure. The Roberts family took things in stride contending that Tom did not take care of himself and let the diseases get hold of him. Tom's premature demise was not unexpected and simply accepted by the Roberts boys. Ma and Pa grieved. Jauan was devastated. Another "brother" was inexplicably taken from him. No opportunity to say goodbye, no final words.

The Roberts' large white, two-story frame farmhouse was situated on acreage reminiscent of Cuban plantations. Sugar cane and tobacco crops were replaced by stalks of green corn, yellow fields of hay and a multitude of Texas Longhorn cattle grazing in lush pastures. Pa Roberts' contempt for Jauan did not diminish, yet he recognized Jauan's work ethic as superior to his own sons, older sons. Jauan recognized that Pa had little reason to acknowledge and accept Jauan as a member of the Roberts family. Jauan continued to develop his skills as a farm hand and a cattle rancher by doing and working the Roberts farm and for neighboring farmers, raising all types of livestock, including the Longhorns.

The in-fighting continued between the older boys as he increased in stature, strength and weight. Jauan was fearless in his fight with the siblings. On occasion, Jauan instigated and antagonized the older boys as if this combat was a progression in a rite of initiation. Jauan could not contain himself as he brazenly left a sibling battle victorious, with his head held high and shaking his fist daring or demanding a second skirmish. The fights became less frequent as Jauan grew stronger, more aggressive and the older boys approached manhood, capable of inflicting all manner of injuries on each other, some quite severe.

Ma Roberts continued in her maternal role doting on Jauan, emphasizing nutritious meals of farm grown meat, potatoes and vegetables. Over the years, Ma had retained the best of the hand-me-down clothing from the ten boys as they got older and outgrew sizes. Why she kept the best of the smaller sized clothing could not be explained. Perhaps it was a premonition, an unexplained sense that decent quality clothing should be kept for future purposes. Jauan was the end recipient and regaled himself in fine farm clothing, including footwear, for the time he lived with the Roberts family. On one hand, Ma welcomed him and made Jauan feel at home as one of the family. On the other hand, Pa's snide remarks, made with insensitivity, along with the older boys' abusive attacks, left Jauan feeling the outcast, a black sheep with little to look forward to other than a weekly fight with an older, stronger opponent. It was due to Ma's kindness that Jauan managed to forge his way upward in the Roberts family. He was indebted to Ma for all she had done for him, although Jauan often thought he would have fared much better in a smaller household or in a more favorable orphanage with fewer children. Things may have been different for Jauan coming up; perhaps he would have been offered more, entitled to more. Such dreaming was mere fantasy. Jauan's formal education progressed as Ma anticipated. He was much more mature and responsible than any of Pa's sons. Over time, Jauan considered himself one of the Roberts family, although he did not identify with the Roberts surname, nor was he fond of the name, Jim. Jauan's contentment and relative security with the Roberts family, however, would soon be in jeopardy.

* * *

A.D.'s recollection of these horrific past events gave him pause, as he sat tormented with unspeakable grief. A.D. inhaled deeply to calm his racing heart and clear his head. He shook his right hand vigorously to restore circulation. The cramping in his scarred left hand impaired his ability to steady the tablet as he wrote. Unaccustomed to writing lengthy documents, A.D.'s right hand, which had tightened and cramped, began to relax as he peered through the west window of the library at the array of colors in his botanical garden. Resting his right hand on his lap for a moment provided the necessary relief to restore control of the ink pen and tablet. A.D. described in prose his journey of words with acute accuracy...

When we landed, one of the boys by the name of Rofarts taken me home to his mother. A kind sad faced woman with 10 children of her own but room in her heart for a little orphan boy.

The soldier boy had seen my sister and gotten my name and age but they gave me this name and I was soon called Jim Roffarts. And let me say right here, mother, as I learned to call this kind old woman love me or ? vicied ? me which is the same and done all she could for me but she could not do much.

And Pa would not do anything and would not give me the chance he gave the others. The love that poor old ma and the boy brought that brought me home with him gave me was all the love I knew in my boyhood.

And the boy Tom, I will call him soon died of exposure in the rough mountain country, folks did,

When he died I was broken hearted I had no one left to take my part in that rough family of boys all older than I.

I came to depend on fighting my way and what little attention ma gave me made me worship her. I went to school when Pa would let me.
Learning the English language as well as read write and Arithmetic.

I have come to think they would have been kinder to me had they sent me to an orphans home or gave me to someone with fewer children of their own that I might have gotten more.

More education and better home training.

Chapter 13

Although she aged to a saddened face, Ma's blue eyes sparkled when she spoke of her "little boy" she named Jim. Her eyes expressed gratitude as she thanked the Lord for the orphan child placed in her care. This blessing was God's answer to continued prayer. Ma Roberts assumed the responsibility as Jauan's mother, aware of his material needs from experience, anticipating his emotional needs from intuition. Fading vigor, accompanied by middle-aged, adult stress over years, fashioned coarse furrows around and to the edges of her eyes, enhancing the drooped corners of her thin-lipped mouth. Ma's exposed skin was tanned as leather from exposure to the elements working daily in crops and livestock. She applied facial makeup only once or twice as Jauan could remember. She brushed her face with light powder causing her skin to luminate as it contrasted with the dark hue of her hands and arms. Ma's painted, pale facial complexion offset her usual sad expression. A touch of rouge on her cheeks and a line of red lip color applied to upper and lower lips gave Ma the appearance of comfort and sophistication. Ma's life at age sixty-something was purposeful again; she possessed drive and perseverance, with highest priority given to her boy. Jauan looked beyond Ma's saddened face as he dwelt on her inner beauty and genuine happiness. Despite his study and appreciation for her, Jauan sensed an inexplicable disturbance within Ma Roberts which was not objectively defined. Yet it was readily apparent, at least to Jauan. There was something foreboding ahead.

Ma and Pa Roberts and their eight rough-neck, wild-mountain sons packed necessities and left Texas, charging "Jim Roberts," then nearly fifteen years old, with the responsibility of overseeing the San Antonio farm, raising cattle and harvesting crops. Pa was not concerned in the least about Jauan's ability and responsibility for the Roberts farm. Jauan had demonstrated his talent and skill in all aspects on the ranch. The Roberts family left San Antonio for some reason, unknown to Jauan, relocating to the southern outskirts of Oklahoma City. Pa placed the San Antonio farm on the market for sale with no set timetable or need for a particular sale date. Possession of the Roberts farm would be conveyed when sold to the new owner, and when Jauan was notified the Oklahoma City farm was prepared to receive Jauan's herd. His livestock consisted of 127 head of Longhorn cattle, four horses, one rooster and twenty-three laying hens. Jauan would ship his Longhorn cattle and one horse by rail to Oklahoma City leaving the remaining livestock with the new owner.

Although Jauan ended his formal education at age sixteen, he was fully accomplished in farming, cattle ranching and raising livestock of all kinds. His herd of Longhorns would provide a fair living for himself, but his goal was to develop his cattle raising business into a large industrious enterprise. At nearly seventeen-years-old, Jauan received a telegram from Pa that the Oklahoma farm was ready to accommodate his 127 head of Longhorn cattle. The herd had now increased to 154 head while Ma and Pa and the boys were in Oklahoma City preparing their new farm as a cattle ranch.

The telegram Jauan received from Pa was brief, direct and troubling:

"Ship cattle now. STOP. Farm is ready. STOP. Ma was bad sick a few months back. STOP, STOP."

Jauan made arrangements with the rail station to ship one horse and his cattle to Oklahoma City, signing a bailment contract that was not of insignificant expense. With the assistance of neighbors, Jauan drove his herd to the loading station in San Antonio for shipment. All cattle survived the four-mile uneventful, open-range drive. Once the herd filled the cattle cars, Jauan purchased a one-way passenger rail ticket for Oklahoma City. Pa and several of the sons met the herd at the Oklahoma Stockyard unloading station and drove them to the new farm south of town. As they approached the farm, the double gates to the largest pasture were fully open to receive Jauan's Longhorns. With the cattle watered and secured, Jauan bolted for the farmhouse to greet Ma Roberts. He anticipated a grand reunion with Ma. He had not seen her in the better part of two years, fondly recalling her sparkling eyes, kindly mannerisms and genuine care for a child who was not of her own. This reunion would occur in mere moments. As Jauan entered through the front doorway of the main house, he called out expecting Ma to be near the entryway anticipating his arrival. She was not. Jauan called again as he searched the lower level of the house. To his dismay, still no response. He walked out to the front porch and inquired of Pa and the boys, "Where's Ma?" Pa replied definitively, "She's in the backyard," as each of the older boys silently scattered at the job's completion. Jauan met Pa at a small fenced-in grassy area at the back of the house. Evincing not the slightest despair, Pa wiped his hands on his trousers and told Jauan that Ma died merely two days into her episode of bad health months ago. The family buried her the day after she died, on a rainy Wednesday afternoon. Jauan was in shock as he fell to the grass on both knees. He peered through the openings in the white picket fence and focused on the wooden cross and a small, flat gray stone marking Ma's burial place. He could not comprehend this reality; a surreal wave enveloped Jauan as he continued to kneel in reverence to Ma Roberts. He didn't know whether to exalt Ma for who she was and what she had done for her youngest boy or lash out at Pa for being the insensitive brute he was. Jauan could not collect his thoughts under these circumstances. His heart had once again been ripped from his chest, as he felt the grip of near unconsciousness. At that moment, Pa spoke up and told Jauan that Ma called for her "little boy" with her last breath. This statement was of little comfort. Jauan was distraught and could not comprehend what he had just learned during the last two minutes.

Pa was stoic in his recitation of facts concerning Ma's death. Jauan wailed like a three-year-old in shock and grief at the loss of the "mother" he had grown to know and love. Pa explained that Ma got "bad sick" and just could not recover. "She died peacefully." Pa spoke with no emotion, with no acknowledgement or consideration of empathy for Jauan in his loss.

At the age of seventeen years, as best he was able, Jauan mentally processed the deaths and disappearances of close family over the last ten years. Kneeling in the dry grass peering through the fence, heaving and in near convulsions, sobbing at the foot of Ma Roberts' grave site, Jauan experienced reality, the finality of death once again. The abrupt disappearance of two brother-figures was shocking, as if the absent W.J. had died just the same as brother Tom. The loss of Ma Roberts was incomprehensible. However, just as with the others, Jauan was denied the opportunity to speak his piece prior to Ma's departure.

Now, the shocking, unexpected death of this kind old woman left Jauan alone once more, as in the past. His heart ached. Juan lay in the back yard trying to make sense of tragedy. He could not do so. Jauan's last friend was taken from him with not so much as a goodbye or an apology from anyone. Jauan's youth was filled with sorrow. It seems happiness for Jauan Fernandez will be denied with the Roberts family. Grief and despair had been his constant companions for nearly a decade.

* * *

A.D. collected his thoughts concerning this recent reflection on Ma Roberts, picked up his pen and spilled his heart out on the next blank page of his tablet...

When I was about 14 years old Pa moved to another state and was moving back again. Ma was in bad health, I was left with some stock and while I was taking care of the stock and getting it shipped.

Ma died they did not let me know of her death until after she was buried when I arrived with the stock. But I was told she called for her little boy (she always called me that) before she died.

I was left alone with another grief. Death had taken the last friend and loved one. It seemed my childhood was nothing but sorrow.

Chapter 14

After Ma's burial, Pa Roberts continued in his belligerent ways, harsh and contrary to those with whom he conducted business, offensive to his neighbors, antagonistic to the sons he raised, uncooperative to those he met. Pa was a selfish, hard man with a bitter disposition. He remained unchanged over his lifetime. The rumor was that Pa beat a man half to death for cheating him out of the money he paid for a horse which he later discovered was injured and became lame. With mercy, he shot and killed the horse and went after his money. He appeared unaffected by Ma's death, and now, unaffected by her absence. Outwardly for Pa, it was business as usual. He conversed with few people outside of his clan. His inner thoughts, even if formulated, remained silent, shared with no one. An emotionless man, he expressed himself only rarely, but then only in dark, angry terms. Perhaps his dreams of life as a youth remained unfulfilled. Worse yet, perhaps he had no dreams, no goals and little aspiration. As each of the eight remaining sons came of age, they left the Roberts farm choosing to take wives of their own, escaping the dictates of Pa Roberts. While the sons knew little more than growing crop and raising cattle, they fled the domination of an irrational and angry father. Ironically, they had no desire to venture too far from Pa Roberts' farm. The sons and their wives bought and leased acreage nearby Pa's ranch for their own operations, and security.

Jauan, anticipating no assistance from Pa, continued to raise his cattle on the Roberts' farm. Jauan gazed out as far as he could see over the vast pasture land. He would become a cattle baron someday, he predicted, with so many Longhorns one could scarcely count his herd, raising the purest breed of cattle in all of Oklahoma. Unfortunately, Jauan's eight "brothers" remained jealous and intolerant of his success. They never accepted him as family. Upon Jauan's surprise arrival with W.J., Jr. from the infantry, Jauan was immediately branded an outcast, an outsider, taken in by charitable Ma who has passed from this life into death. Ma's desire to love and raise Jauan as her own was now of no account; an earthly dream that ended her time on this planet. Despite their jealous contempt for Jauan, each of the boys sought his skills and labor on their respective farms. Compensation for Jauan was an occasional home-cooked meal, a place to sleep overnight accompanied by the foulest of language and derogatory ridicule. To Jauan, this was reminiscent of the mulatto and slaves on the sugar cane plantations in Matanzas, occupying subhuman slave quarters and given meager provisions which could not sustain life.

"Jim Roberts," as Jauan Fernandez was dubbed, built his reputation in the area of south Oklahoma City as an experienced farmer with natural talent, with accomplished skills raising crop and livestock. Neighboring farmers and ranchers, impressed with his abilities, sought out his services. Pay was handsome compared to what Pa and his sons offered. Jauan's work in the locale necessarily made him unavailable to the Roberts clan, as he planned. Soon, Jauan accumulated sizeable earnings. He was able to regularly purchase new boots and additional work clothes and, on occasion, a long-sleeved buttoned shirt with a pocket on the left chest and trousers fine enough to wear to Sunday school and church, if he was so inclined. Jauan, as an independent farmer in his own right, made progress and profit. He was given no advice, support or encouragement since Ma Roberts' passing. However, the Roberts bunch went out of its way to unjustly demean and ridicule Jauan for his accomplishments. They were offended by Jauan's apparent success and renowned reputation. Collectively, the Roberts boys intended to cause Jauan grave economic harm, while insulting him directly to his face. The Roberts boys, exhibiting unparalleled immaturity, would soon exact their economic fees from Ma's favorite boy.

Jauan Fernandez never grew accustomed to it, nor was he fond of the name Ma and Pa chose for him, Jim Roberts, a/k/a *Jim Roffarts.* While developing his reputation as a farmer and a cattle rancher, Jauan distanced himself from the existing Roberts family. They were of little benefit to him. The notoriety associated with the Roberts clan was a burden that must be alleviated.

The orphan born in Cuba, fending for himself during the Spanish-American War, owed his new life to his "true" brother, his mentor, Private John D. Knight. This orphan would often caress the black leather satchel during times of distress and trouble. The connection he had with John D. Knight was life altering. In furtherance of his separation from the Roberts family name and to continue in his new beginning at age nineteen, Jauan informally adopted his new name, "Andrew Danos Knight." He would, henceforth, be identified as Knight and known by the name "Danos" or "A.D. Knight" for all purposes in honor of his brother, Private John Knight. A.D. "Danos" Knight, newly invigorated and liberated, had made this monumental election for this practical name change. Jauan's mental stature was emboldened by his new name. He spoke with clarity and reassurance when dealing in business affairs. The name "Danos" rolled off his tongue as if the ever-present spirit of John D. Knight anointed him. It was a momentous day, a day of utmost significance and import.

Within the next year, turning age twenty, the long-range plan Danos envisioned required additional working capital. He labored tirelessly acquiring significant wealth sufficient to rent forty acres of farm land. Danos purchased two teams of American Cream work horses, specifically bred for planting, hauling and harvesting. With a soft, cream-colored coat, the American Cream horses were hard working and mild-mannered. Purchasing such teams epitomized Danos' challenge and confidence in farming, profitability and success. A.D. also purchased necessary tools and used farm equipment from his neighbors. Soon, he hoped, he would have enough land rented to accommodate his herd of Longhorns.

Danos remained productive and gained financial independence. Economically, he did not falter, but was unable to heal from the twelve years' experience of death, destruction and distress. His emotional scars remained intact.

Over time, Danos made the acquaintance and developed a friendship with two neighbor boys in Oklahoma City, Tom and Arthur Blackstone. The boys were one year apart in age but looked so alike they were often mistaken for twins with dark brown hair, purposely cut short, and brown eyes. Exhibiting fraternity, both spoke with a noticeable lisp when they said any word beginning with or including an "s." Beefy boys, they were large enough to intimidate any foe by squinting an eye and nodding their heads. So it was with the Roberts boys; they kept their distance from Danos for the most part. Danos and the Blackstone brothers became quite good friends and neighbors, assisting one another planting and harvesting crops, tending to the cattle. Work days often turned into evenings of rabble rousing as the Blackstone brothers had invited rather crude acquaintances of their own. After any given work-day or on a weekend, two chicken thieves would join the boys. Two of Arthur Blackstone's third grade classmates, having minimal formal education, learned through worldly experience that possession was nine-tenths of the law. They frequently pilfered chickens from a nearby brooder farm for their contribution to a neighborhood chicken fry. The few stolen chickens would not be missed from the large flock and would not be heard as the classmates rung the necks of the fowl as they ran through the fields. The remaining chickens, having escaped capture at the henhouse, sounded their thief alarms. But the wild squawking signaling thievery went entirely unnoticed. Arthur Blackstone's classmates easily provided two or three or more recalcitrant victims from the neighboring brooder house without leaving a shred of evidence.

As Danos soaked work clothes in a metal tub of soap and hot water, the Blackstone brothers obliged the Wednesday work-day by soaking and rubbing their pants and shirts on the ribbed washboard with the sufficient force to scour out the dirt and rinse the soap from their clothing. Wednesday became a regular washday which routinely developed into an "impromptu" chicken-fry social event.

Although A.D. believed this episode to be somewhat frivolous, he entered it into his memorandum for completeness and accuracy…

Until I was eighteen or nineteen years old, I worked around for the other children now all married, getting a place to sleep.

They didn't seem to think I needed any other pay and I was too young to care. I would work out for strangers enough to buy my clothes.

When I was 20 years old I found I needed more money so went to work and soon had teams and tools and rented a farm and made crop for myself.

I done my own washing and cooking I often had a bunch of boys in on weekends and had chicken fries. The boys robing the neighbors hen house for the chickens.

Chapter 15

During his teen years in San Antonio, uninitiated and inexperienced in female relationships, Jauan Fernandez, now Danos Knight, fancied himself to be an aspiring ladies' man. How he came to this self-assessment about his masculine prowess was quite the mystery. His introduction to female companionship was largely by observing the loveless marriage of his parents, Don Pedro and Carlita, followed by the business-like union between Ma and Pa Roberts, equally as loveless. These two legal unions were void of any emotionality, absent any evidence of passion or love between the married couples. Husbands were occupied with their working lives, while wives engaged in mundane tasks managing households and raising children. Developing skills in the art of "love" would be no more difficult than planting crops, Danos concluded. Unfortunately, his understanding of love was undefined and without description, although he did consider a relationship necessary to satisfy his basic desire for female companionship. Danos was attracted to gentle, feminine attributes; delicate female features caused his passionate arousal. His seduction by a young woman would be wholly pleasurable. Perhaps engaging in a relationship of fiery passion would be his style, uncontrolled and with no commitment.

Danos' teenage attraction to girls and young women came as a surprise at a rather mature sixteen years of age. The attraction he experienced was largely based on female sensuality and physical attributes, an emotional, physical relationship.

Now in Oklahoma City, Ann Meadows' long brown hair, piled and coiffed into a crescendo before she appeared in the store or on the public streets, caught his attention. She was a pleasant, carnal diversion to the many necessary chores occupying his schedule. Ann Meadows clerked at the Oklahoma City General Store, primarily a seed and feed store frequented by Danos Knight. At his first encounters, Danos was utterly smitten by Ann's physical qualities; once captivated, he could not take his eyes off her beauty. She was immaculate, impeccable. Simply dressed in everyday work clothes, she was spectacular. Ann's sultry stance at the counter, with left hand on her hip in an "I dare you" fashion, was purposely displayed for Danos' enjoyment, he believed. He was mesmerized by her brunette hair accented by a pink ribbon holding her hair behind her ears, her blue eyes, shapely curves and soft skin, all proclaiming perfection. As he approached, he was overcome by the faint hint of lilac signifying her outward cleanliness and inward purity. Remarkable. Her female physique was enhanced as she bent to retrieve a bag of seed from a lower bin. As Danos exhaled, he could barely control himself. He played coy, engaging in small talk about the weather and the price of seed with Ann. Danos purposely frequented Ann's store for a chance meeting and the opportunity to draw in the full depth of her beauty. Ann was a sixteen-year-old with the physique of a young woman. Scintillating. Danos, the ladies' man, was prepared.

At an appropriate time during their acquaintance, Danos overcame his nerves and fear of rejection. He invited Ann Meadows to have dinner with him at Arthur Blackstone's home on Sunday afternoon. Soon he would learn Ann was just as attracted to Danos as he was to her. Danos drove his mule and buggy to the feed store at 1:00 p.m. on Sunday afternoon calling for Ann as they had arranged. Ann made the excuse informing her parents she would be at a friend's home for the remainder of that Sunday. This excuse conveyed to Ann's parents raised no suspicion. Danos arrived. Ann sat next to him on the buggy seat holding his left arm as Danos controlled the reins directing the mule for the twenty-minute ride to their Sunday afternoon dinner engagement.

"Ann, I love when you hold me by my arm, directly attached to me. We make a lovely couple, don't you think? I'm convinced you fully complement me with your presence and grace."

"Danos, I enjoy being with you. You are so manly. So self-reliant. So independent. I feel so protected when I'm with you. I can face anything when you are with me."

"I think we should spend more time together deepening our relationship beyond just physical attraction," Ann encouraged.

"Being physical is human nature," Danos responded.

"You understand that I made the excuse I'm spending the afternoon with my friend's family?" Ann queried.

Danos characterized the nature of the lie told to her parents as a reasonable alibi.

"Your parents will have no knowledge of the afternoon we spend together," he assured Ann.

"You will find Arthur Blackstone and his wife to be hospitable and entertaining. They will give us the liberty to be free and alone for a portion of the afternoon."

Ann held onto his left arm securely for the remainder of the ride to the Blackstone farm, her body pressed tightly against his side.

Arthur Blackstone and his wife prepared a sumptuous meal of ham, black-eyed peas, corn grits and cool water from their nearby brook. Throughout the meal, Ann continued to look into Danos' eyes and, by her body language, indicated she wanted to have her way with him. Ann's nonverbal communication was accurately interpreted as Ann and Danos proceeded to the Blackstone barn for their after dinner "conversation." In reckless passion, in the privacy of an old hay barn suitable for their intended purposes, they both ripped each other's clothes exposing nakedness. Danos, unable to think clearly, could only hold Ann next to his body embracing and touching her soft skin, feeling the contours of her perfect body as he whispered in her ear, "I love you." Ann reciprocated, "I love you, too." Their passion culminated in an explosion of ecstasy. Exhausted after their "conversation," they both dressed and gave their regards to Danos' friends thanking them for dinner on this significant occasion. Danos returned Ann Meadows to the feed store from where she walked the fifteen-minute distance to her parents' home. That night, as he lay in bed, Danos recounted the day's activity. The sensuality and sexuality he experienced with Ann was indescribable. He would enjoy this relationship; he was quite sure.

By Friday afternoon of that week, Danos stopped by to see Ann at the general store. To his disbelief, Ann informed Danos that her parents discovered his Spanish ancestry and Cuban background, that he had lived with a man named Roberts and his renegade, ill-mannered sons who were no more than a lawless bunch engaged in the most egregious, immoral lifestyles. Ann was forbidden to see Danos socially again. Ann, at sixteen years of age, was committed to obedience to her mother's wishes. Danos could only speculate that the Roberts bunch had somehow informed Ann's parents of their social friendship intending to destroy his relationship with Ann. The affair was over just as quickly as it began. Ann was ripped away and disappeared from Danos' life. Another loss. Another tragedy. Another disappearance. The most perfect girl he had ever met, the only girl he had loved, whatever that meant, had been taken from the poor orphan boy.

Collectively, the Roberts boys, driven by their malevolent intent, ridiculed and chastised the former Jim Roberts for his failure to capture the heart of this sixteen-year-old. Their comments, "Sissy Boy" and "Casanova" and "Cradle Robber" were piled on Danos, hoping the emotional assault would destroy his ego. Their spoken words punctuated their contempt for Danos, expecting the "ladies' man" to be crumpled in a heap of despair and embarrassment. Danos kept his confidence, relying on his toughness, countering the brothers just as he held his own fighting with the renegade bunch. Danos would stand as tough as those boys thought he was.... as tough as they knew he was. The Roberts boys dared Danos to just get "hitched" as they each did. By getting married, he could simply escape the dominating environment of cranky, old Pa Roberts.

Over the next months, Danos reflected on his prior encounters with other women in Texas that he believed could satisfy his need for female companionship. In fact, he could take a woman in marriage if he had the mind to marry. The "brothers" compelled Danos to reignite the relationship he had with an old Texas girlfriend. Danos recalled a girl he had known in the past, a girl with whom he had corresponded for a short time. While his version of "love" for this old flame may have existed in the recesses of his mind, or may not have exist at all, Danos could be convinced to marry this girl from his past merely to demonstrate his manhood to the world. He was in the mood to do so.

With the encouragement of his "brothers," Danos prepared to leave Oklahoma City for a rendezvous with marriage, commitment and destiny. In an effort to assist Danos with his future marital plans, the brothers conceived a scheme to take control of his livestock during his absence. It was understandable that Danos required assistance raising his livestock while he was pursuing passion and commitment to his soon-to-be bride in San Antonio. Planning his trip and expecting to be unavailable for an indeterminate length of time, Danos was unable to decipher the integrity of the Roberts' offer to look after his livestock. With their undisclosed agenda, the Roberts boys had been presented with an opportunity to add to their wealth by connivance and deception. Theft of livestock and equipment from their brother was harmless. In fact, the theft was justified. "Jim Roberts" got his start in the farming and cattle business largely due to the Roberts' reputation in San Antonio and Oklahoma City. Dividing up the livestock among the brothers to raise during his absence, for the future theft and sale of the livestock, together with possession of his farm equipment, were unannounced but warranted in the minds of the boys. Stealing his entire herd of livestock in some states was considered larceny, grand larceny. In Oklahoma, this was not stealing, so they determined. This was an act of brotherly love. Caring for his livestock was a purposeful mission with little consequence. The Roberts boys considered it their obligation to take the day-to-day responsibility for raising this herd of cattle. Would young "Jim Roberts" even return to Oklahoma City? Or would he carry his new bride off in horse and buggy to parts unknown while embarking on a lifetime of commitment to his new wife? Predestination they concluded.

Danos impressed the Roberts family that he was a manly individual, knew his own mind and had the authority and maturity to act on his decision to engage in formal, contractual marriage. He was, however, relying on this irresponsible, evil plotting bunch to care for his cattle and safeguard his equipment. Enchanted with fulfilling his dream of marriage, Danos was unconcerned about the brothers' scheme to become owners of his livestock. While he suspected this possibility, Danos set on his journey to San Antonio, reminiscing on this vision of loveliness, hopefully now of the marrying kind. The experience of raising cattle and farming fields to produce crops were no longer the priority for Danos. His ego was filled with manhood and virility, bent on taking this Texas woman as a wife of his own for no reason other than he could.

His journey of words was enhanced by the inclusion of Ann Meadows. A.D. realized how fragile a relationship could be. He wrote…

I had met and loved a girl by the name of Ann Meadows. She said she loved me but when her parents objected to my nationality and upbringing, I had to see her turn away from me because she could not go against her mother's wishes. I decided to be as tough as they thought I was.

So when my brothers advised me to go back home and marry a girl I had grown up with I was just in a mood to do it and decided I would marry just to show the world I could regardless of love.

And that just suited the boys as they wanted my stock and seen a good chance to get it for nothing. They offered to keep it for me but I was soon to learn they were keeping them for them.selves, but I had been so used to doing as they told me I did not recognize any selfishness in the offer.

Chapter 16

The boys wasted little time dividing up Danos' Longhorns among themselves as equitably as they could without engaging argument and ensuing fisticuffs. Danos acquiesced to the tenancy of his livestock, expecting the herd would be properly cared for by the boys during his absence while he experienced and enjoyed marital bliss in Texas. The wagons, harnesses and other tack and equipment which Danos had acquired over time, including one mule and several horses, were likewise divided fairly as part of the brothers' intended scheme. His mind clouded by details concerning his proposal for marriage, Danos underestimated the selfishness of his ruthless siblings. Despite growing up laboring alongside the brothers, Danos remained the outsider. Designated the runt of the litter, he was entitled to little, if any, respect and certainly not entitled to any details of their plot against him.

Arthur Blackstone pulled through the gate into A.D. Knight's sandy drive and redirected the team to stop next to the barn, prepared for departure. His worn but reliable farm wagon, outfitted with a cushioned brown leather seat fixed atop a pair of oiled leaf springs, would transport Danos to the rail station. Two large, black work horses hitched to the wagon tongue would pull Arthur and Danos the distance to Oklahoma City. Danos loaded two bags of luggage into the wagon. Arthur commanded the team with a slap of the reins and a "Giddy up!" as they left Danos' farmhouse. The tails of both horses whipped side to side with each step beating the flies from their hind quarters. Regularly passing gas as required, the aroma was acceptable as a common occurrence indicating healthy horses with no digestive problems.

During their ride to the station, Danos and Arthur discussed various topics, the most critical of which was his upcoming marriage to Jane Clark. Arthur, not trying to dissuade Danos from this marriage, was concerned and hoped Danos had rationalized through this decision. True, Danos had not seen or corresponded with Jane in a while, but Danos assured Arthur he knew what he was doing in consideration of the commitment. As an independent individual, Danos considered himself mature enough to make this important decision, especially as such decision would change his personal status from carefree independence to responsible permanence in marriage.

"I'm twenty years old and ready to settle down, ready to make a commitment to Jane and intent on raising my family here in Oklahoma City," Danos retorted.

"My brothers are caring for my livestock until my return."

Arthur, more concerned about Jane than the status of the livestock, questioned whether Jane was suitable for Danos.

"I know you were madly in love with Ann Meadows a while back. She was young, pretty and in love with you, too. She was the marrying kind and mature for her age. I'm sure you recall how passionate she was about you."

"That's old, spoiled milk. Ann's parents, particularly her mother, found my Spanish descent and foreign ancestry offensive and must be accorded the greatest amount of prejudice. In addition to my background, she contended, I've been raised by an ill-mannered old man together with an illiterate bunch of ruffians. I was an unacceptable choice for their daughter's hand. We didn't discuss marriage. It just would not be. There's a special place in my heart where I'll always keep Ann as part of me, but we were just not meant to be."

"Jane's a mature woman. Attractive, genuinely pretty with experience in the fields and with livestock. She's suited for bearing children, giving us a family to raise so we can grow crop and increase our livestock. She is perfect for me in this sense," Danos remarked.

"I wired her three weeks ago informing her I'd be in San Antonio and wished to see her. Jane indicated she was looking forward to our meeting."

"I arranged for accommodations at the Longhorn Saloon, just a mile or two from Jane's home. We are scheduled to meet at her home on the afternoon of my arrival. This is the beginning of a mutually beneficial relationship. One of permanence in the family way."

Danos and Arthur spoke no more about consequential topics and decisions. They remained mostly silent occupied with their own thoughts as Danos contemplated his upcoming marriage. He envisioned Jane just as she was before when they went their separate ways three years prior. An independent, yet needy woman, desirous of a man to provide and support her, a man to fulfill her maternal role with a family of five or six or more kids. She was capable of nurturing the children and managing the family unit from a domestic sense, as well as working the crop field and tending to the livestock. Jane was the woman Danos required, with or without love.

As the team and wagon pulled into the station, Danos thanked Arthur as he grabbed his black leather satchel and a slightly larger case. Danos decided to bring sufficient clothes and essentials should he be required to remain in San Antonio for more than a day or two. As Arthur turned the team in the opposite direction, he wished Danos well that his plans come to fruition for the good of both involved. Danos headed to the ticket counter, purchased a one-way ticket to San Antonio and boarded the second passenger car while the coalmen stoked Engine #73, raising the steam pressure preparing to leave the station. Danos chose an unoccupied double seat next to the window. He would pass his time viewing the scenery of Oklahoma and Texas and reflecting on his marriage proposal to Jane Clark.

This second passenger car in coach had eighteen rows of double seats on either side of a narrow aisle. Danos chose the third row of seats as that row appeared to have slightly more leg room aiding maneuverability in and out, with ample room for stretching. His black leather satchel was securely stowed under the seat in front of him. He placed his larger case above the seats in an upper baggage compartment. More passengers continued to board stepping into the car Danos had chosen. To his surprise, the car filled with passengers. Apparently, the San Antonio destination was significant and of compelling importance for reasons unknown to Danos.

The conductor, in a commanding voice, announced the train's departure with "All aboard!" ordering those late arrivals to get on board or be left standing on the boardwalk. Engine #73 declared its departure with three blasts of its steam whistle. The cars rolled slowly, picking up pace. As Danos observed the station fading in the distance, as the niceties of urban life and commerce were replaced by pasture, livestock and crop fields, a mature man with gray hair and matching mustache settled into the open aisle seat next to Danos. Attired in a dark three-piece suit, complemented by shiny black oxford shoes, Danos' seatmate carried a brown, expensive-looking, soft leather briefcase with gold clasps and lock. A conversation would ensue, Danos was quite sure. Probably a talkative lawyer with all the correct answers, he surmised. Danos was half right. He was talkative. He had the correct answers. But he was not a lawyer. Danos' seatmate for the next twenty plus hours, perhaps prophetically so, was a preacher, the Reverend Archibald Jennings. He introduced himself as Archie Jennings, with just a hint of Reverend attached to his given name. Jennings' southern drawl was comfortable and soothing, yet Danos believed Jennings could call down fire and brimstone when his congregation required admonishment. His dark suit was complemented by a crisp white shirt and a solid black tie, set off by the neatly trimmed mustache lining the contour of his upper lip.

Archie, as he insisted Danos address him, was more than eager to talk, that is, to win another soul for eternity. Archie was passionate about life everlasting, expressing every man's need to ask for forgiveness, repent by turning from his evil ways and following God's commands. As Archie's conversation turned to preaching, Danos abruptly changed the direction of the discussion informing the preacher his job was confined to the pulpit on Sunday. Danos did not care to hear Archie's sermon for the next twenty hours.

Thus, their conversation continued on the subject of worldly practicality. In the span of a short minute, Danos learned Rev. Jennings was educated at the Moody Bible Institute in Illinois, has been married for thirty-two years and has two adult daughters, both married who have thus far provided Archie with three grandchildren.

"So, son, what is your full name?' asked the Reverend.

"Andrew Danos Knight," he stated proudly.

"What takes you to Texas this fine day in the middle of the week?" Archie inquired.

Danos was reserved and somewhat reluctant to tell the whole truth, so he stated he had a large wedding ceremony planned in San Antonio with his longtime sweetheart. Reverend Jennings was impressed and joyful for Danos' commitment at a youthful age. Jennings noted that such life-long commitment was of great importance.

"What is your bride's name?"

"Jane Clark," Danos replied.

"How well do you know your soon-to-be wife?" Archie inquired, determined to confirm this match would have proper chance for survival. Danos squirmed in his seat and said,

"I know her quite well. We are a perfect match. We've been seeing each other for over three years." Not quite a lie, just a manufactured fib of insignificance, he justified in his mind. The Reverend was attuned to Danos' discomfort. He inquired further.

"How many people will be attending your wedding ceremony?"

"Well, the invitation list has not yet been finalized," stated Danos. "The final count of expected guests will not be determined for another several weeks."

"What's the date of your wedding? Perhaps I can join you on your momentous day." Danos wanted this line of questioning to end. The Reverend was pulling Danos deeper into a complexity of lies making escape impossible. At this instant, Danos recalled Ma Roberts' words of wisdom that honesty is required at all levels. However, Danos continued his charade for a while longer until Archie pressed him into this corner.

"The wedding date is set for the thirty-first day of June," Danos stated matter-of-factly, believing this date would satisfy Archie's curiosity. The Reverend Archibald Jennings confirmed Danos' discomfort with his given response. Rather than confront Danos directly about the erroneous date, the Reverend proceeded to tell Danos what he had learned of marriage over his adult lifetime. Danos listened half-heartedly, hearing only bits as Reverend Jennings spoke his piece.

"Marriage is a commitment between a man and a woman, in the eyes of God and with God's blessing, to live as husband and wife, loving each other as God has commanded each generation, that the husband has the responsibility to support his wife in faithfulness, in good times and in troubled times. The wife is to be the helpmate to her husband and remain subservient to his authority in the family unit. Unconditional love is the ingredient required to maintain this solemn commitment to each respective spouse. Without such mutual commitment, without faith in God Almighty, without forgiveness, without respect for each other, a marriage contract is doomed to fail," Archibald Jennings emphasized.

Embarrassed to speak frankly and honestly, Danos agreed with Reverend Jennings, announcing he will keep this good advice for reference and for use in the years to come. Danos expressly heard that his "wife is to be the helpmate to her husband....the bride was to remain subservient to his authority in the family.... that without such help and subservience, "a marriage contract is doomed to fail." Danos' selective hearing and comprehension would eventually convert Jennings' message into a fatal flaw.

Arriving at the San Antonio station, Danos parted ways with the Reverend Archibald Jennings. Despite traveling twenty hours as his seatmate, Danos did not know the purpose of Jennings' visit to San Antonio. Danos did suspect that he answered all of the Reverend's questions honestly and without arousing any suspicion. Of course.

* * *

His upper left leg began to cramp. Mid-way up the underside of his leg, the thigh muscle stiffened with extraordinary pain. He rolled the padded oak chair from its matching desk as he stood to relieve his discomfort. He had been sitting motionless in locked position for over two hours. With both feet planted on the wooden floor and back slightly bent over his writing tablet, his leg muscles eventually objected and required stretching. Danos peered out to the garden, taking in the full breadth of reds, pinks, and white flowers which he had cultivated and planted years ago. The beauty of the botanical varieties decluttered his mind at least momentarily. A nondescript brown finch perched itself on the sill as Danos continued his observation of the manicured lawn and garden exhibiting waves of color. The finch, too, admired the flower garden, but it had no obligation requiring he perch in such place for any specific task or length of time. At that moment of thought, an aggressive blue jay swept to the sill startling the finch, demanding he relinquish his sill spot to the jay. The finch conceded, left reluctantly but without incident. Danos, standing, unable to appreciate the fragrances of his garden, pulled out a Partagas from his vest pocket, bit the end of the cigar and lit the seven-inch-long, hand-rolled Cuban with a Diamond kitchen match. A robust smoke, a maduro with heavy body, gave Danos the sense of well-being. Sipping a glass of blackberry brandy would enhance the pleasure of his brief break. He poured brandy from a decorative decanter into its matching crystal glass. He relieved his legs further by walking in an exaggerated gait across the library floor. Danos stopped and bent at the waist, stretching with full purpose, relieving the tightness of his upper left thigh as he reflected on Ann Meadows. At the age of nineteen years, it was his "conversation" with Ann Meadows that Danos attained his manhood. That Sunday afternoon, years ago, spent with Ann at Arthur Blackstone's hay barn was beyond comparison, sheer ecstasy A.D. recollected. He thought about Ann's future, her beauty and what could have developed had he been patient and persistent.

With the cramp in his left leg subsiding, A.D. returned to the desk chair and sat. He reached for the black satchel and retrieved an old letter he received from Jane Clark two decades ago. The fragile, slightly-yellowed paper envelope which remained undisturbed and still wrapped in wax paper, was identified by faded, but legible, black ink on the front side. A.D. opened the envelope to reveal the contents. A two-page letter in Jane's handwriting. A.D. would skim the letter at the oak desk before he resumed his writing. A.D. began to read…a portion…

My Dearest Jauan:
Our togetherness over these last two months will be my most treasured moments of eternity. We have become joined in a spiritual sense and will so remain in spite of the passage of time. We are inseparable. I long for your return to hold me in your arms once again……

A.D. stopped reading, as he could continue no further. There was no point to reading such a display of immaturity and fantasy. Reading the letter conjured only negative feelings from someone he once thought he loved. As the quality Partagas burned, it filled the library with an aroma fit for nobility. The sunlight filtered through the crystal brandy glass illuminating the essence of freshly pressed berries, perfectly fermented for his sole satisfaction, aroma and enjoyment. A.D. continued his journey of words…

So after all my things were distributed amongst them, I took a train for our old home to see the girl I had corresponded with for sometime.

With the expectation of marrying her at once, I knew I would not love her as I had Ann. But my affair with Ann had made me see I could not have my choice.

Chapter 17

As the San Antonio Line arrived at its destination, Danos grabbed his larger case from the upper bin and his black leather satchel from beneath the forward seat. Sitting, talking, dozing and sleeping for the twenty-hour train ride was exhausting. However, Danos felt relieved and somewhat refreshed once the interrogation by Archibald Jennings concluded. He took four steps to the front of the car, stepped down to the station's boardwalk and looked for familiar landmarks to set his bearings. Jane's address was written on a dirty note card and committed to his memory; she was his priority: a marriage proposal.

Danos rented a room above the nearby Longhorn Saloon on Main Street. A bath, shave, short nap and change of clothes were necessary preparations for his upcoming meeting with Jane Clark.

He strode downstairs and entered the nearly full dining room, seating himself at an open table for two topped by a clean white cloth. The attractive and attentive waitress recommended the cook's lunch special of beef stew and biscuit. Danos consumed his meal in a rush, as he was famished having last eaten nearly twenty-four hours ago. The capacity lunch crowd at the Longhorn was a testament to the quality of its menu. He would return. He washed down his biscuit with a tall glass of sassafras tea. Today is an important day and his mind would not be distorted by alcohol and spirits.

He is to meet his bride in just hours, walking the distance of about twenty city blocks to Jane Clark's home. Danos, familiar with the city geography in general, particularly downtown San Antonio, cared little about strolling the city observing notable changes of the last few years. He did note that the San Antonio population had apparently increased over the last three years. He took a seat in a well-worn, unpainted, wooden rocking chair situated on the porch of the saloon facing the congested street. Danos spent time observing weekday activity and human behavior associated with the bustle of San Antonio. Unattended children jumping rope on a side street. Dogs congregating outside the butcher shop. Laundry employees delivering freshly pressed shirts and laundered clothing. Men entering the barbershop, leaving with a clean shave, looking civil. Ladies entering the general store, leaving happily with items wrapped in packages ordered weeks ago. His time as a single man was passing by, diminishing as he sat in the wooden rocker, well used by every imagined personality and physique possible. He relaxed as if he had unlimited time to while away. He would soon have his bride, his wife. He would be obligated immediately, as soon as Jane accepted his offer of marriage proposal. His mind raced; his heart pounded. He was confident, pressured by his brothers' insistence that Jane Clark would consent to the proposal. On the morrow, he would return to his home and his herd in Oklahoma City, married to Jane Clark just because he could. Reverend Jennings' words were of little consequence now that he had escaped the confinement of his window seat in row three. Danos momentarily rested his eyes as the sun, overhead at half-past noon, was conveniently shaded by his white, wide-brimmed Stetson dress hat. He considered Jane's ability to produce offspring, to grow crop and to butcher livestock. She would be committed to this marriage as was he.

It was Thursday afternoon, nearing one o'clock. It was time to offer this contract for marriage as he had rehearsed repeatedly. Danos, the self-declared ladies' man, could not fail; he knew she was the right choice, the woman of his fulfillment. Jane would be unable to resist Danos' charm and attraction. Time to get on with the business of life, family and farming he mumbled audibly and confidently. With a spring in his step spurred by apprehension and the unknown, he jumped from the rocking chair with long strides bounding toward his destination and the long overdue rendezvous with Jane Clark. In his mind's eye, he imagined Jane Clark, as she stood coyly, exuding primitive, yet somewhat sophisticated sensuality with anticipation, greeting him at her home's entryway. Danos pictured her dressed in a freshly pressed, yellow, long-sleeved cotton dress, with the hem length falling just low enough to expose Jane's bare ankle. With brown hair trimmed perfectly to shoulder length, freshly brushed, tied behind her ears with matching yellow ribbon, Jane revealed a soft, supple neck begging to be stroked. Her smooth, bare skin would be his immediate gratification for reviving this relationship. Her face was pale but accentuated by a light rose blush radiating innocence and virtue. Her luxurious lips, contrasting with the blush highlight, were prepared to lock with his. Although he was not in love with Jane, he could succumb to arousal observing her natural femininity. He would be physically attracted to her in an instant, Danos was certain. Their hearts will beat rhythmically as one, as they gazed into each other's eyes exploring the possibilities, at the same time wondering why it took three years to find each other's presence. The marriage contract will be a mutual expression of commitment as they will move on to Oklahoma City, as husband and wife. Danos had this all figured out, all planned out without so much as a moment of discussion or input from Jane Clark. He would be the head of the family, the patriarch. He would sweep her off her feet; she would be unable to resist his masculinity and charm. Such was Danos' mental picture of his soon-to-be meeting with Jane Clark.

After minutes of walking, Danos confirmed the address as he remembered it, as it was written on his note card, and as the number appeared on the house where Jane resided. As he approached the residence, Danos double-checked the street and house number to be sure it was correct. He took a deep breath making the three steps up to the porch and to the front door. Danos knocked emphatically announcing his arrival and presence. No answer. He knocked again on the wooden portion of the screen door, hanging precariously by one loose hinge, only to be greeted with "Come on in," as a loud voice echoed from the rear of the house indicating the respondent was inconveniently interrupted from a pressing task.

As Danos took his first steps into the home, he was assaulted and overwhelmed by the pungent odor of human waste. Foul human infant waste. Baby clothes scattered about, filled with defecation and strong urine, took his breath away. Someone appearing to look like Jane entered the front room from the kitchen, toting a six-month-old child on her left hip. The putrid smell of vomit filled the air. This person, with straggled, unkept, uncombed hair, was a striking sight. Her drab gray housecoat was filthy, stained by all matter of puke and food spoil, noticeably tight-fitting, refusing to adequately accommodate her obvious fondness for cakes, cookies and sweets. She wore no shoes, but freely roamed barefoot in the filth and clutter disarranged throughout the front room of this hovel. The flooring was made of wood, racked with filth, as determined by setting aside the litter to reveal the construct.

Danos, himself not the tidiest of men, could not comprehend the magnitude of this disarray and refuse. Nearly all floor space, as well as furniture, was cluttered with baby paraphernalia and miscellaneous trash. Jane's physical appearance and environment shocked Danos back into reality. If Jane's residence had shelves and cabinets, they were no doubt empty, as it appeared all possessions Jane owned were fully displayed as unmatched floor and furniture coverings in this place she called home. The underlying clutter was rubbish, urine and diapers filled with dried excrement. Jane obviously had no demonstrable skills for homemaking, caring little about cleanliness. It took Danos less than a few split seconds to calculate the enormity of his error regarding this marriage proposal. Jane reacted. She groped for Danos, pushing baby to the side, kissing him squarely on the lips so suddenly he could not avoid nor deflect her slobber. On up-close recognition, this was, in fact, Jane Clark, albeit three years removed from his mental image. This rendezvous did not unfold as he anticipated. The six-month-old baby stuck to Jane's hip, dressed only in a soiled diaper, was hot, sweaty, unclean. It was apparent the child was uncomfortable. Just as he considered this observation, the baby began to cry, wailing at an ear-piercing pitch and volume. Danos could hardly hear his conversation. Jane invited Danos to sit on the sofa, as she cleared clothing, dinner plates and all other matter of debris from the sofa for a place to sit. The baby continued to wail as Jane tried to explain the circumstances regarding her youngest child. She mentioned the baby's name, but Danos could not hear nor understand above the baby's penetrating wail. Such formal introduction was inconsequential, as the six-month old continued to screech for attention, demanding its diaper needs changing. Any attentive mother could not mistake this child's plea for help. Jane ignored the child as she continued to shout over its incessant cries.

Danos was prepared to bolt. He prepared to run for freedom, but he did not wish to appear rude, for it was he who initiated this rendezvous. His marriage to Jane Clark would not happen. He made the decision to withhold his offer of marriage proposal in a fraction of an instant, withdrawing it before the offer was made. Danos had been blindsided by today's revelation, an eye-opening epiphany of a problematic future lifestyle. Wholly unacceptable. As he was about to excuse himself, he observed from the corner of his eye, two toddlers, just as filthy and unkept as their mother and their six-month-old sibling. One child was crawling on hands and knees through the floor coverings, the other walking unsteadily. The two children were both attired in nakedness. The older child, about two years old, displayed a hand print on his left cheek and a strap burn on his right buttock, evidence of disciplinary correction, warranted or not, meted out by his mother or other irresponsible adult.

Oh! My! What a predicament in which Danos found himself. He thought about his recent encounter with the Reverend Archibald Jennings in which he told only half truths. Danos was at this very moment concocting a bald-faced lie to tell Jane Clark to justify his escape from this dose of family realism. Danos stood up from the sofa prepared to express his goodbyes when, unpredictably, but timely, a rather familiar, lovely young woman entered the living room. Her familiarity was due to the prior meeting of Jane's sister, May Clark, three years earlier. She was then merely age eleven. What a difference three years make! May Clark had blossomed into an incredibly endowed, mature young woman of fourteen years. Reminiscent of his first meeting with Ann Meadows, Danos could not be distracted from May's splendor and allure. He took in as much of her beauty as his eyes could comprehend in a matter of minutes. He looked into the depths of her soul and outwardly at her physical attributes. He was stricken by her innocence and beauty. Although she may have been only fourteen, she looked every bit of eighteen. Mature and irresistible. Smitten again. Purely a physical attraction, no question. May wore a clean, long-sleeved yellow dress, freshly pressed. Her light brown hair was tied in a pony-tail held by a single, matching yellow ribbon. This vision of loveliness is what Danos had conjured for his expectant meeting with Jane Clark. It was actually May Clark who Danos previously envisioned as he walked through the streets of San Antonio toward the address listed on his note card. How fortuitous? Marriage to Jane would not work. Marriage to May Clark is the fateful alternative and to his good fortune. Danos instinctively made the decision, based on physical attraction alone, a two-way attraction, as May was drawn to Danos as strongly as he to her. Fate cannot be avoided or discounted. Meeting May was due solely to a twist of fate. Not a fluke, but an inexplicable occurrence with unquestionable providence and the need to be joined together. Love or no love; such does not matter. Danos can marry a woman, any woman, even May Clark, just because he can do so. Pressured by the insistence of the Roberts boys, this venture to marry was more than a taunt or challenge, it was the expected way of life for Ma Roberts' boy, Danos. He was, therefore, justified.

With an inconspicuous wink of his right eye and an indicative nod, May understood that she would leave the room and join Danos outside after his meeting with Jane concluded. Danos tipped his Stetson to Jane, thanked her for meeting with him and excused himself as he was required to leave immediately. His sudden departure was necessary to make his appointment with the Reverend Archibald Jennings, his preacher. Jennings was the hallmark of punctuality, he explained to Jane, and he must leave to get across town in less than one hour. As Danos stepped off the porch and bounded down the three steps, he considered this bald-faced lie about Rev. Jennings. Few observers knowing this excuse would feel Spiritually comfortable with such string of untruths abruptly excusing Danos from Jane's presence. Danos escaped. Now at liberty to run free again, that is, until he met May Clark just down the street. Danos grabbed her right hand, as May, awash in a flood of tears, announced her need to get out of that house. She could live there no longer. Jane's sexual appetite was never satisfied. She latched on to a man that gave her the first two children. Then, when Jane became pregnant with this six-month-old, the lazy vagabond snuck out the house one night and hasn't been seen since.

"Jane's a terrible, inattentive mother with no patience."

"She expects me to clean after her three bastard children, as if I'm somehow responsible for her being in the family way."

"I watched many times as Jane lost patience with those two boys and couldn't control herself. She slaps them constantly and beats them with a leather strap," May said erupting in anger and fear.

"Jauan," as she knew him, "I cannot stay here living with Jane and those three kids in that hog pit she calls home. Our parents avoid Jane and me because they expected so much more of us. I'm sure we disappointed Mother and Father. They still live in San Antonio, but we rarely see them, and they never come to Jane's house."

Danos accepted the emotional outburst from this woman six years his junior. May trembled in Danos' arms as she sought his comfort and strength. Danos invited May to join him in his room above the Longhorn Saloon. They walked together, holding hands, as Danos informed her of his life with Ma and Pa Roberts in San Antonio and in Oklahoma City. He also explained his new name. May loved the name, "Danos." She began addressing him as Danos immediately. Approaching the Longhorn, they decided to enter the hotel above the saloon going up to the second floor by the rear stairwell, undetected. They removed their shoes and boots and stretched out on the bed for comfort. May touched his clean-shaven face with her left index finger. She traced the contours of his lips, cheek bones and chin. Danos did not object. His manhood, his ego, were fortified as this fourteen-year-old woman softly stroked his skin and told him she needed him. She could stay with him forever. Providence, he was convinced. It was the right time, the right woman. Danos looked into her eyes, held her left hand and made his proposal for marriage. May, overcome by his words, began to sob. "Yes," she said. "Yes, I accept. I will marry you. I will be the best wife you could ever have," as she sobbed uncontrollably and kissed him all over as her sign of acceptance. They made love to each other, further fulfilling acceptance of the commitment to one another. As day turned to night, May and Danos held each other in their arms and fell asleep in bliss.

Overnight, as she considered her future, May devised a strategy to bring this marriage contract to fruition. May explained to Danos that, as a fourteen-year-old, she would be unable to legally marry without the permission of her parents. Not being of legal age, May needed parental consent to marry in Texas. Danos had previously inquired about the legal age for marriage but was unaware of the minimum age. May would consult her mother tomorrow morning, explaining that she had been reacquainted with the former Jauan Fernandez and that he asked for her hand in marriage, to which May accepted. Her mother, most assuredly, would understand and grant the necessary permission for marriage. This strategy would work. Andrew Danos Knight and May Clark will be joined as husband and wife soon; he will have a wife, the wife he sought. For just an instant, Danos thought about asking Reverend Archibald Jennings to perform the marriage ceremony here in San Antonio. On further reflection, such idea was stripped of value. Reverend Jennings had already been made the subject of an intentional lie. There was no point in demonstrating that it was so much more than an insignificant fib.

May began the walk to her mother's home the next morning in anticipation of obtaining the necessary consent for a simple, unencumbered marriage. May indicated to Danos she will return in a few hours with the required permission. Then they'll discuss their future in detail. He agreed and bid her well. Danos, now accustomed to the disappearance, rejection and death of persons of significance during his short life, had faith in May's commitment to marriage. He did note that circumstances can fall outside of one's control. He pondered an alternate strategy if May's plan met with failure. Or if May failed to return to him. Such would not be unexpected, but, rather, would be consistent with the life he has been dealt in Cuba, Texas and Oklahoma City.

* * *

Danos shaved, bathed and made himself presentable for May's return. He went downstairs to the dining room for a bowl of corn grits or beef stew and biscuit. This morning he was entitled to a treat, a celebratory shot of whiskey, maybe two, followed by a half pitcher of water. Last night's engagement should be cause for merriment, Danos believed. A festive occasion, indeed. After his meal, Danos stepped to the porch at the front of the Longhorn Saloon. He sat himself down positioning in the rocking chair he occupied yesterday. It was nearly the same time of day, just past noon, with the sun hovering directly above. His eyes, shaded by the brim of his hat, squinted as he looked down the street for his fiancé's return.

He spotted May at a distance easily identified by her yellow dress. She hurried toward the Longhorn taking steps which appeared to be a near run. As May drew closer, Danos detected disappointment on her face. Upon her arrival, May's face was red with obvious anger. She had been crying. She was distraught as she got to the point directly. "Mother and Father refused to grant their permission for our marriage. Let's go upstairs to your room to discuss this," she suggested. "I do not want to stand in the middle of San Antonio crying my eyes out for all to see." She brought a small brown duffel with her, clothes and personal items, for her overnight needs. She intended to stay.

As they entered the room, May further displayed her anger, kicking the wooden bedframe with her right foot, ripping the bed covers off and throwing them to the floor. It was exhibition of a continued reaction caused by her parents' refusal to listen and understand. She couldn't help herself, nor control her reaction. As her anger dissipated, she sat on Danos' lap and asked him to make love to her. They napped in peace together, May Clark free from fighting with her parents and the yelling, crying, screaming and filth of the hog pit; Danos free from the orphanage, fighting with Pa Roberts and the boys and disappearances and deaths. They had the safety and companionship of each other.

As Danos woke, the position of the sun indicated it was late afternoon. He kissed May on the cheek, told her to continue to nap, and he would return in less than one hour. She had faith in his strength and determination. They will be married, she knew.

Danos left the Longhorn and took a buggy for fare to the San Antonio rail station. He purchased two tickets to Lake Charles, Louisiana, departing San Antonio at 6:30 a.m. the next morning. As part of Danos' strategy, to be shared later with May, they planned to board the train at the St. Hedwig, Texas whistle-stop, twenty-two miles east of San Antonio. The conductor and engineer were made aware of this scheduled whistle-stop.

As Danos returned to his room, he told May they will be married in Louisiana. They were to commence their plan in two or three hours under the cover of darkness.

A.D. made his journal entry…

And when I met Jane I was prepared to propose at once but she had changed so much I hardly knew her and decided I was not in such a hurry to show the world I could marry.

She had a sister, they were Jane and May Clark. I liked the little sister May. But my proposal of marriage met with the same objections I had with Ann. It seemed the boys I had grown up with even denied me the right to marry as they were doing.

So May and I decided to run away and met one dark night to carry out our plans.

Chapter 18

May secured her last few personal items in the small brown duffel, flung the strap over her left shoulder and tucked the bag between her left arm and torso. She wore a pair of old brown, leather half-boots, well-worn and comfortable for fast travel. Her hair was tied back away from her eyes for unobstructed vision. She was prepared to escape from her sister and her sister's kids. From the abuse. From the chaos. From the filth. From her parents and from San Antonio. Danos, held his black, leather satchel by the long straps with his dominant right hand draping them over his shoulder. He carried the larger case by its black handle as they both quietly disappeared from the Longhorn down the rear staircase. Darkness concealed their exit; they left undetected and determined. They were confident the Clark family had not discovered their plan to leave the city. Danos reasoned that anyone who might suspect their departure from San Antonio would surveil the train station for an early morning departure. Trains were scheduled daily for Houston, Dallas and points beyond. May and Danos, alone on the dark streets of San Antonio, walked briskly to the public livery. Danos had reserved a horse and buggy for their twenty-two-mile ride to the St. Hedwig whistle-stop. He calculated a buggy ride of approximately three and one-half hours to their destination. With their bags stowed behind the seat in the wagon bed, Danos cracked the whip against the back of the lone mare; she flinched and jolted pulling the buggy into darkness. Danos, familiar with the dirt road to St. Hedwig's running parallel to the rails, was aided by a cloudless third-quarter moon illuminating the night sky, identifying his route.

Danos' Lake Charles plan began without a hitch; no one saw them leave the Longhorn as they headed to the livery. Danos was pleased by the simplicity of the plan he hastily put together. If May's parents, or her sister Jane, show up at the train station in the morning, May and Danos will be presumed still in San Antonio. No one would be the wiser as the two eloped to Louisiana. This risk of being caught by her parents added to the romance and excitement for this fourteen-year-old girl. Danos, however, had endured a lifetime of risk. Such was an integral part of his rebellious life. He did not elect this lifestyle; it was thrust upon him. Perhaps he was predestined to suffer for his disbelief, his lack of faith. The tragic events in Cuba were merely a premonition, a foreshadowing of continued pain, suffering and failure in this new land. As Danos matured, he grew to believe that he was in sole control and responsible for his own success and equally responsible for failure. Instant self-gratification was the measure of his success. He relied on himself exclusively. He would blame himself alone and accept accolades alone. Relying on others, or on a Supreme Being for that matter, resulted in disappointment, always. Along with the tragedy he experienced in Matanzas, he routinely acknowledged and accepted failure as a product of ill preparation or factors out of his control. He gained experience in the ways of this new world, the Texas lifestyle, living with Pa Roberts and his delinquent "siblings," which maintained and bolstered his desire to be free and wild. This day's adventure, adding to his prior experiences, was his challenge for fulfillment, for success. He sensed the same exhilaration now as he did when escaping from the nuns vaulting over the black iron fence surrounding the Matanzas orphanage. This Lake Charles adventure could end in failure, but he did not believe failure was a possibility this day. His plan was in full progression, indicating success.

During the buggy ride to St. Hedwig's, Danos revealed the remainder of his plan to May. "Louisiana has established the minimum marrying age for a female of merely twelve years to legally obtain a license to wed," Danos confidently announced. "When we arrive in Lake Charles, we'll quickly make our way from the rail station to the courthouse," a short distance walk he was told, "and apply for our marriage license. The clerk will be vested with the authority to perform the marriage ceremony at that moment. Once married, we will begin our new life in Oklahoma City." May was gleeful, excited to be a bride, embarking on married life with Jauan Fernandez, now unceremoniously known as Andrew Danos Knight. The two arrived at St. Hedwig's well in advance of the scheduled whistle-stop. They napped in the wagon padded by two thick blankets covered with gray and black horse hair. There was a distinct aroma of sweaty horse intertwined with the smell of an old mule. No matter, they rested their eyes until the sun rose and waited for arrival of the Louisiana line.

At 7:10 a.m., on schedule, Engine #1813 and the Louisiana line, pulled into St. Hedwig's with the engine's cowcatcher stopping precisely at the yellow, thickly painted line on the weathered boardwalk. The conductor jumped down the two steps of the third passenger car, positioned a wooden stool to assist boarding passengers and assisted Ms. May Clark up into the aisle of the passenger car with Danos stepping in directly behind. The signal was given by the conductor; the brakes released. The engine powered forward increasing its speed, accelerating as if the train had not even come to a stop, heading to its Lake Charles destination. As Danos found an open double seat, May perused the passengers in cabin car number three. Finding no one she recognized, or finding that no one recognized her, May moved forward to the second car coupled directly to the front. She observed each passenger from the rear of the car as the train swayed side to side picking up steam; she made a thorough inspection. May confirmed no familiar passengers on this second car and proceeded forward to the first car, viewed the passengers from behind and moved to the forward portion of the car. She once again perused the passengers, this time from frontal facing, as May Clark made her way back to the third car occupying her seat with Danos. There was no one on board whom she recognized, or recognized May, confirming they had not been discovered nor followed. A.D.'s plan was falling in place, almost too perfectly. Danos regarded their arrival in Lake Charles uneventful. Their stop would be brief, but for the time required to fulfill the final act of their plan.

They gathered their personal belongings and luggage as the train pulled into the Lake Charles station. Weary from lack of sleep over the last two days, the couple fought drowsiness. Bright sunlight on this Louisiana Monday morn helped as they focused on the task at hand: race to the courthouse, meet with the clerk of court, get married and depart Louisiana heading for Oklahoma City, leaving little demonstrable evidence they were even there, save for the recorded marriage certificate, after which it would be too late for any valid objection.

As they disembarked with the others off the #1813, they mingled with passengers of other trains, as well as train employees and passers-by. This mass of indistinct humanity made identifying one particular person in such a large maze difficult, if not impossible. Shoulder abutting shoulder, jostling one another unintentionally, the mob collectively moved to the exit up the five-step wooden staircase located at the east end of the rails to the street. This level accommodated the station waiting area, ticket counter and appealing brass bracketing providing complimentary maps of the City of Lake Charles, along with printed advertisements of local businesses. Uniformed policemen and constables milled about the station in a pretentious exposition assisting passengers and, at the same time, discouraging the ilk of society, pickpockets, panhandlers and thieves. Buggies for hire stood empty at the north exit of the station offering transportation to new arrivals headed to their choice of destinations. A view of the downtown map indicated the courthouse was a brief walk from the station. No point to hiring horse and buggy. They left the station in a hurry seeing no familiar faces. They were obscure passengers arriving in Lake Charles on a fine morning, prepared for business and pleasure.

Having walked merely thirty paces from the station, May noticed a man following closely as they increased their pace toward the courthouse. This smallish looking man had a moderate muscular definition with no distinguishing marks or features. His hat obscured his hair and face to an extent. He was unrecognizable with a glance lasting just seconds. The man sprinted toward the couple as they sought to carry out their plans. May's heart pumped to pounding. She breathed deeply expanding the depths of her lungs inhaling as much oxygen as possible. She prepared to fight or take flight. Her brown eyes shifted toward the open street prepared to bolt in all-out escape. He was now an obvious "tail" lengthening his stride as he closed the gap approaching May. Danos, glancing over his shoulder, assessed the diminutive, but solid, size of the "tail" and chose confrontation. Danos was accustomed to fighting the older and stronger Roberts boys. He was able to take a punch and defend himself against larger opponents. Likely a thief hanging around the train station, the "tail" was looking for a mark to transform into his victim. It was somewhat ironic the "tail" would shadow them toward the courthouse to commit a robbery, but that was his intention, Danos concluded. "Grab my black satchel and hold on tight. I'm going to take this guy out right here," Danos instructed May. The "tail" was just a stride from May and Danos as they neared the bottom step of the courthouse. As Danos intoned manly instructions of strength and power, May became emboldened. She would offer her physical assistance to overpower the "tail." Danos commanded, "Stand aside!" as he whirled around blasting the assailant with a ravaging right hook. It happened so quickly the assailant did not know he had been struck. Danos threw his punch with the full power and accuracy of a crushing, dominant right-handed fist, landing squarely on the assailant's left eye. His head jolted to the left. Then reflexively to the back. His hat dislodged off the side of his head and fell to the street. His knees buckled. He wobbled. He fell to the ground landing on the sidewalk face-down. A curious passer-by rolled him over. Danos and others inspected the "tail" seeking to identify the man. Did anyone know this troublemaker? He was recognized by none of the townsfolk; likely a vagrant intent on thievery was their consensus. All passers-by observed the instigator as he remained motionless on the ground. His breathing was shallow. Danos knocked him unconscious with one blow. A.D. Knight felt instant gratification as he took May by the hand and made their way up the courthouse steps searching for the clerk's office with little time to squander.

They left the crowd on the street, milling around, peering at the lifeless-looking man. His left eye began to discolor. Red and yellow, then black and blue. With his eye swollen, puffiness consumed the entire side of his face. Blood gushed profusely from his nostrils and drooled from his mouth mixed with saliva. Climbing up the granite steps and into the courthouse, May and Danos were victorious. A helpful employee, unaware of the recent knockdown at the foot of the courthouse steps, directed them to the office bearing the sign, "Marriage Licenses." They hurried down the hallway. Their heels announced their presence on the stone floor echoing throughout the corridor. As they approached the clerk's open office door, several constables and sheriff deputies grabbed Danos by both arms, threw him to the floor and locked his arms behind his back, immediately restraining him with handcuffs. Within seconds, Danos was stunned and overpowered. He could not react; he was shackled with black, chain-linked leg irons. Any escape or offensive counterattack was impossible. As he looked up from the cold floor, restrained by uniformed men sitting on his back and legs, he heard May screaming for help, "Danos, Danos!" as she was whisked away by two female attendants. He was subdued. Unable to come to her defense, May disappeared down the hallway in an instant.

After several minutes lying restrained and captive on the first-floor hallway in the Lake Charles courthouse, far from San Antonio and Oklahoma City, Danos considered his plans disrupted. He could only speculate what might have gone awry to cause this major predicament. The officers continued sitting on his back and legs with their full weight. Getting up, even changing his position on the floor, was impossible. With his left cheek pressed to the cold stone, Danos' vision was restricted. The uniforms were soon joined by an authoritarian sounding man bellowing instructions to take Danos to the basement level and place him in the first available empty cell, "Be sure to station two guards outside his cell. We'll deal with this criminal tomorrow." Danos was helped to his feet, still tightly handcuffed and shackled. Two uniformed police officers, Cpl. Davis and Pvt. Willings, escorted Danos down a flight of ten stairs, as Danos counted since the leg-irons made it impractical to descend steps. Then around a corner and down a dark and lengthy corridor to a block of eight dimly lighted holding cells. All cells were unoccupied. Danos would effectively spend his time in solitary confinement until he was afforded an explanation for his rude welcoming to Lake Charles. He was shoved into the cell as the black iron cell door clanged locked behind him. Davis ordered Danos to come near the bars of the cell perimeter and stick out his hands. Davis unlocked and removed the handcuffs. The leg-irons would remain so long as Danos was a "guest" in the holding cell.

Davis and Willings advised they would be down the hallway at their desks. If Danos needed anything, he should just yell down from his cell and the guards would ignore him from their station. "How cordial," he thought. Danos could not imagine such treatment.

In the quiet of the holding cells, the sound of voices traveled easily throughout the basement. Danos could hear Davis and Willings talking and laughing from their guard station. As they conversed, Danos could hear and understand the gist of their discussion. They laughed loudly. The facts surrounding Danos' predicament, as they pointed out, were quite hilarious. It seems the fourteen-year-old girl, May Clark, was the daughter of an influential man from San Antonio, Maurice T. Clark. Maurice Clark was not naïve as Jauan Fernandez believed, Jauan Fernandez, or Danos Knight, or whoever he was. The guards howled loudly. Davis and Willings had not seen this much excitement in Lake Charles since July of last year when crazy Fannie Dobbins shot and killed the local druggist, Herman Staid, for openly embarrassing and defaming her at a Tuesday night town hall meeting. Fannie was sentenced to a mental institution in New Orleans, until she got well. If she got well. As Danos listened, he discovered the assailant he knocked unconscious at the courthouse steps was one, Jeremy Solomon, a private investigator hired by Maurice Clark to "tail" his daughter, underaged May Clark. "Tomorrow will be interesting," they agreed with boisterous laughter.

Danos sat on the edge of a rustic cot positioned against the brick wall at the back of the cell. He stared straight ahead at the black iron bars with the locked cell door. It reminded him of his days in captivity at the Catholic orphanage in Matanzas. This stay in the Lake Charles courthouse jail would be brief he hoped. A lengthy stay could not be tolerated and would be unhealthy, possibly triggering nightmarish visions of the orphanage. Possibility of escape was dismal. Danos was provided a bowl of what they called "stew" and water for his evening meal. His pocket watch displayed the hour of 8:00 p.m. when the lone light at the far end of the eight cells was extinguished. Danos was left in the dark to himself and his thoughts, as the laughter and discussions from the guard station trailed to silence. As he sat on the cot, both legs stretched to the floor, he felt a critter rub against his right ankle. It was too dark to identify the creature. Probably a long-lost cousin of the rats he fought in the trash heap at Port Matanzas. Be assured, Danos would sleep uncomfortably tonight, considering the "interesting" day ahead.

This May Clark episode was quite painful for A.D. Just reminiscing about May Clark caused emotional swings that terrified him. He captured few details, but made his next entry…

We made our way in to a City in another state where they were not so particular about a girls age.

But May's Parents had discovered her affair and had the police watching exit and entrance into the city. We were caught before we could get the license and put in jail to await her father.

Chapter 19

Cpl. Davis appeared at Danos' cell early the next morning with a cup of hot black coffee, a tin plate of four thick slices of fried bacon and a biscuit. A breakfast to rival the "stew" he was served the night before. Danos was afforded a trip to the privy to relieve himself and freshen up for the day. The accommodations were spartan. He was wide awake finishing breakfast as his day began.

Later in the morning, he heard a grouping of footsteps, multiple persons, bounding down the ten basement steps, turning the corner and marching down the hallway toward his cell. Danos recognized one of the voices but could not believe his ears accurately identified this man. As the group arrived at the front of his cell, the sheriff identified himself. He introduced the group: Maurice T. Clark, May's father, attired in a dark brown business suit and looking formal. He did not fit the image of coming from a clan of mountaineering people. He dressed more like a business man of sorts, perhaps a lawyer. He saw May standing still and silent to the side and rear of her father. She said nothing. She did not wish to make eye contact with Danos. Her father obviously coerced her out of fear into realizing she had made an error which was in the process of being corrected. Cpl. Davis and Private Willings, dressed in their formal, dark blue Lake Charles uniforms, stood in their official capacities as witnesses to the proceedings which they were thoroughly enjoying. Just as the sheriff was about to read the charges brought against Danos by May's father, another man stepped from the back of the group to get a closer look at Danos in the cell. To his surprise and dismay, Danos recognized the Reverend Archibald Jennings. Too much to be a coincidence that Archie Jennings would just happen to be in Lake Charles, Louisiana and run across his seatmate from row three mere days ago. Rev. Jennings and Maurice T. Clark were old acquaintances and had been friends for decades. In fact, Maurice asked the reverend to accompany him to Lake Charles to retrieve his daughter and, hopefully, talk sense into the fourteen-year-old. Archie found this to be his immediate calling, to straighten this young girl from a wayward path with a grown man she barely knew but with whom she desired to elope. Archie now discovered the identity of this man engaged in criminal conduct with his friend's daughter. Reverend Jennings requested that the sheriff permit him fifteen minutes or so to "chat" with the prisoner after the sheriff finished reading the charges against him. Permission granted.

Sheriff Walter F. Johnson, Calcasieu Parish, Louisiana, read the charges as brought by Maurice T. Clark against defendant, Jauan Fernandez, of San Antonio, Texas. "By and on behalf of the state of Texas, Bexar County, on the petition of Maurice T. Clark, on behalf of the minor child, May Clark, age fourteen years, does hereby levy the charge of kidnapping a minor under the age of sixteen years, by and against her will, absent the required consent of a lawful parent, crossing state lines for the purposes of marriage to an underaged female child, so says the state of Texas." Danos stood in silence, glancing at May Clark whose eyes were riveted to the floor, not looking up, nor giving Danos any confidence she would come to his aid and defense. It was clear Danos was on his own. He did not fear the repercussions of his actions but was sorely disappointed in May's denial of her desire and commitment to marriage. The blame lies with Danos. He accepts sole responsibility for failure of his Lake Charles plan. Later in the day, Danos will travel back to San Antonio by rail, accompanied by Davis and Willings. They were prideful when their names were announced for all to hear their assignment to escort this criminal back to the state of Texas. Their chests swelled with pride as the assignment was proclaimed. Twits, both of them, Danos thought.

The visiting entourage turned and headed back up the hallway toward the stairs leading to first floor. Reverend Archibald Jennings remained looking at Danos. He explained he had known Maurice Clark for over twenty years. They had business dealings together and became friends, family friends. He knows May and Jane Clark, both troubled girls. Jane, more so, as she is in a family quandary with little possibility of extricating herself from the responsibilities of three children. Her indiscretions have marked her a loose woman with no scruples. Her life will be difficult. Reverend Jennings pulled a stool close to the jail cell. Danos was able to see Jennings' trade-mark: his neatly-trimmed, gray mustache which he sported for the past two decades. In his soft southern drawl, Archie asked,

"Is it Jauan Fernandez or Andrew Danos Knight?"

"Honestly, both are correct, Reverend. Jauan Fernandez is my given name at birth. My parents were executed in the Spanish-American War. I escaped from Cuba with the assistance of an army private, John Knight," he replied.

"I recently took on the name 'Andrew Danos Knight' in honor of my friend and mentor, Private John D. Knight."

It then dawned on Danos, throughout his conversation on the train, row three, from Oklahoma City to San Antonio, Reverend Jennings knew Danos was fabricating a wedding tale that was not planned and would not happen. He was confident Jennings and Maurice Clark discussed Jane Clark's "marriage" to Danos; quite sure they found that to be amusing. They were unaware that Danos was prepared to marry any woman who would have him just because he could marry. What they did not know was the depth of May's dissatisfaction and misery living with Jane and her three kids. May was ready to make a change. They feared Danos' actions were unpredictable, so Maurice Clark engaged the services of a private investigator, Mr. Jeremy Solomon.

Maurice Clark's fears became realized when Solomon reported that May had run off with Jauan Fernandez. Maurice has a multitude of friends and acquaintances in San Antonio. He learned of the whistle-stop planned that morning for St. Hedwig and the purchase of two tickets to Lake Charles, Louisiana. The plan was too simple to be effective and not complicated enough to succeed. Maurice's daughter, May Clark, had been kidnapped by a twenty-year-old man, who the Clark family knew as Jauan Fernandez. Danos felt the verbal noose being slipped around his neck by Archie Jennings. Reverend Jennings had a way with words, intoning, inflecting as he spoke to make one feel ashamed of his conduct, drawing the evildoer into remorse for his illegal, sinful conduct.

"You know what you did was illegal, don't you? You know what you did was commission of a crime, a criminal violation of the state code of Texas, don't you?"

Danos was back in "row three," held captive in the holding cell in the basement of the Lake Charles courthouse, with no escape available, as Reverend Jennings chastised him mercilessly.

"Are you aware of the penalties which can be assessed against you if you are found guilty at your criminal trial in San Antonio?"

"Are you also aware that you have sinned in the eyes of God Almighty? I cannot forgive you for your transgressions, but God can," so Archie stated emphatically. Danos was staring blankly over Reverend Jennings right ear, giving the appearance he was listening to the foundational beatdown by Jennings in the dimly lit cell. Danos could respond and defend himself, but, at that moment, grappled for an explanation of a sophisticated defense which did not materialize. He was unable to defend himself against a man of God, a man of conviction. Perhaps he could defend himself in a court of law and escape a guilty verdict. Surely May Clark will vouch for him and substantiate it was a consensual agreement to elope and get married in Louisiana. He was confident in May's goodness and willingness to tell the truth. Ma Roberts' words would haunt him on his return to San Antonio, "honesty is required at all levels, my little boy."

"God is merciful, my son," Jennings went on. "He will forgive you if you ask Him. If you repent and desire to change your life, He will forgive. With His grace all things are possible," Archie stated with hope and joy in his voice. Danos swallowed, cleared his throat and stood.

"Reverend Jennings, thank you for coming to visit, I appreciate your effort. I have significant things on my mind which I need to sort out. Perhaps we will see each other again one day," Danos stated sounding less than credible. Reverend Archie Jennings stood and left Andrew Danos Knight alone in his dark cell with his thoughts, exiting the basement as had the others.

The next morning, Cpl. Davis and Pvt. Willings instructed Danos to approach the cell door. Davis secured the handcuffs on both his wrists, unlocked the cell door. After being allowed his brief time in the privy, all three started up the hallway heading to the first floor of the courthouse. Danos could only shuffle, restricted by the leg-irons. Ascending the stairs to the courthouse main level was awkward. Danos took one step at a time and counted to ten going up, just as he descended down the ten steps days ago. Once outside, Danos could only squint to reduce the volume of sunlight entering his pupils. Having been locked in the basement for what seemed to be at least a week required adjustment to the open air and bright sun. They walked to the train station, two uniformed officers encouraging a shackled prisoner to move faster. A.D. cared little for their authoritarian attitude and continued at his own restricted pace, as he was the downtown spectacle walking the streets in his black and white stripes.

Once situated at the rear of the second passenger car, row eighteen, the leg-irons were shackled and locked to the seat struts as Danos was figuratively incarcerated by a manner of restriction. He would sit, captive, in row eighteen for the duration of his trip back to San Antonio to stand trial for kidnapping. His black satchel and case were under the seat of row seventeen directly ahead of him. Davis and Willings took turns watching Danos in his discomfort, unable to stretch his legs or lay across the double seat. Willings kept an eye on Danos as Davis stepped back to the smoker car to "freshen up," with a shot of whiskey or two. Danos thought this was enjoyable duty for Davis and Willings. The train ride back to San Antonio was without incident. They stepped out of the second passenger car on to the boardwalk of the San Antonio central train station. Within minutes, Danos was back in jail, at the Bexar County Jail, incarcerated. He hoped the judge assigned to his case would set bond quickly so he could secure release from jail to facilitate trial preparation.

May returned to San Antonio with her father and Reverend Jennings. May, Danos later learned from reliable sources, fabricated stories for her father that the kidnapping was just that, a kidnapping. Danos took her against her will, promising to pay her for her assistance as she helped him escape an untenable situation in Oklahoma City. She did not wish to live with Jane any longer and desired to move back home to safety with her parents. Danos learned May testified to the prosecuting attorney all manner of crimes committed by Danos within the state of Texas and in Louisiana. She testified Danos tried to kill Jeremy Solomon after she told him she knew the man. The litany of potential crimes allegedly committed by Danos was staggering. He would not get out of jail anytime soon, she hoped.

Danos expected May to stop by the jail to visit him and to let him know she cared about him, perhaps that she loved him. She did not. She did not attempt to contact Danos, although she knew exactly where he was...incarcerated. Danos soon realized May cared nothing about him. Likewise, he confessed to himself, he cared nothing about May, she was just a marriage proposal who got lost in his shuffle of life, once a brief attraction, then on to another. May's disappearance was not unexpected, for she was quite young. Immature would describe her accurately and more fully. At fourteen years of age, her commitment for a lifetime was an excessive risk. Danos did not love her. She was an attractive girl, emphasizing a girl-child, incapable of making an adult decision. Justifying his plight, Danos considered the loss of May was, in disguise or in reality, his gain. He was free to run wild again. Not shackled to a wife and a life of commitment. Free to do as he pleased. The iron shackles linking his ankles to one another in the Bexar County Jail had been removed, as he was at liberty to rest his feet up on his bunk and clear his mind, contemplating his next move in the fast-paced life of Andrew Danos Knight, cattleman, rancher, farmer, eligible bachelor. He wrote…

Her father and the Sheriff arrived next day. She was turned over to her father and I to the Sheriff. Her father had placed a charge of kidnapping against me as May was under aged.

When we arrived home, I was placed in jail again and May was subjected to all kinds of examinations and questions. She told a lot of things on me that I was not guilty of.

But I always thought she done it through fear of her father as they were a rough sort of Mountaineer people.

She never tried to communicate with me or see me afterwards. So I will never know the truth and as I was just marrying her for a wife and home and not because I loved her it did not hurt me to give her up.

Chapter 20

As Danos grew accustomed to the surroundings of the San Antonio courthouse holding cells, he was comfortable in his familiarity with this geographic area, the city in which he received his start in a new life, in a new world. Whether he would find a wife to raise a family, farm the fields and butcher livestock was still his priority, but not as urgent as he once believed. Danos needed to secure his release from jail to prepare for trial defending against these trumped-up kidnapping charges. He managed to send off a telegram to Pa Roberts in Oklahoma City. After weeks of not hearing from Ma Roberts' little boy, Pa assumed he just ran off and would not return. The telegram caught Pa by surprise. Danos requested bail money be posted with Bexar County so he could secure freedom, at least temporarily. Judge set his bail at $300.00, a tidy sum guarantying Danos would return for trial on the kidnapping charges. The following week, the deputy sheriff unlocked his cell door and said, "You're free to go. Stop at the clerk's office to reclaim your belongings and receive instructions concerning setting trial in your case." Danos was surprised, but relieved. The clerk said bail had been posted by a "Mr. Roberts" from Oklahoma City. "Here are your personal items. Check to be sure all items have been properly accounted for, and sign this receipt," the clerk stated simply. She added, "Keep us informed of your mailing address. You will be notified by post at least thirty days in advance of your trial date. If you hire an attorney, our communication to you will go through your lawyer." Danos signed the receipt, left the mailing address of a friend, and walked out of the county jail, a free man.

After he changed out of his prison garb and as he walked down the streets of San Antonio, Danos inhaled the familiar and not so familiar smells of city life. The aroma of baking bread and biscuits in the early hours of the day was tantalizing. Countering the smell of freshly baked bread was the overpowering smell of horse manure and urine from drawn carriages and wagons combined with fumes from the new invention, the manufactured automobile. San Antonio had only a few automobiles driving on its streets in 1911, a previously uncommon sight, but now predicted to be the wave of the future. Why he was bailed out by the Roberts bunch he would never know. They surely did not care about his wellbeing. Perhaps they posted bail because they had a trifle of respect for their deceased Ma Roberts and the care she showed for her little boy.

At nearly twenty-one years of age, Danos temporarily moved into an unoccupied farmhouse owned by his longtime friend to get back on his feet. Beauregard (Bo) Shockley, actually more of an acquaintance than a friend, agreed to assist Danos with lodging for a while. His possessions were few. They all were contained in his black satchel and the slightly larger case. His intention was to remain at the farmhouse, working jobs for neighboring farmers and ranchers for a while, then slipping back into town to get May Clark for his wife. He would necessarily be more creative and inventive in his scheme to entice May Clark away a second time. Foiled in his first attempt, another opportunity to capture May's heart would present again.

* * *

After a month or two had passed, Danos checked with the clerk of court at Bexar County Courthouse. He discovered the kidnapping case had been inexplicably, but fortunately, languishing in the clerk's office. Danos' case had not been assigned to any judge nor had the case been formally designated a prosecuting attorney. The clerk informed Danos that the status of the case against him now had low priority due to the withdrawal of Maurice T. Clark's incident report and petition to prosecute. Why Maurice withdrew his claim the clerk could not say. Perhaps May had discussed the matter with her father. Perhaps tempers subsided. Perhaps things merely returned to a normal status and they didn't want the case to fester, erupting into an emotional brawl six months down the calendar. This would renew the psychological trauma between the litigants and interrupt the healing process on both sides. Perhaps Reverend Jennings had exerted his influence on Maurice Clark. The clerk informed Danos that if the case was not assigned to a judge and prosecutor within the next ten days, the case would stand dismissed based on Bexar County local rule. The kidnapping case described in the petition for prosecution, sounding severe and formal, would not go forward without Maurice Clark's further endorsement. Danos could not believe what he was hearing from the clerk. Might the case against him be dismissed..... based on procedural considerations? Could the case be dismissed and vanish as if it had never commenced? Perhaps May Clark was preparing herself for another elopement with the blessings of her father. Doubtful. Danos would assess his chances for the next opportunity. It was strange, however, that May Clark did not attempt to contact Danos, did not attempt to visit him while he was in jail nor while residing at Bo's farmhouse. Danos must evaluate the risk necessary to entice May Clark to become May Knight. His goal to marry a woman remained unfulfilled; he would press on.

Danos, staying busy working on neighboring farms and ranches, was invited to Bo Shockley's home and ranch from time to time. These visits were in the nature of social events. Bo enjoyed hosting hog roasts, chicken fries and neighborhood social gatherings. On the following Friday evening, Bo prepared to roast two hogs in his firewood pit. He extended personal invitations to his neighbors, their families and friends. It had all the markings of a gala celebration for no reason other than to meet and greet at the Bo Shockley ranch.

Danos cleaned his black Frommier western boots, shaved and bathed and dressed in new shirt and trousers for the occasion. Pretty May Clark clouded his head as he remained mindful of the troubling kidnap charges, at least until that tenth day expires according to the clerk. He would continue to monitor the case status with the Bexar County clerk's office. Andrew Danos Knight's refined appearance this evening was not a true reflection of himself. Over the years, he developed a colorful vocabulary and a penchant for strong drink that rivaled a drunken sailor. He had no one to scrutinize his choice of words, continually ripping vulgarity off the tip of his tongue that most assuredly would have embarrassed Ma Roberts had she still been alive. The routine of imbibing strong drink to intoxication was a matter of course, not so much during the work day, but frequently afterwards to calm his nerves by letting nature sink in as he came into a state of relaxation, as he called it. Fortunately, he was not a belligerent drunk, but a docile creature, merely demanding services and compliments from his associates. Church? Oh no. Not for Danos. God had little place in his life, actually no place in his life, for God permitted him to suffer a young life of indifference which should not be required of any child. His life in Cuba remains tragic; he was ill-prepared for life in Texas and Oklahoma, despite the opportunities established through John D. Knight's benevolence. Danos would enjoy the food and fellowship with Bo Shockley, meeting and greeting his neighbors this Friday evening. A stranger is met only once, he anticipated.

Danos Knight arrived at the Shockley ranch just a bit tardy as he entered the sprawling back yard and decorated porch. Tables and chairs were plentiful and placed in a gathering area away from the firewood pit, yet close enough to the porch making spirited beverages conveniently accessible. As he surveyed the backyard, he recognized those with whom he had worked, nodded a greeting and continued his sweeping view until he locked eyes with a dark haired, dark eyed beauty. Here he goes again, with May Clark still stuck at the forefront of his mind. The virility of this twenty-one-year-old Danos Knight permitted his mind to crater to the ditch in an instant. He must meet this beautiful girl who has the looks of a mature woman. His eyes remained locked on her for a forever. Within moments, Danos considered he could get this beauty; thus, he could put fourteen-year-old May Clark out of his mind for good. It was obvious from the crowd around her she was a magnet of attraction. Her hair, her dress, her smile, her posture, her beauty, all breathtaking. Danos was mesmerized, struck by her command of the neighborhood audience. Her name was, simply, Helen. Too common, Danos thought. Too ordinary, he concluded. But the name, Helen, could take on a new and deeper context when they became better acquainted. The thought of May Clark would eventually vaporize into a terrible experience which will end with insignificant damage, so long as the charges are dropped against him. Danos would be free to run wild with this girl named Helen. The joy, the excitement, the availability of this beauty filled his inner being as he began his courtship in earnest.

Helen was born to a rather poor family, but they were honest and respectable people. She was an only child, born to Phineas and Claire Simmons. At age seventeen, Helen Simmons was physically mature, actively seeking a complimentary mate with whom to share her life, Danos presumed. Helen did not divulge she was searching for a perfect husband. Rather, she played reserved and acted unconcerned about the prospects of marriage. The Simmons family was church going, which, while not completely offensive to Danos, was a minor detractor based on his own personal experience with a merciless God; a God who permitted Danos to experience unspeakable things as an orphan. What Phineas and Claire Simmons derived from Sunday church going was not evident to Danos. Helen was raised in this religious upbringing, attending church regularly with her parents, to save her soul she believed and confirmed regularly. Danos was occupied with a less than spiritual agenda, but it did include Helen Simmons.

Danos continued in his drunken ways, cursing, fighting and refusing to attend church. He declined Helen's invitations to attend with her family. Always too busy with crops, ranching and personal chores. Yet, he enjoyed Helen's friendship and presence.

This relationship had the prospects of developing into permanence. It appeared San Antonio would provide the perfect woman for Danos Knight. He must merely remain persistent and maintain a façade of respectability.

The tenth day, now come and long past, required the Bexar County clerk to dismiss the case. Danos, focusing on Helen Simmons for the last two months, arrived at the courthouse as if unconcerned about his legal predicament and asked the clerk for the status of his case. She stated, "Maurice Clark failed to timely renew his petition for prosecution within the final ten days; the case has been dismissed." So relieved by this announcement, Danos thanked the clerk profusely. The clerk handed Danos an official "Notification by Clerk of Bexar County Court" which confirmed the dismissal of his case. Pursuant to the Judge's entry of record, the claim against Jauan Fernandez, based on alleged facts of kidnapping May Clark, was permanently dismissed; the case could not be reopened by Maurice or May Clark, so the clerk explained. Danos neatly folded the "Notification by Clerk of Bexar County" and stuck it in the breast pocket of his shirt. The notice would be placed in his black satchel when he returned to the farmhouse. Items of significance found their way into the satchel given him by Private John D. Knight.

During the first months of their courtship, Danos considered meeting Helen's parents but felt it was too early in the relationship. In addition, he regularly engaged in the intemperate behavior of cursing, fighting and drinking alcohol to excess; activities unknown to Helen he believed, and certainly unknown to Phineas and Claire Simmons. His religious views were inconsistent with those of the Simmons family. Danos believed he would be required to improve somewhat in these areas to transform himself into a desirable husband.

San Antonio was a fairly populated town of intermediate size which continued to grow. Yet, it was small enough for word, rumors and colorful stories to get around town regarding promiscuity, public drunkenness and gambling. These were fanciful and salacious topics discussed among the men at the barber shop and repeatable fodder for the church ladies' gossip groups. Although they had yet to meet, Helen's father knew she had been seeing Danos Knight, who was more commonly known as Jauan Fernandez in Bexar County and equally identified as "Jim Roberts." Although Phineas did not run in the elite social class, he did frequent the men's barber shop on Main Street once or twice a month for a hot shave and hair trim. These timely visits to the barber shop provided ample opportunity to engage in local chatter and a convenient forum to discuss a subject's background in colloquial terms. Over the past number of shaves and hair trimmings, Phineas learned of Jauan's sordid relationship with May Clark. He learned most recently that Jauan had been raised by a rowdy bunch of brothers and a belligerent father, the Roberts family, and that he was also known as Jim Roberts. On his most recent trip to the barber, Phineas learned of Jauan's adventurous spree to Lake Charles, Louisiana with May Clark. He was shocked as he learned the details of the kidnapping of this fourteen-year-old girl. Phineas may have been supplied inaccurate and exaggerated facts, half-truths and outright lies about Jauan's adventure with May Clark. Nevertheless, he would accept these facts as truths and gospel, including the reputation of the ruffian Roberts family. Details clearly described Jauan's arrest and incarceration for kidnapping, even though eye witnesses were lacking. He kidnapped an under aged fourteen-year-old forcing her across the state line to marry against her will. He did not know the case had been dismissed. Phineas Simmons had no other option but to have Jauan Fernandez (or Jim Roberts or Danos Knight) arrested by the Bexar County Sheriff after Helen refused to stop seeing him. Mr. Simmons was convinced his daughter had no knowledge of the destructive background of this twenty-one-year-old. Many of the circulating rumors about Jim Roberts were true as they were corroborated by reputable sources. Jim Roberts cursed like a sailor, had unequaled propensity for strong drink, no doubt an alcoholic, and was a godless unbeliever who ran free on a whim. Given the opportunity, Roberts could easily convince Simmons' seventeen-year-old daughter to slip to another county or state for purposes of marriage just as he did with May Clark. Thwarting

Jim Roberts' courtship by incarcerating him in Bexar County before he had the opportunity to elope with Helen was appropriate. From the barber shop on Main Street, Phineas Simmons headed directly to Sheriff Stanley L. Howe's office, swore out a warrant for Jauan Fernandez's (a/k/a Jim Roberts, a/k/a Andrew Danos Knight) arrest. Within an hour, Jauan Fernandez was incarcerated in the county jail. Jauan was not informed of the charges levied against him but was advised Mr. Simmons wanted him kept away from Helen. Jauan Fernandez was locked up, not in a dungeon-like holding cell, but in the regular county jail which provided filtered light into each cell. Iron bars covered the widows permitting a prisoner to maintain touch with the reality of the day by casual observance of the outside world. He was again relegated to wearing black and white striped prison garb while incarcerated. Despite his request, Jauan was refused paper and pen intending to write a letter to Helen. She did not know his whereabouts; to Helen, it was as if he had inexplicably vanished..

On his second day of incarceration, the court's bailiff called for Jauan Fernandez to be brought to the county courtroom. To Jauan's surprise, a deputy appeared unannounced at his cell door to escort him to Judge McCrary's chambers. The judge's chambers were just as formal as any courtroom he had the pleasure of entering. Centering in the judge's chambers was a light oak conference table surrounded by six matching wooden chairs, presumably for meetings and consultations with other judges and attorneys. Judge Julius McCrary occupied the high-backed chair at the head of the table. As Jauan was positioned at the conference table one seat removed from the judge, his hands were handcuffed, leg irons were shackled to both ankles making escape impossible. Any retaliatory movement toward the judge would be considered an assault and met with swift action by the two sheriff deputies standing immediately beside Jauan. They both were prepared to use their clubs and pistols with the slightest move perceived to be a wrong move.

The national flag of the United States and the flag of the Great State of Texas were proudly displayed at the front of the chambers.

Judge McCrary wore a distinguished looking black robe, validating the authority vested in him by Bexar County and the state of Texas. The Judge had a thin paper file on the conference table. He opened it in front of Jauan displaying the contents of the kidnapping case summarily dismissed against him. "May Clark," he mused in a whisper upon perusal of the file.

Judge McCrary asked, "What is your name, son?"

"My birth name is Jauan Fernandez. I'm also known as Jim Roberts. But I prefer to use my every day name, Andrew Danos Knight," he stated.

"Mr. Knight, do you have any proof or document or paper of any kind that identifies you as any of these three persons?"

"No, your Honor," Danos said softly and ashamedly.

"Are you a resident of San Antonio?"

"Well, your Honor, I live here, and have been living here for some time now. Approximately eleven or twelve years," Danos replied.

"Where were you born, Mr. Knight?"

"Judge McCrary, I was born on May 15, 1891 in Matanzas, Cuba."

"Do you have a certificate of birth from Matanzas?" "No, sir. All documents of public record in Matanzas were destroyed when the rebels burned the government buildings to the ground. Our plantation home in Matanzas was also burned to the ground. The revolutionaries took command and control of Havana and Matanzas. If there was a record of my birth, I'm quite certain it was destroyed in the fires."

"How did you get from Cuba to San Antonio, Mr. Knight?

Danos reflected on his past twelve years and knew Judge McCrary had a purpose in posing these questions. Before he could formulate his response, Judge McCrary spoke again.

"The state of Texas has many opportunities to offer people, honest people, who want to work here, live here and raise a family here. Looking at this file before me, it appears you may not have the proper credentials and integrity to be welcomed in San Antonio. So, how did you get here?"

"Judge McCrary, I lived with my parents on a sugar cane plantation in Matanzas. At nearly age seven, during the Spanish-American War, the Cuban rebels executed my parents, along with other members of my family. I was spared but lived as an orphan on the streets around Port Matanzas for many months in fear, starving, naked, and fighting with other street kids for food. I was placed in an orphanage run by Catholic nuns but escaped back into the streets. When the United States Army arrived to assist the Cubans, I was designated their mascot and sailed with them as a stowaway to Galveston in March, 1899. I have been living in San Antonio and Oklahoma City since then. I am an orphan, sir." Judge McCrary sat in silence for a long moment looking directly into Danos Knight's eyes, as though peering into his soul.

"Mr. Knight," said the judge, "I, too, was orphaned at the age of eight years old. My parents were lost at sea on a steamer ship that was caught up in a hurricane. I was staying with a family friend while my parents sailed from Corpus Christi to Spain in September that year. The hurricane was unpredictable and violent. It took months for my parents to be declared missing. Finally they were declared dead, lost at sea. I was raised by an intelligent, moral woman who saw to it that I receive a formal education. I miss my parents to this day."

Danos bonded and connected immediately with Judge McCrary. McCrary emphasized the necessity of becoming a legal resident. Judge McCrary had connections in the Department of Statistics in San Antonio and proposed to create an original certificate of birth to be recorded in the public records of Bexar County, Texas. Danos confirmed he wanted his legal name to be shown as "Andrew Danos Knight," with the birthdate previously provided. His parents' names were Don Pedro Fernandez and Carlita Fernandez. Judge McCrary emphasized this was a bit of a stretch of his authority, but he would see to it that Danos became a legal resident of Texas with documented papers authenticating his legal name and residence in Bexar County. Why would Judge McCrary do this for a poor little orphan kid, he pondered? There was an affinity between the two based on their immediate connection and on the life without parents each had experienced as orphans. They continued their conversation about the process of establishing Danos' birth certificate, with judge indicating he could receive the Texas Certificate of Birth within two days. Perhaps his life was beginning to turn for the better, thanks to a caring judge. Legal status in San Antonio with a documented legal name was the best news Danos had received since arriving at the Port of Galveston on the transport *MICHIGAN* so many years ago. Even better news came at the end of that same week. Andrew Danos Knight was again summoned to Judge McCrary's chambers.

On his arrival, Judge McCrary stood from his chair to greet Danos. Standing tall, Judge McCrary shook Danos' right hand, applying a manly grip indicative of the strength of the state of Texas and instructed Danos to change out of the black and white stripes into his civilian street clothes which occupied the chair next to him. The deputy removed his handcuffs and shackles. Danos excused himself, went into Judge McCrary's empty personal office, changed clothes and returned to chambers. Judge McCrary instructed Danos to read and sign a Document of Intent to become a United States citizen. Danos signed and dated the prepared document which would be filed with the clerk of court. Judge McCrary asked Danos to repeat this Oath of Allegiance if he desired to become a citizen of the United States. Danos indicated his assent. Judge continued as Danos repeated the oath:

I, Andrew Danos Knight, declare on oath, that I absolutely and entirely renounce and abjure all allegiance and fidelity to any foreign prince, potentate, state or sovereignty, of whom or which I have heretofore been a subject or citizen; that I will support and defend the Constitution and laws of the United States of America against all enemies, foreign and domestic; that I will bear true faith and allegiance to the same; that I will bear arms on behalf of the United States when required by law; that I will perform noncombatant service in the Armed Forces of the United States when required by the law; that I will perform work of national importance under civilian direction when required by law; and that I take this obligation freely, without any mental reservation or purpose of evasion; so help me God.

"Congratulations, Mr. Knight," Judge McCrary said proudly. "I hereby present you with a copy of the Oath of Allegiance and a copy of the Document of Intent which I will have filed in the public records of Bexar County today."

"I am also presenting you with an authenticated Certificate of Birth for Andrew Danos Knight for your personal records. This document has been duly filed in the records of Bexar County, Texas. Additionally, in reviewing this kidnapping file, the matter has been legally dismissed against you and is officially closed with no additional action required or permitted. You are a free man, Mr. Knight." Danos gratefully thanked Judge McCrary for his assistance and kind words. Danos was overwhelmed with pride. He is now officially Andrew Danos Knight, a United States citizen, a Texas resident, thanks to the efforts of another orphan, an orphan who became the sitting judge of Bexar County. Danos was free at last. His life would continue in the United States legally, but he would also remain an orphan, scarred by his ordeals, forever more.

"You are free to go. Remember, honesty is required in all situations. But let me add, 'As a legal citizen of Texas, stay out of trouble. Contact me whenever you find difficulty.'"

* * *

His chance meeting Helen at Bo's mixer was a fateful evening. A.D.'s emotions gyrated while he recollected the events of the past. He jotted his entry…

I stayed in jail a few days until the boys could fix my Bail. Then, I went to visit an old friend intending to wait awhile, then slip in and get the girl again as they did not finish the charge against me as it never came to trial.

While I was at a friends house I met a dark eyed dark haired girl that would have put May out of mind if I had been completely sure I could get her.

Everyone was crazy about her and I was afraid to give up the thought of May until I was better acquainted with Helen.

I was sure Helen's people would object to me as I cursed drank and did not go to church or anything her husband would be expected to do.

They were poor but nice refined people and as I expected as soon as her father heard of my affair with May, he had me arrested and returned to jail after he had tried to get Helen to stop seeing me.

Chapter 21

Unaware that Judge McCrary planned to free him from jail, Danos penned a letter to Helen Simmons on the morning the day before his release. Explaining his predicament, Danos directly blamed Phineas Simmons for causing his reincarceration. Whatever Phineas had learned about Danos Knight was most assuredly untrue and certainly did not merit additional jail time. Helen met with the clerk of court when she received his post. The clerk informed Helen that Danos had been released. Helen sent a return post in care of Bo Shockley, making excuses for the actions of her parents which got him locked up for a third time. Although Danos had become intimately familiar with the Bexar County Jail, the deputies, and the jailhouse food, he was happy to be free again. Helen expressed disbelief that her parents could do such a thing to a friend of their daughter. Mr. and Mrs. Phineas Simmons voiced objection to Danos, describing him as irresponsible and uncultured, to state it mildly, even though they did not know him and had never met him. Despite Danos' insistence, Helen was convinced his incarceration was due to the efforts of someone other than her parents. Notwithstanding Helen's disbelief, Danos learned from the clerk of court that Phineas did file a complaint against him, and he was incarcerated on the request. Convincing Helen otherwise would only cause friction between the two, a minor issue which need not turn into argument or hostility. Danos had made progress in this "relationship" with the dark haired, dark eyed beauty, as was his objective. The issue was put to rest as far as Danos was concerned.

He viewed this conflict as self-aggrandizement, assisting Helen in feeling a sense of remorse and empathy for him. This ultimately could be advantageous. Arranging times to meet with Helen must be strategic; proposed meetings were challenged by indifference and scheduled with difficulty. Phineas kept his eye on Helen's every move. Excuses for Helen to leave the house to meet Danos required creativity and plausible alibis; the few meetings they did have were on the sly. Covering her tracks with solid, invented excuses attested by her friends made such meetings whimsical and romantic, but always of short duration. Eventually, Danos agreed to begin attending church with Helen at the First Baptist Church of San Antonio, just so he could meet with her. Church attendance was by design, with no expectation of Spiritual redemption or salvation, at least for Danos. He was excited to put on a clean shirt and trousers for Sunday services, as Helen dressed in her finest. Helen explained to her parents that she was participating in First Baptist's ladies choral ensemble and felt called to serve the Lord in this manner. The excuse worked for a while. They met each Sunday attending the worship service, then enjoyed each other's company for an hour which Helen passed off as the ladies' choral group practice time after the morning service. Claire Simmons bought into Helen's logical and realistic story until Phineas took to investigating. He easily discovered there was no ladies choral ensemble at First Baptist of San Antonio. Henceforth, Mr. Simmons forbade Helen from attending church alone; he required they attend their local church as the Simmons family, as they had in times past.

On the following week, Helen and Danos met at the edge of Bo's cornfield, a perfect cover to avoid detection among the thick green, but now browning, stalks behind Bo's weathered hay barn. They laid together stroking each other, unable to keep their hands off each other's bodies. As he had already planned, Danos escalated their short meeting asking Helen for her hand in marriage.

"Helen, we've been together for some time now. I'm sure you feel the same about me as I do about you. Will you marry me?"

Helen anticipated this moment that his marriage proposal would come soon. It was not shocking, just a matter of course and timing. She was prepared.

"Yes, I will marry you. I have been waiting for you to ask me. Yes. Yes."

Although she was forthright in her response, she expressed her desire with clear reservation, articulated in the sound of her voice, complemented by resistant body language. Danos perceived her hesitancy as he attempted to emphasize the immediacy for marriage.

"Let's elope, now, tomorrow, this Friday. Let's get married now."

Despite Helen's assent to his proposal, Helen objected to eloping and declined marriage before she spoke with her father. Danos believed nothing good can come of a meeting with Phineas Simmons. Phineas knew Danos was no longer in jail and his objections to Andrew Danos Knight continued based on the defamatory information he learned months ago. Helen said yes to marriage but would not leave her parents without Phineas and Claire giving her their blessing. So it was, Danos, the orphan, unknowledgeable of the formalities of offering a proposal for marriage, inexperienced in the proper etiquette of courtship and inexperienced in discerning what is of great import to his betrothed, began sensing the pain of rejection and loss. Helen's refusal to marry at this instant was perceived as failure. Patience was a virtue he never acquired. His goal remained immediate self-gratification. Was it immaturity that caused his stomach to tighten with her refusal? Was it his lack of culture and formality? Perhaps he did not understand a daughter's respect and need to observe the will of her parents. Danos was sullen and in despair. Nonetheless, Helen was determined to exercise personal control over her destiny. That destiny would bear fruit when her parents consented.

Danos pressured Helen nearly every day they saw each other.

"Are you ready to run off with me so we can be married?"

The subject became repetitious and bothersome to Helen. She understood that Danos could not help himself. He was driven to demand elopement until she agreed, yet she would not agree. She believed Danos was sincere in his requests, but she also noted he was persistent to the point of exerting unreasonable control over her. Was this an intrinsic attribute he could wield in other aspects of their married lives? she pondered. Not overly concerned, Helen believed Danos would be patient and act only on her timely decision. Danos, on the other hand, asked himself if Helen was struggling with his impatience, with his immaturity. Perhaps she sees a peculiarity in Danos that may be unfixable. Will she change her mind and renege on his marriage proposal?

Over the next weeks, Danos, as best he could, inwardly engaged in profound soul-searching. Having proposed marriage to Helen, Danos admitted to himself he had no understanding of the essentials a husband was expected to possess. In retrospect, he had no credible mentor offering advice and direction as one deliberates a lifetime of commitment. What little Jauan learned from the fleeting period of youthful observance of Don Pedro as husband was of little consequence. As a husband, his father had talents and skills exemplified not in the Fernandez family, but in sugar cane and tobacco production, along with expertise managing the complex plantation. Don Pedro's actual role as husband in the family was imperceptible. Danos received no instruction from his father, either by word or example, as to what functions a husband performed. It was far less obvious to a boy of five or six years who managed to occupy himself in his father's absence. An absence while at work; an eternal absence in his premature and brutal death.

At that age, Jauan was equally displeased by the role Don Pedro occupied as a father. He spent little time, virtually no time, with Jauan. It was a rarity that Don Pedro was even present in the owners' mansion during Jauan's waking hours. How does one determine, if a father spends no time with his child, that a father could establish and develop any type of relationship with his son? It was Jauan's mother, Carlita, but more commonly the domestic servants, who watched and cared for Jauan and his sibling. Young Jauan could not recollect any specific time Don Pedro functioned as father to Jauan in the Fernandez household. Danos did recall the gold necklace, now in his possession, which his father gave to his sister for her birthday. One such kind act of gift-giving, although dear and tender, cannot constitute the entire role of a father in the life of a child. Experience as a son raised by Don Pedro simply did not exist. There was no lifetime foundation upon which to build. The fundamentals of being a husband, a father, were absent from Jauan's memory of Don Pedro Fernandez.

Pa Roberts and his sons, now all married, also demonstrated no such qualities or characteristics as husbands. Their activities imparted no insight into the role of a husband. Perhaps their wives were just as "knowledgeable" with no expectations of their husbands except for a "romp in the hay" every so often. The Roberts wives and husbands lacked the understanding and the ability to define what constitutes "husband." To the naive Danos, the formula for a happy marriage between husband and wife was elusive, perhaps unknowable. Observation of the Roberts ruffians gave Danos no practical insight to wedded bliss if such exists. What role his brothers played as husbands provided nothing to demystify Danos' predicament of determining what Helen required of him. It was, at that time, doubtful that Danos could ever learn what he must offer Helen as a husband. Experience as a father would present additional complex problems which Danos would eventually discover.

Consequently, Danos threw himself into his farming and ranching to clear his mind of Helen's stubbornness. Surely she will reach a point in which frustration with her parents becomes an insurmountable obstacle. Then they will be free to elope and run wild. Danos began to sense that waiting might be a positive sign of the maturation process. How long he could wait for Helen he did not know.

"Mr. A.D. Knight," had a positive ring to speaking his name aloud. The "Mr." prefix added dignity and formality to his character. Danos liked it when he was addressed as Mr. Knight, although most knew of and referred to him as Danos. "Jauan Fernandez" was used infrequently only by old acquaintances. "Jim Roberts" was a distasteful name Danos did not care to be called. His friends in Oklahoma knew him as Roberts, as Ma Roberts informally adopted him as her own. But Judge McCrary solemnized and authenticated his new beginning as Andrew Danos Knight.

* * *

On a Wednesday in the middle of the third week of September, Helen Simmons appeared unannounced at Bo's farmhouse looking for Danos. She had stopped at the farm which Danos called home only to find he was not there. Bo offered Helen a tin of sassafras tea as they sat under a twenty-year-old shade tree waiting for Danos to return from the blacksmith shop. One of his team threw a shoe which needed replacing. Bo and Helen spoke in generalities about Danos but then moved onto his goals in life, previously undisclosed to Helen. But she understood Danos in simple terms. She was aware he did not live a pretentious life and could therefore have no lofty goals. She was not surprised that the plans Danos expressed to Bo included "placing her on a pedestal," as Bo related. Perhaps Danos had developed a degree of patience, along with passing understanding. Helen was pleased. She waited for Danos' return to make her announcement known to both of them. Presently, Danos arrived at the farmhouse. Bo Shockley's team and buggy wasted little time returning with a new shoe for his mare.

He was surprised to see Helen sitting there waiting for him. They did not have a meeting scheduled, but one certainly was overdue. Dressed in a light blue, ankle length dress, Helen had her hair pulled off her neck so as to feel any available breeze in the heat of late summer in southern Texas. As Danos dismounted from the buggy, Helen hugged him and broke down sobbing. Her words were frantic, mumbled and indecipherable. Neither Danos, nor Bo, could understand anything she was saying. She spoke words on top of words, all exploding at once, garbled, meaningless and incoherent. After a few sentences, Helen was persuaded to sit down under the tree once again. She took a sip of tea and calmed down while Danos held her left hand and asked what she was trying to say. Through more sobbing, but with less emotion and volume, Helen began to speak with a degree of clarity. "Father has taken ill. He's in bed with a high fever. Doc Madison came to the house and examined him but doesn't know what's causing the fever. He prescribed aspirin to be taken every four hours which he believes will reduce the feverish temperature. The apothecary is to prepare the medication and bring it out to the house directly. Father is seriously ill. I just wanted to let you know."

Danos still had not met Phineas Simmons since he had been seeing Helen. There would be no reason to make a visit to a sick man whom he did not know. Further, Phineas had a dim view of the person who has been influencing his daughter. Better just to stay at the farm and get his chores done he commented. Helen agreed. She would return home to be with her father hoping his illness will improve overnight. She said her goodbyes and rode directly home in the Simmons wagon.

The following day, Helen returned to Danos' farmhouse and announced her father's fever spiked overnight, despite the aspirin powders prepared by the apothecary. He died at 3:00 a.m. His death was peaceful, despite a brief convulsion just as he gave up his soul to eternity. Helen cried again, a remorseful cry that she tried to be obedient to her parents, but that she failed. It is now too late to make amends to father. She will stand alongside her mother as father is buried. She must be strong and supportive for her mother's sake. Danos had decided he would not attend the funeral of a man he did not know, despite being the father of the girl he would marry. Helen understood and accepted his rationale. Danos advised Helen he'd be gone to Oklahoma City to check on livestock and equipment. He anticipated being gone for no more than two weeks.

* * *

A trip back to Oklahoma City was planned by rail, leaving Friday morning from the San Antonio Central Rail Station. Not knowing what he would find with the Roberts clan, Danos opted to purchase a round-trip ticket which could be used and redeemed for his return trip at any time up to sixty days from date of the purchase. This ticket gave Danos flexibility to see the Blackstone brothers and other friends and acquaintances, with sufficient time to conduct his business with Pa Roberts and his "siblings." Danos packed clothes and another pair of boots all which fit comfortably into his larger, black-handled carrying case. He left his white dress Stetson at the farmhouse in San Antonio but wore a light brown work Stetson which fit snuggly. He intended to ride the range and examine the fields looking for strays and equipment that may have been left out by one of the brothers. Danos believed he would profit handsomely when he disposed of his stock and sold the remainder of his equipment.

The next morning, Danos rode his favorite mare to the train station and spent time observing the ticket master selling tickets for this day's passengers. As he stood watching, he wondered if this was the clerk that provided information to Maurice Clark about May's planned elopement to Lake Charles and their whistle-stop at St. Hedwig's. He had no way of knowing and decided a confrontation with a nosy, loose-lipped clerk will likely have unfortunate consequences. The thought of punching the clerk in his face for divulging his secret plans did, however, gratify him. When the ticket clerk was available, Danos purchased his round-trip seat for the 7:00 a.m. Friday morning run to Oklahoma City. This information, now possessed by the ticket clerk, must be presumed to be a public announcement. Danos did not care. His travel arrangements were made as he rode home to prepare for his trip to confront the Roberts family.

He awoke Friday in the dark of early morning, well before sunrise. Danos scrambled two eggs and made a bowl of corn grits, accompanied by fried bacon and black coffee. Substantial nourishment for the train ride north. He finished packing and took a bag of hard candy and dried beef jerky. The combination of the flavored sugar and salt jerky would quicken a difficult day of travel ahead.

Bo picked him up at the farmhouse with his team and buggy and drove Danos to the station.

Bo expressed his intention to attend the funeral of Phineas Simmons the following week. Bo and Phineas had business dealings, mostly small, over the past years. Out of respect for Phineas and the family, Bo decided he should attend. Reverend Sears, pastor at the local church which the Simmons family attends, had a Spiritually immature dislike for burying members of his congregation. Reverend William Sears, still in his early calling of pastorship, was burdened and perplexed by the solace needed to comfort the family of the deceased in its worldly loss and, at the same time, freely spread joy among the family and congregation exemplifying the proposition that transitioning from death to eternal life is a genuinely happy occasion. It made little sense to Sears. Therefore, Reverend Sears officiated funerals in quick dispatch. He made few remarks of comfort for the family, while leaving the joyous, or not so joyous, after-life occasion to be considered only by the deceased's survivors, those who possess first-hand knowledge of the lifetime of benevolence, or corruption, of the deceased. The service would be brief; the undertaker would rest Phineas in a six-foot dirt grave. So would be Bo's respect to the Simmons widow and to Helen, the betrothed.

* * *

Danos thanked Bo for the ride to catch his train, told him he'd return in two weeks or less. Danos hopped aboard and found a comfortable seat for the long journey. The cushioned seat he chose, four seats from the rear on the right, appeared to have been recently replaced by the maintenance crew of the train line. This leather cushion had a luxurious look and feel compared to the other seats. The old replaced seat likely had been ripped, worn, cut or vandalized, requiring replacement, he suspected. He placed his large case in the rack above the rows, opened the window seat, permitting the free flow of air to enter and circulate throughout the passenger cabin. He closed his eyes to catch up on the sleep he was denied by this early departure. In minutes, the train was nearly at top pace heading to Dallas, and on to Oklahoma City. The unoccupied seat allowed Danos to stretch out on the double length and lean against the repositioned back seat cushion pressed against the side wall of the car.

As he sprawled comfortably across the full seat, eyes closed, legs hanging in careless fashion, a passenger rudely struck the bottom of Danos right boot which was dangling into the aisle. The ill-mannered passenger demanded he be allowed to occupy this seat. The unexpected companion made his verbal demand again. Danos was about to retaliate but did not when he recognized this traveler. Was this particular seat selection by this passenger coincidental or planned to be a bad omen? Any conversation with this passenger would be uneasy he feared. Twenty hours, or more, on the train with this jackal. What did Danos do to deserve this designed coincidence? As his companion for the remainder of Friday's daylight hours, the occupant of this seat in row fourteen, offered his hand as an introductory shake, between gentlemen. "Mr. Jauan Fernandez, also known as Mr. Danos Knight, I am private investigator Jeremy Solomon." Danos refused his outstretched hand and wished to escape. How is it he gets trapped in the same row and seat with a unique, but relevant stranger? How is it the conversation will turn into spinning falsehoods in order to avoid truth by fabricating devious responses? Danos queried to himself.

"If you recall, I was employed by Mr. Maurice T. Clark to investigate the kidnapping of his fourteen-year-old daughter, May Clark." Danos remained silent, now facing straight ahead as the engine roared and pulled at full power.

"You, Mr. Knight, took me on your escapade to Lake Charles, Louisiana as Maurice instructed me to track May Clark's whereabouts." No questions posed by Solomon yet. No answers required. Danos, looking forward, did not glance at his seatmate. He could not sit with this investigator posing questions for twenty hours, he thought.

"I am certain you had no idea who was following you from the Lake Charles train station that day, did you?" First question. "I truly believed you were a thief intent on robbing me and May Clark."

"Mr. Knight, and I use that title loosely, you made a large error in your calculation in Lake Charles. You see, although I'm an investigator in private practice, I formerly worked in Texas employed by the State as a criminal investigator. I have influential connections on the side of the law, as well as shady acquaintances on the dark side of the tracks. My connections owe me favors from work I've performed over the years which I can call due at any time. My colleagues have few scruples when it comes to returning favors. I suggest you watch your back and over your shoulder, Mr. Knight. You do not know the day, nor the hour." No comment, although this sounded vaguely like Scripture from a sermon he had once heard at First Baptist of San Antonio.

"Also, Mr. Knight, when I return to San Antonio from my present business trip, my attorneys will be filing a lawsuit against you in Bexar County Court for the damages I sustained as a result of your pugilistic actions at the Lake Charles courthouse. My left eye was damaged, my cheek bone was cracked, my nose broken, and my vision has deteriorated to the point it affects my ability to see clearly, nearly lost my eyesight completely. I will seek monetary damages from you in civil court. Please govern yourself accordingly, Mr. Knight."

"Pugilistic?" What does this word, he had never heard before, mean?

With that, Solomon rose from his seat, turned to the back of the car and sarcastically said, "Have a pleasant day, Mr. Knight," as he exited out the rear access heading to an available seat in another passenger car. Danos was relieved he would be left alone for the remainder of his trip to Oklahoma City. However, he would be left alone with disturbing thoughts concerning this brief conversation. Danos stuck a thick slice of beef jerky into the left side of his mouth. He popped in a hard candy piece positioning it between his right gum and cheek. This, he hoped, would distract him into a brief nap before their only scheduled stop, Dallas, before Oklahoma City.

* * *

It was mid-afternoon as the train wound north of Dallas and neared the Oklahoma border. Danos noticed the sun was still high above the horizon, bearing down with its unrelenting heat, exacerbated by unusually low air moisture. The sun continued to blaze the land as far as he could see. Although the breeze blew through the open window of row fourteen, it was uncomfortably hot and did little to relieve the passengers. As the train traveled further north into Oklahoma, all visible pastures were scorched to a brown hue. Any seasonal green, even in mid-September days, was not to be found in south Oklahoma. The few grazing cattle which Danos observed from his window seat found little grassy substance in the dried fields. The need for moisture was evident but lacking. Cattle languished under sparse shade trees as the livestock sought a cooler place in which to congregate. The southwesterly Texas-Oklahoma gusts propelled dried bushes across open fields, rolling as natural spheres of brittle stalk, twigs and branches. The steady wind continued without relenting. Just south of Oklahoma City, the winds whipped with ever higher velocity without regard to man, livestock or crop. The strong breeze and gusts made visible by billowing, gray dust from dried topsoil, continued to rage mercilessly. Sand and dust permeated every inch of the engine and passenger cars and found its way into every exposed orifice of each passenger. The sting and grit of this sandstorm was unique. The few cattle remaining in the fields sought protection from the pelting sand driven by persistent winds. As the train pulled into the Oklahoma City station, the velocity of the constant wind seemed to subside a bit. Danos caught a wagon for fare and proceeded to Arthur Blackstone's home. He would spend the night there before looking for his livestock and equipment. Danos was exhausted from this trip and fell asleep in an instant.

At breakfast, Danos inquired,

"Arthur, I need a horse or a team and buggy to explore and visit Pa Roberts' farm, and the ranches of all the Roberts boys. I plan on rounding up my livestock and equipment and selling it all to prepare for my life with Helen Simmons."

"Of course, Danos. I'll hitch up the team and wagon directly after breakfast. I'll throw a saddle, halter, bit and reins into the back of the wagon if you want to saddle out into the fields."

"Thank you, Arthur. We can discuss all of this when I get back later this evening. About Helen, too. I'm sure you will be interested in what has transpired."

Danos climbed aboard the wagon, pulled a red bandana over his nose and mouth, and took off for Pa Roberts' farm. Despite his low expectations, Danos would be surprised.

* * *

A.D. Knight paused his writing. He looked through the glass pane, spotlessly cleaned by the housekeeper two days prior. He peered toward the flower garden searching for the gray squirrel that competed with the birds for seeds and nuts in his homemade feeder. The gray squirrel, a frequent guest in the garden, was not visible from his vantage point, but the blue jay and brown wren apparently had put aside their differences as they amicably shared access to the seeds and nuts in the trough. Perhaps the furry friend decided to be complimentary this day.

Danos pulled the black satchel nearer to the edge of his desk. He retrieved the three documents which declared Andrew Danos Knight official. He unwrapped all three papers, examined all, and read the Oath of Allegiance aloud to hear himself speak those significant words. As he finished, ".....so help me God." stuck in his throat. He swore allegiance to the United States of America based upon a profession to a God he now believed existed, but still could not attest to this Supreme Being's power, love and mercy freely given, as his wife, Martha, manifested. He sat a moment and held the Oath of Allegiance with both hands, thankful for the opportunity provided by Judge Julius McCrary. He continued his writing…

Helen did not know I was in jail until I was there about a week. Then she was so hurt at her parents that when I wrote her she wrote me saying she was sorry her folks had caused me trouble if they had but she did not believe they had done it.

Although they had objected to me she did not think they would do that to me. I did not try to convince her that they did as I could see that as long as she wasn't sure about whether her parents had done it.

It made her think more seriously of me and that is what I wanted. I will skip over the time I had seeing her. I even went to church to get to see her until they stopped letting her go alone. And

I proposed to her and she accepted timedly and I coward that I was immediately begin to urge her to elope with me insisting on a talk with her father.

She did not want to leave without the consent of her folks and kept putting me off. Finally her father taken sick and died without me ever meeting him. I had gone to see about disposing of my stock and things I had left with my folks.

Chapter 22

Danos' borrowed team was weak and faltering, thirsting for water, fighting against the winds in stages as if pulling its load up an incline. With sun beating down on the backs of the two mares, the team stepped through chunks of dried, cracked clay under hoof. Danos rounded the slight leftward curved drive onto Pa Roberts' property. The exterior of the house had markedly deteriorated since he was last there. The white paint was weathered and chipped. All windows on the second story were unused and boarded. Vibrant flowers normally in planters on the front porch were now brown and lifeless. A somber, vacant air enveloped the farmhouse. The garden was dry. No vegetables, no corn, beans, tomatoes. No okra. Nothing green but resilient weeds of a persistent variety. Just not like Pa Roberts to let his garden spoil. Danos helped himself to surveying the outer house and barn. He saw only six feeble chickens, dried and dusty, roaming erratically, scratching and pecking in the dry earth with little energy or purpose looking for who knows what. Doesn't appear the chickens have been fed or watered lately. No feed in the trough, no water in the metal tins. Before entering Pa's house, Danos scanned the pasture as far as he could see. No livestock in sight. Perhaps the cattle were hidden resting under shade trees and obscured from view. Danos walked the grounds with purpose, around the house and into the backyard. He focused first on Ma Roberts' cemetery plot. The white picket fence had been removed, stacked neatly near the far side of her marked grave. Next to Ma's burial site, Danos observed a recently dug plot aligned parallel to Ma. A small wooden white cross was planted indicating the head of the grave with the simple inscription affixed, "Pa." Despite the animosity between Pa and Danos for over ten years, the youngest "Roberts" son, Ma's "little boy," was sickened as he realized Pa had been laid to his final rest next to his mate. Danos fell to the ground for Pa just as he had for Ma Roberts. Such was Jauan's expression of honor and respect for his "parents." Both taken from him unknowingly; no warning, notice or explanation. With angst, he speculated Pa could just not live without Ma. After Ma's death, Pa must have finally realized how much he had relied on Ma's continuous presence. And on her rock-steady stability, love of God and family, and her ability to present a calm temperament despite the outrage of the siblings as they cursed, fought with each other and with outsiders, and drank themselves into oblivion. Danos logically deduced Pa died soon after Ma of a broken heart. His will to go on without Ma was shattered at her death. The fight which once occupied Pa's being and released as reaction or on command, was exhausted. Danos was mistaken.

Danos left their gravesites with an ill feeling. These two people graciously took him in, an orphan, as one of their own for ten years. Although the Roberts environment was far from ideal, Jauan had food, shelter and clothing, despite being largely ignored by Pa and in a constant state of sibling rivalry with the older boys.

Danos entered the unoccupied farmhouse with apprehension examining its condition and contents. The floor-length draperies had been removed from all windows, presumably taken by the boys for their own use. The sunlight filtered into the living room unobstructed making thorough examination possible. As Danos explored from room to room, it became obvious any usable furniture, bedding, cookware, linens, clothing, anything of value had been removed. The farmhouse was vacant but for unwanted junk, valueless remnants of the long life shared by Ma and Pa. Their legacy of sixty plus years on this earth was reduced to worn out furnishings and an empty, fifty-year-old farmhouse in desperate need of repair. Inspecting the entire house was too great a task for Danos at the moment. His heart would not allow it. When these raw events and visions temper over the next few days, Danos may summon the fortitude necessary to complete his assessment. He turned and walked out the front door, closing it securely behind him. Feral cats, rats and chickens do not deserve to occupy this homestead. What will happen to this farm he pondered? Danos would meet with the Roberts boys individually to uncover the facts and discuss the property.

* * *

He climbed aboard the buggy, jerked the reins guiding Arthur's team down the curved drive into the road leading to the youngest Roberts farmhouse. Danos anticipated Daniel, and his wife Anna Roberts, would speak with him even though he was not expected or invited. It was a twenty-minute ride to Daniel and Anna's place, a farm with which Danos was quite familiar, having worked there regularly in times past. As he pulled onto the brown grass apron, dried and brittle near the home's entryway, he removed his red bandana. Anna stepped on the wooden porch to get a closer look. She immediately recognized "Jim Roberts," her brother-in-law. Anna was surprised to see him, but not shocked. She invited him into her home and made him comfortable with a tarnished tin cup of cool spring water. She called Daniel advising him of their visitor.

Daniel, too, was surprised by his visit, but did welcome him. There were only seven years difference in age between Daniel and "Jim." They could relate to one another more readily than the other brothers could or tried. First off, "Jim" advised Daniel that he was no longer called "Jim Roberts," explaining his legal name was Andrew Danos Knight, goes by "Danos," thanks to Judge McCrary. Daniel concurred this was acceptable, since he was really not one of the family, but merely accepted by Ma Roberts in her fantasy years ago.

"I just visited Pa's farm. The backyard grave site, now occupied by Ma and Pa, was quite troubling for me. Why didn't one of you notify me of Pa's passing and burial?"

"We had that discussion among ourselves and decided, under the circumstances, it would be best to bury Pa immediately after he died, without any viewing or any formality. Sending notice to you was considered an impossibility. We heard you were in jail again even after Pa paid $300.00 to bail you out once before. We assumed you were incarcerated."

"As another point, the circumstances surrounding Pa's death were quite gruesome. I can explain as this may help you understand."

"Please, go ahead. Explain."

"Pa had a field of alfalfa hay that he was sure to lose because of the drought. Everything was so dry. We had no rain for weeks, months. Crops were burning daily from the scorching heat and no rain. Pa's alfalfa field was sapped of moisture, but salvageable to an extent. He believed he could cut and save much of the hay before it burned completely. Pa let us know on a Monday he intended to cut the field and asked our assistance for the following Thursday. We all agreed to help Pa with gathering, loading and stacking the cut hay into the barn."

"So how does this relate to Pa's death? Danos asked.

"I am getting to it, don't be so damn impatient," Daniel exclaimed.

Anna, seated next to Daniel, nodded in agreement that his full explanation was forthcoming.

"Pa worked that painted, renegade stallion to pull the mechanical grass cutting blade to cut that alfalfa field. It had always been a rambunctious horse, contrary and unpredictable. We discouraged Pa from using that ornery horse for field work. He believed he could manage the paint and it had plenty of energy and drive to get the field cut quickly. Pa hitched the stallion to the mechanical blade. If you recall, the wheeled mechanical blade was outfitted with a low platform where Pa stood just to the rear of the stallion. The best we can figure, as the blade was pulled, it cut a six-foot-wide swath of alfalfa to the immediate right of Pa as he reined the stallion's direction and cutting path. Pa figured it would take a couple of days to cut the field, and by Thursday, it would be ready to gather."

"We all arrived Thursday morning anxious to get the hay out of the field, but Pa was nowhere to be found. It appeared that a third of the field had been cut, with the remaining crop untouched, still standing. We looked all through the house, around the house, yards, barn, everywhere. He was nowhere. He didn't answer our calls. We began to search the fields. First the alfalfa field, then neighboring pastures. After several hours searching, we found Pa lying on a slope, jagged with rocks, next to the dried ravine on the east side of his property. Pa was caked with dried blood, disfigured, dead. It was a gruesome sight. We believe, as he was cutting the field, two leather straps secured to the stallion were wrapped around his legs and waist. This configuration, with rein straps securely attached and bound around his lower body, gave him the freedom to direct the path of the stallion with more ease and accuracy. I've seen him do so many times before."

"We believe the stallion got spooked by something, like a rattlesnake, a band of wolves or wild coyotes, something, and bolted. The stallion's sudden jerk would have whiplashed Pa to the ground. Wrapped in the leather reins and straps, that horse dragged Pa through the hay field, through the pastures, down the rocky slope leading to the ravine. He could not have survived the trauma of being dragged uncontrollably and thrashed about through the hard dried earth, rocks and debris. That stallion, I imagine, kept on running. Still has not been found. The reins eventually stretched and weakened and broke leaving Pa lying dead on the sharp, jagged rocks. His clothing was ripped to shreds. His arms and legs were cut, bruised, broken. Bleeding all over. His head, face and hands were a gory mess when we found him. His abdomen was ripped and chewed open. His internal organs, his guts were eaten by wild animals as he lie there. His eyeballs were plucked, and tongue picked out by blackbirds or ravens. We presumed, we hoped, he was dead by the time the animals and vultures got to him. It was a disgusting sight. A disturbing, sickening sight."

Danos feigned empathy while listening to Daniel's suspected recounting of how Pa's life ended at the edge of the alfalfa field. Such a freakish demise. Danos felt little remorse. Pa's death occurred just over a month ago; little compassion for Pa's life-ending drama. Yes, it was most unfortunate, but life goes on, so Danos expressed to himself inaudibly, as Daniel and Anna sat within earshot.

"So, Daniel, I shipped 154 head of cattle here to Oklahoma City, with all 154 head accounted for, corralled in Pa's largest pasture three years ago. In May 1911, approximately a year and a half ago, you boys divided up my herd amongst yourselves with each of you accepting responsibility for a portion of the herd to look after while I returned to San Antonio to marry Jane Clark. Now, I've come back needing to sell my cattle and equipment for a bank roll of money. My finances are low. So, where are my cattle? Where's my equipment?"

"Jim, er, Danos, your cattle are all gone. Every head of livestock was sold about four months ago. Your equipment has been sold, too. We all had about twenty or twenty-five head each when you got thrown in jail and started on your life of crime. We figured you would be in jail for a long time. Then, when the drought started earlier this spring, crops were failing, not growing, dying and burning in the unbelievable heat. We sold the few pieces of equipment you gave us when you left. Farming was no longer possible, let alone profitable. The once rich topsoil has been blown away by the constant winds. Crops could not grow. It was worse with the cattle. Despite the Longhorns' ability to withstand drought conditions and disease compared to other breeds, it didn't take long for the cattle to become malnourished in the heat with little available grazing. The herd was becoming dehydrated. The cattle began to develop disease and were losing weight. The entire herd was sold to salvage some gain from the sale before all perished."

"So, where's my money you received from the sale of my cattle and equipment?"

"Oh. Well. The money is gone, too. Since we couldn't farm, we had to spend the money on food and living expenses. I'm sure you understand our predicament. We'd never do anything to hurt you, but we were damn sure you wouldn't return. But, if you did, you'd understand."

"You need not visit the other brothers. They'll tell you the exact same account I just related to you. Pa is dead. Farming is dead. Crops are dead. Cattle were sold, or they would be dead. Your few pieces of equipment were sold so we could buy food, or we'd be dead. That is the reality of our life in Oklahoma City. So, you might just as well get on back down there to San Antonio to figure out what to do next, my 'little boy,'" Daniel intoned with sarcasm.

He smirked confidently. Daniel Roberts and the boys had tricked the little runt of the family, the outcast. They had, indeed. All Danos had worked for and accomplished in the last three years and more has been for naught. He knew he could not trust the Roberts brotherhood of hoodlums. But Danos, schooled by the ruffians, would have done likewise if given the same circumstances and opportunity.

Daniel stood up from the sofa and said, "Come, Danos, let me show you the door and you can return to Texas." Danos bid Anna goodbye but looked Daniel directly in the eyes… threatening recompense. He was torn between leaving peaceably or launching an all-out attack on Daniel, purely for purposes of self-gratification. Vengeance really. He chose to leave without incident. Danos already had an altercation with the private investigator which is now percolating into a lawsuit in civil court. He would return to Arthur Blackstone's for the remainder of the day. Perhaps he can work for Arthur for a week or so to earn spendable cash. Danos exited the house with eyes riveted on Daniel Roberts, but with no further comment.

* * *

Exhausted from the day in the Oklahoma drought, shocked by the news about Pa's demise, and infuriated by his argument with Daniel Roberts, Danos pulled Arthur's rig into the barn. He sat in the buggy, his spinning head buried in his hands, as the horses drank what little water was left in the rusted, metal trough. Danos dwelled on today's events; he was horrified as they replayed draining him of all vigor and strength. No one to console him. No one to offer advice. No one to consult for explanation. No one to make sense of his predicament.

As a perfect host, Arthur had beef grilling on the outdoor firepit. The wind continued to blow late in the afternoon sun. They sought refuge inside the doorway of the barn blocking the full force of the wind and sand, as Arthur tended to the evening meal. The aroma of cooking meat on an open fire gave an illusion of normalcy, albeit tempered by the hot dry air and blowing sand. Arthur had placed two potatoes he had salvaged on the open coals and prepared them to go with the meat dish. He brought the meat and potatoes into the kitchen and carved generous portions of beef brisket for each of them. The potatoes were burnt black on the outside and cooked thoroughly within. They ate their fill and washed the meal down with tins of water.

They sat on wooden rocking chairs in the living area of Arthur's rustic home, casually observing the sand collected about the house, having penetrated through every crack, crevasse and point of entry.

"Are you aware that Pa Roberts died a month or so back?" Danos queried.

"I heard a rumor to that effect, but I don't know for sure that he did die, nor do I know any details."

"I just came from Daniel Roberts' place. He gave me the gruesome details. Pa was dragged through the fields by his wild stallion and died as his head was bashed against the rocks. Wild animals and vultures picked his carcass clean left dead near the ravine when the boys found him. At least that's what Daniel claims. I don't know whether to believe him or if I should try to find out the truth. Whatever actually happened, Pa is dead and buried next to Ma. Let's talk about something else."

"Sure. Are you heading back to San Antonio, or going to stay here in Oklahoma?"

"I may stay a week or so to earn some money. Have you any work so I can earn wages?"

"Danos, I wish I did. This drought and continuous wind have killed nearly all of my herd. Crops are ruined, there will be no harvest. I am barely getting by. The few cows that survived the longest I had to butcher before they all died. I can manage for a few more months, but I don't know what I'll do after that. The other farmers and ranchers around here are in the same position. I doubt you'll find much work in central Oklahoma."

"That settles it then. Those Roberts boys beat me out of everything I had. They sold all my cattle, equipment and spent all the money. I will probably go back to San Antonio this week and marry Helen Simmons. She is a beauty. She agreed to marry, I just need to convince her Ma to let us get married. You would like her if you ever got to meet her."

"I'm sure I would. Are you in love with her?"

"Strange you would ask that because I do not know. I don't know what being in love is like. I don't know what a husband is supposed to do. But I do know I can marry whoever I want, whenever I want. I was prepared to marry Jane Clark, and ready to marry her sister, May Clark. But none of that worked out for me. Now that Helen has come around, I feel I'm ready to get hitched. I'll just follow her lead and she and I will get along just fine. I know that's not much of a plan, but I can get her away from San Antonio and we'll be on our own, get a house, have kids and I'll have a job. Helen can take care of the kids and I'll work like I've been doing. Somewhere we'll make a home."

"I'll take you to the train station tomorrow morning if you want to get back."

"I accept. I'm ready to get back to see Helen."

As he lie in bed that night, Danos considered he was not man enough to take care of himself, yet he was arguing with and pressuring this young girl-child, Helen Simmons, to marry him. Things will work out. He was convinced.

He noted with difficulty…

I let them beat me out of everything I had.

Chapter 23

After the passing of her father, Helen appeared to have lost her best friend. Quite understandable. She became even more closely attached to her mother and insisted she would not elope and would not marry Danos without Claire Simmons' approval. When Danos returned to town, he picked up with Helen just where he left off. Unclear about the truth and meaning of love, Danos was attracted and committed to this seventeen-year-old dark haired, dark eyed beauty. He had a discerning eye for attractive women. Danos was infatuated by Helen as she put all the others out of his mind. Helen Simmons told him she loved him. Countless times. Danos, unfortunately, could not comprehend the depth of truth in this statement. Naivety and inexperience. He considered Helen to be his girl as they regularly discussed one another's needs and desires. How much of these discussions Danos absorbed would be evidenced in the early days of their marriage. Helen did trust Danos, relied on him and followed his direction. However, Helen was clear and adamant that Claire must consent to their marriage.

Soon, Helen invited Danos to visit at her home Monday, Wednesday and Friday evenings each week for supper, desert and coffee. This invitation also included mandatory attendance at church every Sunday morning. Despite Helen's professed trust in Danos, Claire Simmons remained wary of this renamed "Roberts" boy as he and his kind came from the stock of villains. Danos was raised by old man Roberts, associated with hoodlums and, even though they no longer lived in San Antonio, there was no question that Danos had acquired traits and skills of criminality. Whether Danos is a perfect husband, even an acceptable husband, Claire Simmons is doubtful. Danos struggled to purge himself of his old baggage as best he could. He desired to present himself to Helen as wholesome and acceptable, to be confirmed by Claire's reassurance. Suppertime during the week was an opportunity for Danos to impress Helen and her mother, for Claire would dispense or withhold her consent. Unexpectedly one evening, Claire Simmons inquired of Danos as to his intentions with her daughter. Danos was unprepared to furnish a response but recognized the query to be a valid question. A question which must be satisfactorily answered if consent would be granted.

"Mrs. Simmons," as he addressed her, "I am twenty-one years old, mature, experienced in farming, ranching, growing crop, raising livestock. I can provide a decent, stable life for Helen without worry. And we can provide you with five or six grandchildren for you to dote on." Correct answer!

"I would love grandchildren, and I can keep the children whenever you needed me to do so." Claire stated with enthusiasm.

"Your daughter is my motivation," he stated with conviction. At least in his current state of mind, Helen occupied the "pedestal" on which he had placed her, and as Shockley disclosed to Helen just before her father passed.

"I know you are industrious and a diligent worker. There is no doubt you can adequately provide for Helen's material needs. My concern is whether you, Mr. Knight, possess the qualities necessary to be the perfect husband for my daughter. I am concerned that you may choose to associate with the wrong types of people, like you did with the Roberts bunch. I'm concerned that you remain unchurched. You understand that Spirituality is the only way to eternal salvation, don't you? There are rumors that you have a tenuous upbringing, born in Cuba, but of Spanish descent, with a life on your own as an orphan. Is all this true?" she asked.

"Mrs. Simmons, most of what you said is true. But I have become a U.S. citizen, a resident of Texas and plan to get back on my feet after those no-good Roberts boys stole all my cattle and equipment. It won't take long to get financially prepared and to provide a place for Helen and me to live. You just wait and see."

Claire Simmons listened to his representations regarding his background and her daughter. His Spirituality was lacking, however. Perhaps attending church regularly with Helen and Claire each Sunday will be a positive influence. Claire was concerned about Helen's soul, as well as the future souls of any children they might bring into the world. Not so much about Danos, but she prayed daily that he would treat Helen with love and respect and be the proper head of their family. It would take much prayer, but with God, all things are possible.

Mrs. Simmons queried further, "What is your timeline with regard to taking my daughter's hand in marriage?"

"I am prepared to marry Helen today, tomorrow, this week. My current plans are flexible, but beginning a life with Helen can be soon. I'm prepared to take care of her and be responsible for her. I've been on my own for quite some time and understand Helen's needs."

Danos continued to work in and around San Antonio earning and saving his wages for a bank roll to start his family life with Helen. He did, however, partake in frivolity regularly after work. Danos socialized with young ranch hands, just like himself, who enjoyed drinking spirits when the work day was completed. Danos joined them after his supper visits with Helen and drank to the late hours of the night. To say these young ranch hands were a bad influence on Danos was inapposite. For it was Danos who was the instigator, the leader of this intemperate group of youths. They were secretive about what they did and when they engaged in such adventures. Helen would never know his activities, nor would Claire Simmons. Disclosure or exposure of this repulsive, immoral behavior would be the surest way to kill the marriage proposal, withdraw acceptance by Helen and be denied the consent of her mother.

Three months after Danos had returned to San Antonio, Helen had a serious conversation with her mother. Helen had accepted Danos' proposal. She loved him. She wanted to spend her life with him. Mother must give her consent.

"Mother, it is time that you give your blessing on my marriage to Danos. He's a decent man, a good provider and he'll be good to me. He is a Texas resident, and he has disassociated from those Roberts people. We'll live here in the San Antonio area not far away. We can give you many grandchildren. I will see to it that Danos goes to church with me every Sunday. Papa would approve, I'm sure."

Claire Simmons was reluctant, but she told Helen to arrange for Danos to meet with her this week. They would have a private discussion on this topic. Claire Simmons must clarify specific terms with Mr. Knight.

On Wednesday evening, after supper, Helen excused herself from the dinner table and went out of doors, leaving Danos and Claire to talk in private. Danos realized what was about to take place. He summoned courage and was prepared to make his case for his marriage to Helen.

"You realize Helen is my only daughter and I care for her deeply. I love her and worry about her continually. Asking for my consent to this marriage is a difficult decision for me because, and I will be frank with you Mr. Knight, I have reservations about you and about your sincerity in this relationship. I wish you were from a Godly family, but that can be rectified easily enough if you turn your life around and repent. The Roberts bunch has influenced you negatively; such lacks quality and sincerity. You have had a horrific experience as far as I am concerned. Phineas felt the same way. He was not only reluctant, but he was opposed to you as Helen's choice of husband. This burden is now left to me."

"Mrs. Simmons, I will take care of your daughter. She will be my wife if you consent. I promise you will not be disappointed with me, or with us."

"I am expressing my reluctance. I am warning you. Your commitment to Helen and this marriage is of the highest priority. I do not want you hanging around the Roberts, or any people like them. If you falter, I will assist my daughter by all means available. Do you understand? DO-YOU-UNDERSTAND? Based upon your representations and promise to me that you will take care of Helen, I give my consent for your marriage to Helen and do accept you as one of the family. From now on, I will call you 'Danos.' I have confidence in you, but still have reservations which I am unable to fully explain." Claire Simmons embraced Danos as confirmation of her consent and acceptance as Helen's husband into the Simmons family.

"Mrs. Simmons, you won't be disappointed in us. I promise."

"You may call Helen back into the house and we will celebrate with desert and coffee."

* * *

Helen and Danos were married at the Bexar County Courthouse, the same courthouse with which Danos was so familiar, by the Justice of the Peace the following week. One could only surmise why Claire Simmons did not insist on a large church wedding officiated by Pastor William Sears and attended by church members and her many friends. Perhaps deep inside Claire did not give this marriage much chance. Perhaps she did not wish to be embarrassed in her church when the marriage failed early on. Nevertheless, whatever her reason, Claire insisted on a courthouse wedding. A handful of guests, including Claire Simmons, a few neighbors and Beauregard Shockley, witnessed the brief but memorable ceremony. The couple exited the courthouse, showered with rice bags and petals of flowers, as Mr. and Mrs. Andrew Danos Knight were joined, *"....for richer or poorer, in sickness and in health, until death do you part....."* Those words rang clearly and loudly this wedding day for all guests to hear and witness. Danos soon realized that love was intertwined with commitment. He was capable, for he chose this girl as his bride, his wife. If Ma and Pa Roberts could commit for fifty plus years, so can he and Helen. Danos believed he had changed, deep within, in a profound sense just by reciting those vows in the presence of all to hear and affirm. Danos Knight considered himself the perfect husband. He perceived life with Helen would be similar to the life he had been living, except remaining true to his vow to this marriage would require his constant vigilance and patience.

Despite his representations, and the promises he and Helen made to Claire Simmons, the newly wedded couple packed two suitcases with minimal essentials, caught a rail and headed to Oklahoma City, free to run and do as they please. Running with no restraint and with no plan offered the couple a taste of liberty and freedom, not yet experienced by Helen, but first nature to Danos. There was, to a large degree, romanticism experienced by the new couple, free to roam at will, free to stop and enjoy the possibilities, and free to make a home. Such "plans" were implemented on the fly, with little consideration or forethought.

* * *

".....for richer or poorer...."

The hastily created, ill-advised plans were anything but secure. Helen, as the young bride, was negatively affected by this spontaneous escapade returning to Danos' people. The Roberts clan cared nothing for the outsider. Why Danos went back to the boys was not understood by Helen, nor adequately explained by Danos. Perhaps Danos thought the boys owed him a favor since they stole his herd and equipment. Untrue. The Roberts clan owed Danos nothing. But for the stability of working two weeks with the Blackstone brothers, Danos dragged Helen from one Roberts farm to the next, working for just slightly more than a mere pittance, a sleeping room and board consisting of one meal a day. As Danos plowed and prepared the ground for crop after the drought ended, Helen remained captive and assaulted by continual verbal abuse at the hands of the Roberts women. Crass and foul, these sisters-in-law were most vile creatures. Helen, a meek and caring soul, was tormented unceasingly by all manner of insults, cursing and name-calling. She could not comprehend the impetus for such hatred of her by people she did not know and whom she cared not to know. Each night, as Danos returned from the fields exhausted and filthy, caked with sweat and dirt, he showed little interest or empathy for Helen as she recounted the most miserable days of her life. The sisters-in-law gathered together to insult and belittle the new bride. She could no longer accept the verbal abuses as normal conversation; it was a verbal slug fest, beating Helen from dawn to dark. Cordiality and hospitality were not considered, perhaps unknown to the wives of the ruffians. It follows that the Roberts boys would marry women of such ill repute, lacking any suggestion of dignity or civility. Danos offered little sympathy for her endurance through such a gauntlet. Helen cried each night as Danos cussed and drank with each of his "brothers." Helen cried herself to sleep, as Danos bathed and joined in a meal with the siblings; he must keep his strength up to labor in the fields. Helen begged that they leave the Roberts and get a place of their own. Eventually, after he had saved a little more money and his bank roll became significantly more than modest, Danos conceded and agreed that he and Helen should change their living and working environment. The change would be a positive one with planned direction. Danos and Helen agreed to find a farm to buy and grow crop as their independent way of life. The taste of freedom they initially experienced in Oklahoma City would continue as it began, free to do as they pleased.

* * *

Danos had been sitting at the library desk writing for hours. Yet he had much more to record and explain. He must stand for a brief while. As he stood, he stretched his legs, touched the fingertips of each hand to the tops of his black oxford shoes and felt the muscles in his back and legs gradually pull and loosen. The tightness from being restricted to one position eased as he continued to stretch. He did not realize how physically demanding it would be to write the pages of his personal story. He considered the writing necessary to pass along to family generations, or down to any soul who might have an interest in the record of his personal endeavors. However, the physical toll on his body this day would not compare to the mental trauma of recollecting and writing, further depicting and emphasizing the wretched life he had lived. Continuing on will be torturous, agonizing.

Danos left the library trudging down the stairs to the main level of the house just to break for exercise, stretching as he encountered each step. He cleared his mind as he thought about his next adventure with Helen and how he might structure the coming sentences into acceptable prose. He also considered how one must carry on rational deliberation with oneself to record a descriptive journal entry. At the bottom of the stairs, he turned to the right and walked down a short hallway. He unlocked and opened the door onto the patio adjacent to the back lawn and flower garden. The usually friendly squirrel, startled in the corner, scurried away; the wren and jay flew to safety in higher branches. Danos looked at his favorite green and white striped lawn chair which had a natural, relaxing sway built into its construction.

He strolled through the flowers, inhaling the sweet essence of azaleas, gladiolas and lilacs, roses and peonies. The abundant pallet of colors and hues exploded into his appreciation as if he had just observed the profusion of a magnificent bouquet. He sat in the lawn chair, believing a change in seating contour would invigorate his legs and torso.

The coming sentences and paragraphs would be mentally exhausting, as he came dangerously face to face with Helen (Simmons) Knight after more than a decade's absence. Danos feared recollection of this portion of his life as it was a segment of repugnant reality. Independent. Irresponsible. Inconsiderate. Immature. Irreconcilable. Inexperienced. The thought of recounting the dark details of his relationship with Helen was "guilty as charged." He began to sweat and shake uncontrollably in his favorite outdoor chair, a chair which normally provided comfort. Not today. Not this coming hour. The dreadful past will converge with the present. It will be terrifying to relive and nearly impossible to record. Danos must summon every measure of inner strength to continue this feat. He sat for a long moment regaining a semblance of composure. He stood, walked up and down one row of the flower garden, pivoted and entered the house, up the stairs and resumed his position at the library desk. He continued his record…

I was not man enough to take care of myself, yet I was arguing this little girl child to marry me.

She loved and trusted me and when I went back she persuaded her mother to let me come to her house.

We were together about 3 nights a week and Sundays for about 3 months. I was with her feeling the only decent safer ones.

I spent during the week often getting drunk after I would leave her house on the nights I seen her.

I managed to keep her from knowing this of course. Finally she agreed to marry me at once if I would get her mother's consent.

After while I got up courage to speak to her mother and soon we were married. With her mother warning that she could expect any kind of treatment from me and my people as we were a tough bunch.

Helen left with me for the home of my people. I was expecting to drag her from one to the other working for our board as I had done until I could get started again.

So after I had done this for awhile and she had been insulted and resisted by marrying one of them, even the women.

Chapter 24

"....for richer or poorer..." (cont'd)

After losing all his livestock and equipment to the Roberts brothers, Danos embarked on his new beginning with Helen Knight. He experienced early success marked by the sizeable bank roll he saved through arduous work and perseverance. Danos believed he could negotiate the purchase of an existing farm which would meet his requirements. Helen, thankful for the merciful split from the demon-possessed Roberts kinfolk in Oklahoma City, was prepared to run free with her husband. They packed their bags and left for Arkansas, an exceptional corn and cotton producing state with remarkable opportunity. Helen cared not which state nor how far she was from her mother in San Antonio. She insisted only on great separation from Oklahoma City and the Roberts brothers. Little Rock met this singular requirement. Unfortunately, Danos would become unforgivably confused in his vow and role as Helen's "desirable husband" and falter in his promise to Claire Simmons.

As they disembarked from the train in Little Rock, each carried two cases of possessions. Helen, energized with optimism, stepped off the train with a bound carrying one black and one brown suitcase. She had packed the black case with her finest clothing and personal essentials, bathing, cosmetics and grooming. The brown case contained everyday work clothes, as she would assist Danos in preparing and planting the field, weeding and harvesting. A successful marital enterprise would come to fruition as the couple joined forces building a crop farm in Arkansas, from little of nothing to greatness. Danos carried his black leather satchel and the larger case, both packed with work clothes. Danos did bring one long sleeve shirt and dress trousers for meetings and church, should he decide to attend. His bank roll was discreetly tucked in the satchel along with his memorabilia.

Helen and Danos carried their belongings five city blocks from the Little Rock rail station to the Hawkins Inn on Fourth Street. The room accommodations were sparse but adequate, bed, chair and wash stand. Neat and clean. Breakfast served daily at 6:30 a.m. The inn was centrally located in mid-town. They secured lodging for three nights, believing they could quickly find and purchase an existing farmhouse with sufficient acreage for crop. The inn's proprietor, Reginald Jones, III, was well-connected to the community and provided banking information to Mr. and Mrs. Danos Knight concerning available farm land.

Taking time to freshen up from their journey, Helen and Danos thanked Mr. Jones for his recommendations and proceeded directly to the Pulaski County Bank & Trust of Little Rock. As they proceeded to the bank, they observed the vibrancy of the business district of Little Rock. Just off the pedestrian walkway, streets were lined by sitting benches, made of wood and painted an inviting deep-green color. Street lights, uniformly distanced between one another, made for early evening illumination encouraging social gathering. All categories of businesses were available including Doc Ephingham's apothecary, general stores, William J. Black's funeral parlor, local physicians Doctors Brandon and Remington, the local newspaper and printing company known as the Little Rock Gazette, several other banks and clothing stores for men and women. From the advertising boards strategically placed about mid-town, agriculture, by far, appeared to be the chief enterprise in Little Rock. Danos felt welcomed and at home instantly. Helen followed the lead of her husband, relied on him and trusted he would make the soundest of decisions for their new beginning and joint farming enterprise.

Pulaski County Bank's Vice-President in charge of real estate and farmland introduced himself to Helen and Danos.

"My name is Henry MacFarland, senior Vice-President of the bank. I oversee the land acquisition and mortgage department of Pulaski County Bank & Trust. I sell and finance the acquisition of land and acreage throughout the state, but primarily in the Little Rock area. What can I do for you?"

"I am Andrew Danos Knight. This is my wife, Helen. We just arrived in town, staying at the Hawkins Inn, booked for three nights. We are looking to purchase farmland in Little Rock, intending to grow crop, and raise cattle, eventually."

"What size farm are you interested in purchasing, Mr. Knight," MacFarland inquired. "We have a modest bank roll to invest and hope to find at least thirty, forty or fifty acres of tillable soil to start crop. I'm industrious and work hard, day and night, to be successful."

"I'm sure you have the ability to make a go of it, Mr. Knight. We have a sixty-acre parcel of prime farmland which has just been announced for sale by the owner, Mr. Bertrand A. Smith. He goes by B.A. Smith. The sixty acres is on the northwest side of Little Rock, about one mile out of town on Creasy Springs Road. It has an old farmhouse, somewhat run down, which a young, energetic man like yourself can fix up to livable condition. I can make arrangements for B.A. to show it to you, perhaps as early as tomorrow, if you'd like."

"That would be perfect, Mr. MacFarland. Could we meet with Mr. B.A. Smith at 10:00 a.m. tomorrow?

"I'll get in touch with B.A. this afternoon and send a message care of the Hawkins Inn by tonight confirming the meeting."

"That is fine, Mr. MacFarland," Danos replied.

Danos and MacFarland shook hands as gentlemen, most unlike the Roberts clan. Helen and Danos returned to the Hawkins Inn discussing what seemed to be much good fortune on their first day in town. Hopefully the sixty acres of farmland will be available at a reasonable price. Danos contemplated the need to retain funds from his bank roll to buy a mule or horse or two and a minimum of equipment, most importantly a plow, to break ground and prepare the land for planting, plus living expenses until income is generated from crop. Danos envisioned he would also work as a farm hand or cattle rancher for the neighbors for supplement. Helen agreed as they solidified plans for their joint venture. Helen will cook, keep house and do other domestic chores. Danos would work the field; Helen, too, as she becomes available. Additional income working for the neighbors was Danos' plan. Finally, a workable strategy was devised, agreed by both.

Mr. Reginald Jones, III advised Danos in written message that B.A. Smith would arrive by horse and buggy at the Hawkins Inn tomorrow at 10:00 a.m. and escort Mr. and Mrs. Knight to view his property. Their plan was coming together just as they had hoped. If the acreage was suitable for farming, Danos had made up his mind to purchase the property. The condition of the old farmhouse was of secondary concern, for Danos could refurbish anything into habitable condition.

Mr. Bertrand A. Smith arrived promptly at 10:00 a.m. the next morning calling on Mr. and Mrs. Knight. Danos and Helen made brief introductions as they climbed aboard the spacious two seat wagon, pulled by two magnificent-looking brown mares. The leather halters and harnesses were unmistakably custom made. The brown leather, specially engraved with Smith's personal insignia and bejeweled with decorative, polished brass riveting, projected luxury and extravagance. Such splendid equipment manifested Smith's success. His team of mares were disciplined and well-trained. B.A. Smith wore a brown suit, with western leather boots. His matching brown hat, of high-quality, was impeccable. There is no question, B.A. Smith was a man of wealth and means. His personality, as far as Danos could discover from their initial conversations, was a product of farming, business dealings and turning a profit.

"Mr. Knight, may I call you Danos?" asked Smith.

"Of course you may."

"I farmed that parcel for six consecutive years, and then rested it the seventh year, last year, the year of jubilee. It stayed dormant and rejuvenated this last growing season. The drought and windstorm from the west hurt a little but did not damage us as badly as Oklahoma. This parcel should still be prime earth with healthy topsoil. With rest and rejuvenation for the last twelve months, this sixty-acre plot should result in a far greater yield than the average acreage around these parts. Cotton or corn, either one, my boy."

B.A. Smith was in his mid- to late-fifties, slight in stature, uncommonly thin, but confident in his words of exhortation and enthusiasm. His southern drawl, typical of most in Arkansas, portrayed an air of comfort, integrity and sincerity. His sandy brown hair was beginning to gray around the sides and above his ears, manifesting B.A. had experienced his share of stress and anxiety over his adult life. While his maturity was reflected by rugged facial features, his blue-green eyes unmasked the soul of a youthful spirit, inclined to genuine care for his fellow man. Danos and Helen were both impressed and comforted by this feature. The prominent wrinkles at his eyes' edge and the corners of his mouth indicated Smith tends to smile readily and optimistically, rather than offer an offensive foul scowl. B.A. Smith was just a country farmer turned prosperous businessman.

They arrived at the parcel, near the farthest end of Creasy Springs Road in due course. B.A. assisted Helen down from the buggy onto the field thus far only imagined and pictured in their minds. The parcel was a large expanse of green vegetation, not fenced but clearly marked by the surveyor according to metes and bounds. B.A. pointed out the marked boundaries. The corners and perimeter indicated the sixty acres were dimensioned in a nearly perfect square. Extraneous tree growth was absent from the parcel indicating its prior use for growing crop. Easily accessed from the road, the farmhouse occupied the southwest corner of the geometric plot. However, of chief concern to Helen, the farmhouse was little more than a dilapidated cabin. The metal roof appeared to be in fair shape if it does not leak. However, the doors and windows needed significant work. Once cleaned and repaired, it could accommodate Helen and Danos, the first residence they would call their own.

Helen's heightened body language, interpreted only by Danos, signaled her disproval of this intended living facility. She clearly indicated the cabin was unsatisfactory. B.A. Smith represented it was a furnished dwelling, sold "as-is" with the acreage. Danos brushed off Helen's assessment discounting the condition of the cabin stating, "I can fix this farmhouse into a home, easily." Helen became queasy. Early on, she learned how to recognize and interpret Danos' unwavering commitment in direction once he made up his mind. Danos and Smith haggled and negotiated the price to the satisfaction of both, although Danos knew the agreed upon price was higher than what he intended to pay. But Danos believed the anticipated, above-average harvest, as professed and predicted by Mr. Smith, would more than compensate for this investment. Additionally, he would work for the farmers in the area earning supplemental income. Danos, without discussing the business deal with Helen, his business partner, or receiving her approval, agreed to pay the stated amount. Danos had the funds. Helen became the owner of a cabin in the country, their Creasy Springs Road domicile in Little Rock.

Helen Simmons, the newlywed, now Helen Knight, was thankful and fortunate to have a dwelling of her own, especially far away from her in-laws. Before long, Danos transformed the cabin into a castle to be enjoyed by Knight and his wife. This lady, once a distressed damsel, has been rescued from a life of emptiness, suffocated and controlled by her widowed mother in San Antonio. Helen was transformed into a lady anticipating her husband's return from the fields in the early evening to enjoy the benefits of married life, so she considered.

Danos and Helen soon discovered the disadvantages of a cabin in the country which had remained unoccupied for a full year. The bedding was infested with bugs and other pests which required exterminating. Purchasing necessary extermination and cleaning supplies was outside of their anticipated budget, but required, nonetheless. The cabin soon became a home, as Helen assumed the role of a domestic and cook and was obedient to her wifely duties.

* * *

"...in sickness and in health..."

Danos had cleared one-half of the sixty-acre plot of unwanted, wild overgrowth and vegetation as he began to till the soil with his young two-mule team. Plowing sixty acres with the two-furrow metal plow, purchased second hand, would take considerable effort. The available time needed to prepare the field for planting was quickly diminishing. He required assistance preparing the entire sixty acres. Initially, he *suggested* Helen help clear the growth and debris of the remaining thirty acres. She preferred her domestic role and to rid the cabin of dead lizards, dried frogs and southern scorpions she discovered throughout the day. Further, her time was largely occupied with sewing dresses from simple paper patterns for herself, as she had left nearly all her clothing with her mother in San Antonio. Helen would never impose on her mother to ship anything to Arkansas. Sewing and embroidering were favorite past-times while Danos worked the field. Helen told Danos she preferred not to work in the field; Danos was most displeased. He *politely asked* that Helen help clear the remainder of the field. Helen unreasonably denied his request which Danos found to be contemptable and unacceptable, for he was the head of his family.

As a Tuesday afternoon rain shower unpredictably burst into a downpour, Danos returned to the house unannounced. Helen was surprised by his entry, as she was sitting in silence sewing the hem of a yellow-blue, patterned cotton dress. He stood in the living area; his clothes soaked by the downpour. His gray-colored work hat had been removed to reveal his wet, stringy black hair clinging to his neck and shoulders as water pooled on the flooring. Danos became enraged. He looked directly into Helen's eyes. It was the same look the Roberts brothers fashioned when they were about to lose control. Helen had seen this look before. The familiarity of eyes figuratively beating her was a mere prelude to the rage which would soon follow. She recognized the same degree of temper in the Roberts brothers on numerous occasions. Helen did not know what to do, how to react, or what she could say to avoid his next move. Danos instinctively grabbed the black, cast-iron skillet off the wood-burning stove. He raised it high above his right shoulder and came down with a force that could easily crush a skull. He released the skillet as it launched in a short trajectory slamming into the wall of the cabin, sailing just inches to the right of Helen's left ear where she sat on the sofa, clanging onto the wooden floor. Helen was terrified. In shock. Danos had never reacted this way before. He was breathing deeply, staring at Helen's patterned hem-work and yellow-blue dress. The surface veins exposed on his wet neck were engorged and bulging. His chest was heaving, deeply inhaling each breath. She could hear her heart pounding aloud. Danos was a moment from erupting. Helen had nowhere to go, nowhere to hide, and nowhere to run for safety. Her complete dependence and faith had been placed in her husband. She loved him unconditionally, she thought that instant, but she also feared him. Helen could think of no immediate solution to this quandary. Her dependence misplaced, Danos would explode.

Danos shouted as loudly as he could for no one to hear. Only Helen.

"WHAT ARE YOU DOING, WOMAN?!!" he exclaimed in thunderous volume.

"Did I not ask you to help me in the field?"

"I NEED HELP IN THE FIELD! HELP IN THE FIELD! We have thirty more acres to clear. Only limited daylight to work and you deny me?!!"

"I expect you to move when I tell you."

He grabbed a wooden kitchen chair and splintered it into kindling, driving it into the floor. Breaking this solidly built piece of wooden furniture by hand was terrifying. Danos appeared to have super human strength in his rage. He grabbed Helen's paper sewing pattern ripping it in two. He threw her yellow-blue dress across the floor. Helen feared what he would do next. He looked into her wide eyes and grasped a handful of Helen's dark hair, yanked her off the sofa with one jerk and continued to scream in her face, as she stood inches from destruction. With mouth wide open, teeth and tongue exposed, she felt his hot moist breath shower against her cheek, his spittle sprayed uncontrollably into Helen's eyes, nose and mouth. It was too much for Helen to comprehend. She was bordering on blackout witnessing her husband out of control. Danos shoved her onto the sofa. Trembling in fright and torment from his hysterical rage, Helen curled into a ball and remained on the sofa motionless, defenseless, in silence.

Danos departed her presence and changed into dry clothes.

"Woman, as soon as this downpour stops, I *demand* that you get out to the field and start clearing the remaining thirty acres. We have no time to waste. We have no time for you to cut patterns and sew dresses. We only have time for field work. Understood? UNDERSTOOD?!"

"Yes," Helen whimpered with fear, like a tortured animal, in submission to her husband.

Helen's attitude changed from this attack forward. She feared a repeat of his violent acts. Once Danos reached the crescendo of discontent, he could lose control and explode in a moment, without further warning. This was the first display she witnessed, but it would not be the last. Helen remained the victim, but also his business partner. She walked the thin line set by her husband with no deviation allowed.

Helen worked in the field daily clearing the remaining overgrowth. From sun up until late afternoon, Helen swung a heavy scythe ripping the weeds and thick vegetation just above the root at ground level. The chopped weeds and growth dried and were heaped into piles. As the mounds of weeds were gathered, Helen set them on fire monitoring the flames and watching as billowing clouds of gray smoke rose into the skies. Helen was cautious of the breeze and refrained from burns on days with driving wind.

While they worked together, they spoke about little other than the importance of preparing the soil for planting crop. This silence was preferrable as it avoided spawning arguments about insignificant issues, even though Helen remained frustrated about his lack of concern for obvious domestic problems. Helen made noticeable progress throughout the day while Danos continued to plow. Late in the afternoon and evening, about one hour before sunset, Helen left the field to prepare their evening meal. This schedule worked well until Danos took on supplemental work and tasks for the neighboring farmers and ranchers. With his skills, Danos was in demand and stayed occupied not only on their own acreage, but also at the other farms and cattle ranches into the dark of night. This became the norm for the newlyweds.

While Helen toiled in the field doing a man's work during the day, she retreated to the farmhouse and worked in the kitchen preparing a meal and setting the supper table for Danos. Most nights Danos went to nearby farms, working for the neighbors, often socializing after the workday into the late of night. When Danos did return home, Helen had already retired for the evening, preparing for another physically demanding day at sunrise. On most mornings, Helen made a simple breakfast of coffee, grits and biscuit to start the day. His stamina for field work was second nature, as he had done this type of work all his adult life. Helen had never been physically driven to this extent. She was run down most days even before sunrise. A full day of field work was too much to expect from a frail young woman. Danos decided he would plant corn for his first crop. A corn harvest would be less complicated their first year in crop rather than cotton, he believed.

After several weeks had turned into a month on this demanding schedule, Helen became depressed about her situation. Many nights Helen sat on the worn sofa, alone, while Danos worked elsewhere. Alone with only her thoughts, Helen was unable to consider or solve the problem: lack of friends, no acquaintances and no one with whom to talk and discuss her predicament. Danos had no insight into this real-life problem Helen was experiencing. He could not comprehend that Helen sat on the sofa crying into the night waiting for him to return. His reaction was flagrant insensitivity to his dark-eyed, dark-haired beauty. He scoffed and scolded Helen for her weakness and emotional venting, crying like a child. His answer to Helen's problem was only to work harder and longer in order to expand this little farm into a grand enterprise. That was his vision. Helen's vision of the future had likely changed. It seems she had little control over her life, and no control over Danos.

However, not once did Helen consider leaving Little Rock to return to San Antonio. She could not bear to listen to her mother go on about the shame of it all. Helen married a mountain man from the hill country, having acquired learned skills and traits from villainous siblings experienced in a lifetime of crime. No, Helen had made her own choice by saying "I do" to Danos' proposal. Things would work out, she hoped, as long as she kept her faith in Danos.

One night, after laboring on a particularly challenging portion of the field, Helen became acutely ill. She was in serious pain and moaned throughout the night. She wailed continuously. Danos expressed no concern or sympathy. He only complained that Helen's crying and groaning noises through the night disturbed his sleep. It was Danos, man of the house, that required a sound night's sleep in order to work sixteen or eighteen hours the following day. Just before sunrise, with no concern for Helen, despite her obvious pain and lack of sleep, he demanded that she prepare him breakfast. He would stay in bed until she announced the meal was ready. As Danos fed himself and drank coffee, Helen dressed for a day of field work. She would not disappoint her husband. Helen worked all day on her feet clearing the last bit of land to be plowed and made ready. At the end of the day, he ordered Helen to carry a heavy sack of seed from the field to the barn. His insistence that she work a full day was expected; she pressed on, working in the field and in the home, with no sympathy from her husband. Danos had no experience in this regard; he could not understand that a woman, a young woman, his wife, had limits on what she could do, what she could undertake and finish. He had no patience with her physical shortcomings. The illness which Helen suffered was not simply of a fleeting nature. She remained chronically ill for two years. Danos was incapable of empathy, but he did demand somewhat less of her in the field over this period. He insisted that Helen carry her own weight working in crop, in addition to keeping the home. An impossible task in her condition.

* * *

Danos turned slowly in his wooden chair away from the desk and focused on the copy of the Holy Bible centered on the reading stand; one white, seven-inch tapered candle, unlit, set on a small table next to the stand. The Bible occupied an accessible position. Its placement was an invitation to Spiritually absorb the Word of God. If anyone could expect relief and peace from reading chapter and verse, it was not Danos. He must first overcome his past to make sense of the present. Danos would not deviate from his mission; he would not engage in Scripture reading this day. He concentrated his focus on his life with Helen Knight. As tumultuous scenes from the past filtered through his thought, Danos grasped for objectivity while assessing his own participation in these events. The agony and sorrow he feared in recording these next few pages would terminate in climax marked by fear, dread, shame and irrepressible pain.

The longer he dwelt recollecting, the longer it would take to complete this written journey. The sooner he put pen to paper again, the sooner Danos would reach his journey's end. Agony came from within as he felt the sensation that he was slipping from reality. His eyes began focusing independently of one another. His peripheral vision, now centered around the writing tablet, began to constrict. He had experienced this sensation at times in the past, principally when encountering stressful situations dealing with any number of critical subjects. Such visual disturbances were generated by problems which had no definitive solution, no partial solution. Danos looked out the window into the garden. His usually wide peripheral vision slowly deteriorated into wavy and geometric lines and figures of the outside margins. Depending on the oncoming severity, this episode could last from twenty minutes to well over one hour. Danos knew, from past episodes, he could temporarily lose rational faculties, thus challenging his ability to write and think clearly. He must continue his text to completion…

I found a farmer, ?? something to another state and bought him out. Hellen was glad to get in a house to herself even though it was bedding infested and not much in it in the way of things to keep house with.

She could work in the field with me as long as there was anything to do at home then I went to work for the neighbors leaving her alone from early morning until late at night, in the little cabbin with coyotes howling around. Often I would find her crying when I did I would scold her.

One night she was awful sick and next morning should have stayed in bed But I insisted that she get up and get our breakfast and on account of her keeping me awake I lay in bed until she called me to breakfast.

Her health was ruined as a result and she was sick for 2 years.

I did not have any patience without insisting on her working in the field as there was anything to do.

Chapter 25

"....in sickness and in health...." (cont'd)

As the newlyweds settled in Little Rock and began working their acreage at the end of Creasy Springs Road, Helen complained of mild abdominal cramping from time to time. She was unconcerned, initially, as was Danos. Over time, the cramping progressed to pronounced pain which permeated throughout Helen's torso, into her upper abdomen and, on occasion, radiated in a sharp stabbing sensation between her shoulder blades. The marked positions of attack remained concentrated in these areas, but also radiated into adjoining tissues imparting a sensation that much of her body was involved. Regular attacks varied with intensity, from mild, to excruciating, to unbearable. As the initial months at Creasy Springs turned into twelve, Helen's persistent pain was accompanied by low grade fever and chills; she shivered from cold even when cloaked with her favorite down-filled blanket. Helen found nothing that would lessen these symptoms; this ailment remained mysterious. As their first year of growing crop turned into the second, Helen's symptoms broadened to include bouts of excruciating pain, chills and fever which intermittently resulted in several long minutes of nausea and vomiting. Helen's loss of weight became obvious as she progressively weakened. A thick dampened towel, folded and rolled to twenty-four inches in width, was heated to high temperature on the wood-burner. Helen clutched the hot, moist towel tightly against her abdomen. She discovered this procedure offered brief and considerable relief, yet her symptoms persisted. The frequency of episodes also varied, increasing in random progression, yet the source of these symptoms remained undetermined.

Subsequently, a visit to Dr. Brandon was deemed warranted and an appointment made for Tuesday morning. Helen could no longer cope with the nearly constant pain, always intense. After speaking in depth with Helen, conducting a comprehensive physical examination, consulting his medical books and latest medical journals, Dr. Brandon announced he did not know what was causing Helen's condition and pain. Brandon asked his associate, Dr. Remington, to examine Helen. Remington was likewise confounded. Both suggested Helen consult with a physician specializing in abdominal disorders, as Brandon and Remington were merely general practice physicians. Their experience in this regard was limited. They charged Helen a modest professional fee of six dollars for their examination and services. Danos paid their fee but was offended at their outrageous bill when they were unable to render a diagnosis or recommend treatment.

With her physical condition having deteriorated to the point of debilitation, although not enamored by the prospect, Helen insisted on their return to her mother in San Antonio to seek medical treatment. Danos, apprehensive about Helen's medical condition, yet also concerned about the crops, did consent and made rail arrangements at once. On such short notice, all sleeper cars on this Texas run had been previously reserved and unavailable. Only passenger seating in coach remained. Paying the fare for such discomfort over a two- or three-day trip to San Antonio, with multiple stops and transfers, seemed unjust, especially for a sick woman. They each packed one bag for the few days they anticipated being away from Little Rock.

Fortunately, Danos had just finished planting the sixty acres of farm land. Helen was terribly sick and was unable to help Danos plant the field which she had cleared the prior year. His neighbor, Jackson Allen, assisted by transporting bags of seed corn from Adams' Seed and Feed to the Danos barn, then positioned the bags of seed strategically in the field for planting. While Danos did own a two-furrow plow, harrow, rake and wagons, he opted not to purchase a mechanical planter, thus avoiding additional financial obligation. Rather, he would once again borrow a mechanical planter from Allen. Over the last planting season, Danos learned the key to maximum crop yield was planting straight rows set the optimum distance apart. Jackson's planter, manufactured by the John Deere Company, made of solid cherry wood and tempered cast iron, was sturdy and dependable in its operation. Danos planted a four-row swath as he and his mule team navigated the planter through the rich earth at a steady pace. As he concentrated intently, Danos rode on the single seat of the green planter maintaining the rows in straight, parallel lines. He visually fixed on four-foot-tall white stakes as his reference points at the far end of the first rows. He would not deviate from the fixture as the first swath of four rows he planted required precision in setting the template for succeeding rows. The forward metal shovels of the planter dug four parallel trenches in the earth as the seed corn was mechanically released from the hoppers, dropping kernels of seed corn into the trenches at optimum depth and spacing. The rear shovel devices covered the seeded trenches with sufficient earth to encourage germination and growth. Planting row after row was his dream. His business venture commenced independently as a small crop farm progressing to a successful enterprise. Danos' dream was being fulfilled with this second year of crop, as the mule team pulled through the sixty acres of plowed land, planting row after row. Pride swelled within as he smiled reflectively on this spring planting day as seed corn was deposited in the trenches. Bright sun caused Danos to squint, even though covered with a wide-brimmed straw hat, as he envisioned an abundant harvest in late fall. Danos imagined and visualized success. He could rely only on himself; he felt he could run and jump free with exhilaration. His calling and skill as a crop farmer were innate, borne naturally in a Spanish-Cuban boy plucked from tragedy and disaster by a mentor that gave of himself, caring for this orphan-boy. Just one orphan of the countless many in Cuba. Why would Danos succeed, while others perished? He pondered this question for decades, with nary an answer.

* * *

They boarded the third rail car with assistance from the conductor, a personable, conscientious gentleman willing to assist his passengers to the fullest. What the conductor could not do is assure everyone's complete comfort, nor assure reasonable quiet for those who chose to doze, read or quietly converse. Unruly children had tickets for seats in coach as did Danos and Helen. The scourge of this trip, obnoxious tykes, yelling and screaming, running up and down the aisles like misbehaved, unruly rascals. Are they not accompanied by a supervising adult? Does the adult parent not find this raucous behavior disrespectful and offensive? These little passengers did have an assigned seat with a purchased ticket, but one could not know this detail as the wild imps ran from row to row for over an hour until they became bored with car number three. Pairs of rowdy children then moved their way forward, or retreated, making their way to torment the paying adult fares in adjoining cars. What obnoxious creatures.

Helen had been sitting at the widow seat enjoying the scenery of the Arkansas countryside in apparent peace and comfort. She exercised patience by disregarding the constant uproar of disrespectful children roaming throughout passenger car number three. She seemed not to be bothered by this constant noise and movement. Danos sat in the seat next to his sick wife. How much more of this commotion he could tolerate was unknown. Danos suffered through the first several hours of this trip with little conversation. He finally spoke with a degree of sincerity to Helen, as if he had true concern for her well-being.

"How are you feeling so far on this trip?" he inquired.

"I am fine, at least for the moment."

"I have had about enough of these rude children. I intend to find the conductor and lodge a complaint. It's impossible to spend three days on this train listening to this incessant noise."

"Calm down," she said. "We'll be in San Antonio before you know it."

Danos expressed no concern for his bride but rather was just making idle conversation. Quite strange to be together in close quarters for a three-day journey when their routine called for Danos to be in the field or at the neighbors, sixteen or more hours per day. Danos certainly was not a nursemaid, nor a caregiver. He lacked the experience and patience, training and skill necessary to be of any assistance to Helen in her ill condition. This is the reason they opted to return to Texas, to get a professional diagnosis and treatment by a properly trained physician, not those two inexperienced imbeciles in Little Rock.

Danos was about to make another comment of no importance to Helen but realized she had just closed her eyes and dozed off to sleep, her head propped against the small soft, blue sofa pillow she brought with her. He would not disturb her. And those rowdy reprobates better not come back here making noise, or he would take matters into his own hands. Forget the conductor. Danos cared little for small children, he confessed to himself. How could one be a husband and a father to such rude, undisciplined children? He never considered this to be an eventuality with Helen. Now, with her illness, her excruciating pain, how could she cope with a pregnancy? This is just not turning out to be the life he envisioned. If they had no children, and if Helen improved medically, they could run free again as an irresponsible husband and wife with no ties, no obligations. Perhaps Helen's health would improve.

The screaming kids must have found something with which to occupy themselves in another car, as they had not returned. Perhaps their assigned seats were in another car and their parents decided to discipline them by confinement. Danos hoped this was the case. As the train continued its journey through southwest Arkansas, it approached the first scheduled stop to load or unload passengers. Danos and Helen would not be required to exit the train. A mere scheduled stop.

As the train built up steam and speed once again, Helen woke from her sleep, bending over at the waist in her sitting position as she sensed cramping in her abdomen. She knew the signs and progression of these episodes. Helen's cramping continued, while the pain in her upper abdomen became more pronounced. As usual, this pain became severe causing Helen to groan, moan with each surge of discomfort. Danos did not wish to listen to her audible expressions of grief, for he was of no assistance to her. She requested that Danos get her water, as that sometimes minimized her cramping. Danos assented to Helen's mission request. He rose from his seat and headed to the rear of passenger car number three. He disappeared. Helen waited for his return with her water. He didn't return. Helen continued to moan in discomfort. She began to run a slight fever, as the stabbing pain started in between her shoulders. The conductor happened by and retrieved the water she had previously requested of Danos. Sipping the water did little. The constant motion and sway of the rail car brought on and aggravated her nauseousness. Nothing would relieve this episode but for the passage of time. Rarely a few minutes, frequently an hour or two or more. Danos would not return.

Danos, presumably having gone to fetch water for his wife, got sidetracked in the smoker car. The passengers occupying the smoker were all adults, standing, sitting, engaged in adult conversation with no children allowed. Upon entry into the car, the concierge offered complimentary cigars for the enjoyment of patrons. Danos helped himself to a hand-rolled, Cuban vintage maduro, bit off the end and lit the cigar. He had not had an opportunity to enjoy a quality cigar in many months. As he enjoyed the cigar's aroma and appreciated the wood tone and slight hint of spice in this fine Cuban, a professionally dressed gentleman engaged Danos in conversation.

Mr. Malcolm Chancellor wore a pale blue shirt accented by a black Texan bow tie and brown jacket. His dark blue trousers were neatly pressed, and his brown western boots identified Chancellor as a Texan, perhaps a native Texan. Chancellor was also puffing a quality Cuban and juggling a brandy in his left hand. He struck up a conversation with Danos. Chancellor was senior by at least thirty years over twenty-two-year-old Danos. Malcom

Chancellor looked strikingly familiar. He sported a thick, gray mustache which bordered along the contour of his upper lip and was neatly trimmed. There are no coincidences, situations happen for a reason.

"My boy, my name is Malcolm Chancellor. How do you do?"

"Well, Mr. Chancellor, I'm just fine. My name is Danos Knight." Chancellor put his brandy down on a white cocktail napkin at the edge of the round table, put his cigar in a conveniently accessible glass ashtray and shook Danos' right hand in gentlemanly fashion.

"Let's sit down here in these fine, comfortable seats. We have miles to go and likely several more cigars to smoke."

"I agree. I take every opportunity to indulge in a quality smoke. This Cuban is a genuine treat," Danos confessed.

"This run from Little Rock to Texas is frequented by businessmen of all types. Most smoke cigars and enjoy a brandy or whiskey over the journey. I make this trip about every month, sometimes more often. I have relatives living in San Antonio and I conduct business with numerous railway customers. My companies provide furnishings and equipment of various sorts to major and smaller rail operations. We are always interested in upgrading our line of equipment and furnishings, adding new amenities for passenger comfort on the longer trips and the shorter runs for that matter. Texas has a huge rail system and we concentrate our business in that state. Our home office is in southern Texas, San Antonio. But we also have offices in other states, including the Little Rock office.

"What a coincidence?" Danos blurted out spontaneously. There are no coincidences.

"My wife and I are heading back to San Antonio to see her mother, and to get a medical opinion. My wife has had this medical condition, stomach pain, for quite a while. The two doctors she saw in Little Rock couldn't help her. They suggested she see a specialist. Hence our trip to San Antonio."

"What is your wife's name, son?"

"Helen Knight. She is up in the third passenger car dozing comfortably," as Danos released a little untruth about her current medical status. He would admit to no one that he could not bear to listen to his wife moan in agony. Her episodes of discomfort far outnumbered her times of normalcy. Danos could not help himself. He was just naturally insensitive. No fault of his own, just made that way. He didn't believe his natural tendency towards overt callousness could be disciplined to respect nor control Helen's pain. Why, if he had such pain, he would just contend with it. He would not audibly profess such pain to obtain sympathy from friends and family, or anyone else who might care to listen. That's just life, he thought.

"Well, Danos, I'm not an overly Spiritual person, but I do have a first cousin who is a preacher in San Antonio. He has an open line to the Great Healer in Heaven. I will ask him to pray for Helen's accurate diagnosis and treatment and complete healing when you see your doctor in San Antonio."

"Thank you. Who might this preacher be in San Antonio?" Danos inquired. If Chancellor says Archie Jennings, it will prove this is not a coincidence.

"Danos, my first cousin pastors a small church in San Antonio. His name is Reverend Archibald Jennings."

Shocking. Incredulous, Danos thought. To happen upon Archie Jennings' first cousin in the smoker car on this passage to San Antonio is certainly not a coincidence. Smoking a Cuban cigar with Mr. Malcolm Chancellor is also no coincidence, nor is this conversation. It's as if the stars and the moon were lined up, pushing and pulling the tides, with astrological signs set to confirm these events in the galaxies tonight. Danos was in total disbelief.

"Danos, perhaps you and Helen would like to join us for church services one Sunday for Archie's sermon. He is quite compelling in delivering the Lord's message. It may do you good in Helen's time of medical needs. I don't mean to pressure you, but here is one of Archie's business cards with the address and times for Sunday worship service."

"Thank you." Danos could barely reply but indicated no commitment.

This is why Malcolm Chancellor, with that gray mustache and the Texas suit and boots, looked so familiar. Archie Jennings' first cousin. How could this be?

Danos finished the Cuban and discarded it appropriately in the elegant, free standing communal ash tray. He rose from his seat. Danos had been in the smoker for at least three hours and felt somewhat inclined, perhaps some sense of guilt, to check on Helen back in car number three. Maybe the renegade mob of children had reappeared and was threatening passengers. As he bid good day to Chancellor, Malcolm handed Danos a business card of his own. The business card was of thick stock, rich ivory-colored with elegant gold printing on the face. Mr. Malcolm Chancellor was the owner and founder of Railway Equipment and Supply, Company, San Antonio, Texas. The address and phone number prominently displayed on the lower half of the card. Chancellor expressed to Danos he hoped they would meet again for further conversation on this journey. He was always seeking intelligent young men with solid work ethic to fill employment positions in his company. Danos thanked him and made his way to the third car.

* * *

"...in sickness and in health..." (cont'd)

Helen was sitting up leaning uncomfortably against the unforgiving coach wall. Her eyes were open. Her face was pale, exhibiting exhaustion. The tall glass window was slightly ajar to allow the flow of fresh air. No aggravating children roaming. He was relieved. He asked Helen if she would like to go to the diner car for a bite to eat.

"I'm not hungry," she stated, obviously annoyed with him.

Danos sat next to Helen as they conversed in silence as an old married couple. They would not exchange another word. He would not apologize for his inordinately lengthy absence. She would not apologize for having a painful episode so early into this journey. Danos did not hold her hand. He did not comfort her. He did not put his arm around her shoulders, did not touch her forehead to check for fever, did not ask Helen how she felt, nor did he bring the water he was asked to retrieve. Danos sat there. Silent. Ill-equipped. Incompetent to console his wife. His duty, he believed, was to get Helen to San Antonio to see a medical specialist. This was in the process of being accomplished. This demonstrated lack of concern for Helen came to him instinctively, perfectly defensible and acceptable, at least in his view.

Over the course of the remaining rail journey to San Antonio, Helen and Danos made three more stops and one change of transfer on to another line. Helen suffered two more attacks of abdominal discomfort, unassisted by her husband; unconsoled. Danos spent several more hours in the smoker. He saw Malcolm Chancellor only once again. Chancellor was leaving as Danos was entering the smoker car. They exchanged brief pleasantries and departed with Malcolm Chancellor encouraging Danos to submit an employment application to his company for a position. Chancellor indicated he would receive a favorable interview.

"Just call me for an appointment when you're ready," Malcolm concluded.

* * *

When their train from Oklahoma City arrived at the San Antonio rail station, they were not welcomed by Claire Simmons as they anticipated. Danos missed crossing paths with the disembarking Malcolm Chancellor and was thus unable to bid Chancellor a proper farewell. Danos had hoped to personally express his interest in the RESC job application. There will be further opportunity to discuss employment in earnest. Claire's non-appearance was not surprising, based on her warnings in the past to her daughter and to Danos. Taking a buggy to the Simmons residence was perfectly acceptable. Danos carried both bags, the extent of his chivalry, up to the Simmons home. Claire was expecting them but was not particularly keen on having house guests after their nearly three-year absence, especially after their rude departure to parts unknown. Oklahoma, then to Arkansas of all places. Claire displayed no excitement or joy about Helen's return. Her detached demeanor outwardly expressed disappointment with both daughter and son-in-law.

However, Claire Simmons did find time for significant mother-daughter talks with Helen over the next days. The topic was essentially centered on "I told you so," with no sympathy for Helen's medical predicament, nor her choice of husband. Claire expressed little desire to assist Helen with her problems, as Claire had significant issues of her own. They discussed what it was like for Claire to live alone as a grieving widow. She was still bereaved by the death of her beloved Phineas after three years and refused to declare independence. Claire relied on the largesse of the local church for most meals and socials with the other church ladies, mostly widows of inappropriately youthful ages, unfortunately.

Helen made an appointment with an abdominal specialist for this coming Wednesday at 10:00 a.m. His name was Russell A. Cole. Dr. Cole, now in his late-50s, came from a short line of medical doctors, father and grandfather, both specialists in one medical field or another. Russell Cole had advanced training and experience in gastrointestinal organs and associated abdominal matters. Helen felt relieved once her appointment was confirmed and on the office calendar. She was confident Dr. Cole could definitively diagnose her condition and start her on a prescribed treatment to resolve the cramping, chills and fevers. Intense suffering for the past two years was sheer punishment. For her sins at such a young age? she would ask herself. For marrying this renegade, Spanish-Cuban boy? she queried. For making decisions contrary to her mother's wishes? she wondered. Who knew why she was plagued with this cross to bear? Nevertheless, she was eager to be healed and rid of this ailment.

Doctor Russel Cole conducted a two-hour consultation Wednesday morning questioning and examining Helen Knight about her years of abdominal distress. His examination of Helen was similar to the assessment conducted by Brandon and Remington, but the quality of his inquiry was in greater depth and accuracy, ferreting information from her that seemed inconsequential to the untrained lay person, but of significance to Doctor Cole. Physical examination of the patient required expertise to feel invisible organs tucked away and hidden within the abdomen. Helen had little knowledge of anatomy and physiology, structure and function, of the female human body. She was barely twenty years old, with little education and experience of modern-day medicine. She relied entirely on Dr. Cole, as Danos sat in the doctor's adjoining office waiting for his remarks and conclusion.

After two boring hours sitting in that waiting room, Danos became concerned as he thought about how much money this physician would bill him for his services. Danos brought folding money with him, hopefully a sufficient amount, but he didn't know. The doctor opened the waiting room door and invited Danos to join them in the examination room. Upon entry, Helen was smiling and perky. Her dark eyes were twinkling as she appeared hopeful and relaxed. Unbeknownst to Danos, Dr. Cole previously indicated to Helen he believed he had her ailment figured out. He explained as Helen and Danos listened attentively.

"First of all," Dr. Cole began, "that day back two years ago when Helen was so terribly sick throughout the night, when Danos made her fix breakfast before he got out of bed, was of significant trauma to Helen. She was pregnant with child but was unaware. You both were unaware. Yet Helen obediently did what you, Danos, demanded of her. She dutifully made you breakfast, and then dressed for the field work which you also demanded. Danos, she was ill. She worked the entire day in the field doing the manual labor you required. I believe she did so out of obedience and out of love for you. Having her carry and drag that heavy load of seed from the field to the barn, I am quite sure, was the cause of her miscarriage. That night, she lost the baby of her pregnancy. That would have been your first child had she carried it to term. Nevertheless, it was God's way of letting Helen know she was not ready to become a mother at that time in her life. Miscarriage happens."

Danos sat in silence. He could not look into Helen's sparkling brown eyes. He could not peer into her soul to say he was sorry. He could not ask for her forgiveness. Yet, thoughts rolled through his mind justifying the need for Helen's work in the field preparing the land to sew seed. Absolutely necessary. He would have demanded no lesser action.

"Now, to Helen's current medical issue which brought her to me. It is my belief and opinion, based on the answers she has given, her symptoms, her areas of pain and my physical examination of Helen's abdominal area, that Helen has a faulty and partially functioning gall bladder. The gall bladder is a small organ that produces a product known as bile. Bile is released when the body ingests, and stomach receives, fatty type foods. It aids in the breakdown and digestion of the fatty substances. When the body is functioning normally, bile aids the body digesting those fats. Thus, digestion proceeds normally. If the gall bladder is not producing bile, or is producing an insufficient amount of bile, the fats cannot be broken down, can't be digested and often cause cramping in the stomach, abdomen and intestines with pain radiating in the abdominal area and in the back between the shoulder blades. These episodes are triggered by eating high fat foods. Foods such as bacon, lard, pork, butter, rich cream and milk, to name but a few. I think if Helen can avoid these foods, she can avoid these acute attacks of cramping, fever, chills and pain. I will provide you with a list of foods and substances to avoid. You should plan to eat only vegetables for a week or two and completely avoid the foods on this list. I think this will solve all of your problems."

"Any questions?"

"Will you determine if my gall bladder is functioning at all?" Helen asked.

"I don't think that is necessary. We can conduct testing, which is expensive and not very definitive, to indicate the extent of gall bladder function. But I don't think such testing is warranted. I believe, if you avoid these foods, and stick to bland vegetables for two weeks, you will know that this is the cure to your problem."

Helen and Danos remained in San Antonio for an additional two weeks. Claire remained less than hospitable towards Danos but warmed somewhat to her daughter. Claire Simmons and Helen appeared to have reached a mutual understanding concerning relationships. Helen continued to observe all of Dr. Cole's rules, restrictions and suggestions. During these two weeks of avoiding his list of offending foods and eating mainly grains and vegetables, Helen felt greatly improved. She experienced no abdominal discomfort whatsoever. Danos and Helen then announced to Claire their decision to return to Little Rock after their two weeks in San Antonio. Dr. Cole would send a copy of his medical findings, conclusions and report, together with the recommended treatment to Drs. Brandon and Remington for their information and use. Dr. Cole also provided an invoice to Danos for medical services rendered for Helen. The billed amount was thirty-three dollars for his two-hour examination and conclusions. Danos went to Dr. Cole's office, paid the bill with his folding money, and thanked Dr. Cole for his services and explained he was satisfied. Helen recovered immediately after having suffered for the better part of two years. Helen received no sympathy from anyone, and she expected none.

* * *

Within the first week of arrival back in Arkansas, Danos made an appointment with the managing vice-president of Railway Equipment and Supply, Company in Little Rock seeking employment. On his next trip to the Little Rock office, Malcolm Chancellor scheduled an interview with Danos for a position when one became available. Within a matter of a few days, a position opened, or was created, for Danos. The title of the position was inventory specialist at the RESC warehouse in Little Rock. Although Danos never refined his writing skills, he could read and was excellent at mathematics. He was a qualified candidate for the inventory specialist position. During his interview, Danos expressed his need and desire to continue farming crop. Danos' work schedule at RESC was adjusted to permit flexible time in-season to plant and harvest his sixty acres. Chancellor hired Danos at the conclusion of the interview. The initial position with RESC was a management position and offered opportunity for advancement with Chancellor's company. Danos considered himself fortunate to have met the owner and president of the company on the San Antonio Line. Most fortunate.

With seeds in the ground, green shoots protruding from the soil and an abundant crop anticipated at harvest this year, Danos was elated. Helen's health was no longer an issue while she avoided the troubling foods on Dr. Cole's list. After two additional years continually working the field and as inventory manager for RESC, Danos and Helen increased their savings account and were blessed with the birth of a dark-eyed baby girl. Due to unforeseen complications, the baby was not strong and developed a long-term illness. Danos' hope and expectation of total family health were compromised once again.

* * *

In his grief, reflecting on his miserable life of years ago, A.D. felt inadequate and ashamed while he made the following entry…

She got so bad we decided to go back to her mother and left at once. On the train, she was awful sick all the way. We were not able to get a sleeper. We were on the train for 3 days.

I stayed in the smoker most of the time as there was no pleasure in staying with a sick woman.

When we arrived at her home, we had a doctor after examining Helen, he told her she had lost a child that awful night in the cabin and I even made her get up and get my breakfast, then go to the field I did not feel I had done anything wrong.

Her folks did not pity her much and her mother even had an attitude of I told you so.

At last after 2 years suffering, she got better and I got a better position by that time. Helen had quit expecting sympathy from anyone.

After a couple of years, we had saved a little money a little dark eyed baby girl had been given to our care and an accident of neglect the baby was not strong and my wishes for health was ruined again.

Chapter 26

"...in sickness and in health..." (cont'd)

The daughter, at first considered by Helen to be a blessing, was the product of another difficult pregnancy as the child developed complicated health issues within the first four years of her life. Helen's demanding domestic duties were exacerbated with this sickly child. Helen's routine care for the daughter became extraordinary. Certainly, her first responsibility was to their daughter, with field work and Danos far behind. Danos failed as the paternal role model Helen hoped he would be. Rather, Danos again was overly occupied with earning a bank roll. He worked his required scheduled hours and logged excess voluntary hours as inventory specialist for the Railway Equipment and Supply, Company, impressing the local vice-president, as well as Mr. Chancellor. He continued to raise crop and explored the optimum time to purchase cattle. Adding cattle at this juncture in light of the family situation, however, was ill-timed. Between both jobs, Danos' expenditure of the time resource was similar to his father's schedule. Little did he observe of his father, Don Pedro Fernandez, years ago. Could he subconsciously, but practically, transform himself into a workaholic father, the likes of his own father, the father he never came to know? Focused on work and business, he was oblivious to the needs of his family, especially the need for beneficial relationships.

As their four-year-old suffered in chronic distress, weak and ill, Helen and Danos agreed they must seek comprehensive therapy for the daughter at the West Baden Health and Mineral Spa in West Baden, Indiana. This therapeutic health spa, which came highly recommended, had earned a renowned reputation for the physical properties of its hot, healing mineral waters. The spa was located on a 774-acre resort with physical and mental healing of patients as its chief goal. Together with ingesting a prescribed course of herbs, oral vitamins, natural minerals and a specialized diet, the daughter was prescribed a variety of immersions and soakings in the natural hot spring mineral waters of the West Baden spa. The therapy of immersions was accomplished and enhanced by the stimulating, yet mildly offensive, odor emanating from the waters. The texture and feel of coarseness of the concentrated lime mineral water were offset by the hot waters of the prescribed medicinal soakings. The natural, purified lime mineral water was also used for hydration. The mechanism of therapeutic efficacy of immersions and hydration was not fully understood but provided consistent, positive results for its spa patients. The daughter appeared to have improved over the fourteen days of treatment at West Baden in the Indiana wilderness.

During their trip back to Little Rock, they chanced an impromptu excursion to Oklahoma City to visit the "brothers" and their families. After the initial visit to the home of Daniel and Anna, they realized the seriousness of their error in judgment. Daniel was openly rude, hostile to Helen and Danos, insulting them by calling them "black sheep," stating they were no longer related to the Roberts family. Anna demonstrated her inhospitality by refusing to invite the Knight family into their home. Rather, all five inconveniently and uncomfortably stood outside on the Roberts' wooden porch for just over half an hour. The ill-mannered Roberts brother and his crude wife would never mature to civility. Their lack of hospitality and sympathy should have been anticipated. After standing awkwardly and making small talk for over thirty minutes, Danos announced they would spend the night at an Oklahoma City hotel and leave for Little Rock the following morning.

On their return to Arkansas, the daughter, despite positive early indications, seemed little improved. After his examination on their first appointment, her doctor suggested an operation to remove the child's appendix gland, advising such procedure could be beneficial. Did the physician know such surgical procedure could be helpful or was he just exploring? As the date of the operation was determined and scheduled, Helen gave birth to another child, a son. The daughter's operation was uncomplicated but proved to be of little therapeutic value. The daughter remained chronically ill with a stomach condition, which none of her doctors could diagnose, along with a skin ailment and breathing disorder. The child remained plagued and in constant distress.

Helen expressed deep regret and sorrow that she bore a son to Danos. This newborn male child, most predictably, would be influenced and raised in the ways of Danos Knight, formerly Jim Roberts, thereby imparting the crass lifestyle of the Roberts clan and their ill-tempered wives to the son. Helen was fearful this training in criminality would become the guiding principles for their second child. Helen remained distraught over her Knight family. As much as she tried, Helen could not convince or influence Danos to attend church, read the Holy Bible or take the lead as the patriarch of this family. Danos was intent on earning money, raising crop, buying cattle one day, and carousing with the neighboring ranchers. Danos' lifestyle had not changed much since his marriage to Helen. In fact, his married life deteriorated after the children were born. Having a close-knit family was not a priority, for Danos had no experience or education on this subject. Helen looked after the first-born daughter, while Danos was expected to look after the boy. He assumed no responsibility for raising a son, even if the boy was his own. There was no reason to assume a position in which much was expected of Danos. He routinely ignored the newborn and left the child crying for hours having no patience or desire to care for a new family member.

Helen continued in her domestic role, but the hours fell short to accomplish all that was demanded of her. The daughter became chronically ill with her dermatologic issues and breathing ailment. Her doctor suggested a change in climate for the four-year-old could be beneficial. Helen considered a trip to the dry climate of Arizona for several months. As Helen discussed this change of climate with him, Danos was adamant that he would not accompany his family out west. He did not wish to abandon his crops nor leave his lucrative position with RESC, and he surely did not want to look for another job when they returned from Arizona. Danos was happy with his RESC position and refused to consider a job change.

* * *

Life had become most complicated and complex back then. A.D. sought to recall his family life in his twenties, a nearly impossible task to recollect, yet he wrote from his heart…

She was sick for four years this time and I was as cross and impatient as ever.

We thought she would never be well again. We took a trip to a health resort and an extended visit to my people who of course showed no sympathy whatsoever.

We returned home, she was in very little better condition than when we started. Our home physician insisted on an operation that helped her a little.

Soon there was another baby a boy. She said she was sorry it was a boy as I would be a bad influence for him.

I did not take much interest in the boy often set and let him cry while my wife was cooking me something to eat.

About this time, the little girl got sick, we could get nothing to do her any good. Dr. said she would have to have a change in climate.

I could not leave my job and did not want to quit and hunt another.

Chapter 27

"...in sickness and in health..." (cont'd)

Helen packed several cases of clothing for herself and the children. Sufficient wardrobes for she and her children were required for a lengthy stay of two months, perhaps longer. Her mind raced as she contemplated a difficult train ride with two small children over the next three and one-half or more days to the elevations of Prescott, Arizona for change of climate. They contemplated a stay in the drier air and months of March and April as an intermediate retreat to comply with the recommendation of the daughter's physician. When they arrived in Prescott, Helen detected an immediate, positive change on the touch and feel of daughter's body surface and temperature. Her skin felt cool; the clamminess had dissipated. Daughter's breathing returned to a normal pattern. Gasping for air and her chronic wheezing and coughing ceased. Helen initially planned to stay for two months but extended their stay into the month of October based on the marked improvement of their daughter's health.

Helen dispatched her telegram to Danos. She informed him of the daughter's immediate recovery and progress, seemingly miraculous, and of her intention to remain in Prescott until October. Danos found this wholly acceptable, a true family blessing. He immediately sent Helen additional money for necessaries, and did so periodically, to care for the children adequately. His generosity was not fueled out of care and concern for Helen and the children, but rather, Danos was pleased he would have no responsibility for anyone but himself for six additional months. He could not have been more pleased. Danos' self-absorption and need for independence occupied a high priority throughout his adult life. Despite the obligations of his family, Danos was determined to remain free and unaccountable, to the extent possible. He considered the additional months without his family most fortunate.

During his family's absence, Malcolm Chancellor required that Danos inspect and take inventory of the regional warehouse in Little Rock and review the detail accountings of the RESC warehouse located out of state in Texarkana, Texas, a three-hour train ride from Little Rock. Danos undertook these assignments passionately prompted by his desire to surpass Chancellor's expectations. RESC estimated the assigned projects would take Danos four to six months or more of diligent work to complete. The company made travel provisions and accommodations for Danos in Texarkana. Once this assignment began, Danos enjoyed hotel living away from Creasy Springs Road for a short while, but eating at saloons and family cafes soon turned stale and repetitious. While he focused on the RESC mission and the assigned tasks at the Texarkana warehouse, Danos soon became prone to monotony of routine and boredom away from his Little Rock farm.

During the early days occupied inspecting the books of the Texarkana warehouse, Danos made the acquaintance of a young fellow who had four years seniority working for RESC. They became fast friends finding much in common. His name was James, his wife, Irene, with one child. James and Irene Stinnett. After three weeks living in the hotel, James invited Danos to stay with his family. It would be no intrusion and uncomplicated. Danos would have his own room and own entrance. They would eat together as a family unit. James and Irene had a strange and open relationship. Irene was flirtatious with many of his friends, as James did not appear to be offended nor did he object to his wife's amorous conduct. Danos and Irene also became friends and developed an unusual relationship as Irene playfully engaged with Danos, even in her husband's presence. Danos was physically attracted to Irene but kept his distance, as he valued James' friendship and his position with RESC.

Malcolm Chancellor expressed initial reservations that Danos cancelled his accommodations at the company's preferred Texarkana hotel. Chancellor finally approved of his request to temporarily reside with the Stinnetts, believing this arrangement may assist in providing insight into suspected warehousing issues.

* * *

Helen and the children arrived at the Little Rock rail station from Arizona merely sixty minutes behind the scheduled and posted arrival time. Expecting Danos would meet his family at the rail station was anticipated as Helen mailed him a hand-written letter from Prescott one month earlier advising of her scheduled arrival. She also sent a telegram from Arizona on the day they departed Prescott beginning their return journey to Little Rock. Helen's telegram was specific in detail that the family would arrive in Little Rock on Friday, October 18, 1918 at 9:45 a.m. She expected Danos would be waiting at the station for her with a team and buggy to take them home after their long absence and lengthy train passage.

Helen was disappointed that Danos was not present for their arrival. Perhaps Danos arrived at the rail station on time, but tired of waiting and left when he determined the train was far behind schedule. Perhaps Danos had pressing work to perform for RESC which could not be avoided. Perhaps he did not receive her post or her telegram. Unlikely. Perhaps Danos just did not care to arrive at the scheduled time; it was unimportant to him. Helen secured a buggy for fare.

Helen's scheduled return from Arizona with the children, after having been away for eight months, was anticipated to be a joyous occasion. It was not. She returned home to a distant husband, lacking in concern for his wife and his children. Danos asked no questions concerning Helen's life with the children in the dry Arizona climate, nor did he inquire about the health of his daughter. Danos was rudely unconcerned about his family's life for the past eight months. Instead, he merely accepted them as joint-occupants of the Creasy Springs Road farmhouse. Danos was a husband and a father who had declined to the status of an unmarried bachelor, living alone with no family obligations or domestic duties. The "castle" which he restored for his wife was in disrepair. The roof began to leak last spring just after Helen and the children left for Arizona. It was not repaired. Trash in the home was littered throughout all the rooms. Danos was not prepared for "company." As he recalled looking about the interior of the farmhouse, Danos thought about his repulsive meeting with Jane Clark a number of years ago. Danos' farmhouse had become the image of Jane's "hog pit." Helen was shocked by the filth and clutter. She did not leave their home in such disorder. Having returned, Helen's duty was clear. She must work the farmhouse into livable condition, suitable for raising children and satisfying her husband. Helen, the domestic type, learned from her mother and father. Allowing Danos to live like swine in her absence would not be tolerated.

After a few weeks, Helen, skeptical about his suggestion, finally consented to inviting James and Irene Stinnett and their son to spend the weekend at the farm on Creasy Springs Road. The country life was an opportunity for James to learn and appreciate the responsibilities of raising crop. Danos introduced James to agriculture by relating and discussing his farming experiences. He explained his future plans for the cattle industry to James; the details of breeding, raising cattle and marketing were manly subjects to be discussed over a pint of beer or a brandy and a choice cigar during the visit.

James and Irene were not demanding visitors. However, Irene showed nothing but contempt for Helen from the first they met. What caused Irene's ill feeling toward Helen could not be determined. Irene continued her amicable relationship with Danos, which he enjoyed. After one evening in observation of Irene's loose, overly flirtatious talk with Danos, Helen indicated to Danos that there was something just not normal about Irene. True, Helen had just returned from an eight-month health trip out of town and was preoccupied with tending to the Knight children. As Helen voiced her objections to him about Irene's mannerisms and crude talk, Danos found nothing disagreeable about their weekend guests. Annoyed with Helen's irrational assessment, Danos began to defend Irene, James and the boy, for he and James were not only good friends, but co-workers who must maintain a fraternal relationship in the work environment. That evening, Helen was shocked that Irene mistreated Helen's four-year-old daughter disciplining the child by administering corporal punishment. Danos felt otherwise. Irene was a parent who believed that correction of a child was most meaningful at the moment of infraction. She paddled Helen's daughter with her open-palmed hand on the buttocks. Danos found this correction most appropriate. Helen not so. Irene, jovial and joking as they accepted the Knights' hospitality, Danos defended Irene. Irene was merely a jokester meaning no harm to the daughter.

Danos had been a house guest of James and Irene for months. Why Helen could act in such an obstinate manner on the first day of a simple weekend could not be understood. Certainly, James and Irene were most hospitable to Danos in providing room and board for the time he was taking the RESC audits and inventory in Texarkana. Danos discovered that James and Irene were both from a rough and rowdy class of people. He found a common thread in this type of living that was quite similar to the Roberts clan. Danos could live with such characters; Helen was most uncomfortable and offended. Irene was not just rough on the edges, she was rough to the core, cussing, drinking, telling off-color jokes in mixed company, including in Danos' presence. He was amenable to the crude talk and thought nothing of it. Danos developed the ability to listen to Irene's manly joke and discount it, forgetting the punchline as soon as it was delivered.

After the weekend visit, Danos realized and declared he was much happier socializing with James and Irene than with his own family. Helen was, of course, insulted.

* * *

Danos continued his reflection on the "*Helen*istic" period during his past life as geometric, quasi-liquid-like patterns, strings and lines imbedded his periphery, becoming concentrated and distorted. Undulating forms became profuse with uncustomary hues of primary blues, yellows, reds and combinations thereof. Abstract and incapable of precise description, the configurations permeated his peripheral vision which gradually honed into a bizarre, constricted tunnel. His ability to see on the far right, left, top and bottom margins of his sight line was impaired. He laid down his pen and looked at the fleshy palm side of his hands. They appeared to be unnaturally pale and refused to function as they once had. His fingers pulsed in eerie sensations, sometimes prickly, generally heavy and lethargic, often with no feeling. His lips felt swollen, although they were not; a tingling sensation in both lips, largely in the lower lip, was pronounced as if a portion of his mouth was going numb. He breathed deeply and sighed audibly. His focus on Helen and her physical beauty were effectively countered by her physical weakness, her inability to work in the field as a farm hand and her imperfections as a mother. Helen was also inept at being a wife, his wife, Danos concluded. Sure, Helen was imperfect as are all humans, but her defects were unbecoming and difficult to tolerate. As he sat in solitude, reflecting, Danos could not discover a solution to the problem which evolved so many years ago. Today, at this writing in his library, Helen's problems and failings resurfaced. There were no solutions to the troubles manifested. Danos, adjusting and compensating as best he could for the abnormal peripheral tunnel, was losing his vision. Did he have the strength to finish? To work through these unsolvable problems which plagued Helen Knight? Did he have the fortitude to ask her for forgiveness for his past actions? Must he ask Helen's forgiveness for wrongs committed over a decade ago? Would his lips continue to swell and turn blue before he could finish his story? Danos sensed he could finish; he must do so with urgency. He wrote.....

So my wife said she would take her they were gone 8? (3?) months.

I had that time had met a young couple and the boy and I became good friends. The wife of this boy a wild mixed flooded little flirt included in the friendship.

Upon my wife's return, we had them at our home for a weekend. Hellen entertaining them the best she could with the two children to care for.

Irene (I will call her) showed nothing but contempt for my wife from the beginning. I seen it all but when my wife said she didn't think Irene acted right, I taking up for Irene under the excuse that her husband, James and I were friends.

She had mistreated our little girl while accepting my wifes hospitality yet I was for James and Irene.

I taken a room from them as my work required staying in the town in which they lived ? often.

They were my class rough and roudy. Irene often entertaining her husband and I with dirty jokes such as men tell each other.

I was much happier with Janes & Irene and their baby than I was with my own family.

Chapter 28

Danos found it nearly impossible to continue his writing. This particular episode of tunnel vision continued much beyond twenty minutes. His lips were numb. He could not feel the slight brush of his right index finger. His tongue was dry; he sensed it was swollen. Taking a brandy manifested the physical disability he was experiencing as the first sip uncontrollably trickled down the crease in the right side of his chin from the corner of his mouth, spilling onto his white shirt. His peripheral vision was clouded, muddled. Looking to the sides of his field of vision was impractical. As he focused within the center of his line of sight, Danos realized that his mind could not focus. He was unable to organize his thoughts or to record a coherent passage in the next paragraph on his tablet. He would stop and write no more, he considered. However, Danos sensed he was near the end of his story and hoped to complete the task. As he attempted to write, phrases on the paper appeared as jumbled bits of terms supported by little logic, rationale or organic thought. He continued to transcribe thoughts which came to mind no matter the result. He would take a break in a moment when he had finished. He attempted to go on…

Often going home with such.....that
I would kick the girls furnishings out
....my boy.....little.....he could walk and was.....
Always under foot.

* * *

Danos paused again in his descriptive dilemma. He was losing control of his messaging; losing control of his thoughts. He labored with no satisfaction and no clarity of concept or inspiration. As diligently as he could possibly labor, he became hopelessly lost in his endeavor. Lost physically with the optical disturbance; lost mentally with an incapacity for the smooth flow of thought and story.

In desperate reaction to the dilemma, Danos reached into the black leather satchel and pulled out the pocket Bible which John D. Knight had gifted him. He opened the first page and felt the indentation of the name "Knight" written into the cover page years ago. He leaned back in the cushioned desk chair, closing his eyes. He clutched the Bible to the left side of his chest and maintained his finger, resting on "Knight." This timely deviation from the past hours of writing provided solace and peace. His eyes remained closed as he pictured John D. Knight on the transport *MICHIGAN* handing the satchel and his Holy Bible to Jauan Fernandez, nearly thirty years ago. John D. Knight, smiling in Danos' mind's eye, was about to leave Jauan on the ship's deck disappearing into the uniformed confusion of the regular army on its way to Austin. Danos dozed for a long moment. His breathing became shallow, barely noticeable. His heart beat slowly and rhythmically. Danos could feel the numbness of his lips begin to diminish, returning to normal. His tongue became moist, his body went slack and lethargic as if he could fall asleep. Danos opened his eyes. The wavy, geometric tunnel which had been clouding the periphery of his vision, began to clear and dissipate. Clarity of thought was returning. He would relax for another few moments. These signs of anxiety and stress were disappearing with purposeful mental relaxation. The intensity of reimagination and putting pen to paper over the last hours took its toll. He would recover shortly, but he was exhausted and drained. He continued…

"...until death do you part..."

He re-read the last few phrases he had written. He could not decipher what he wanted to say. He would add no further comment. "What I have written I have written." He was quite sure he heard this saying in a sermon or reading at the First Baptist Church of San Antonio on one occasion with Helen years ago.

Danos was not a caring father for he had no training, either by instruction or observation. He often complained to Helen that the daughter's furnishings and belongings were scattered about the home, and the son was always under foot and in the way. Danos did not possess the virtue of patience and would leave the farmhouse to tinker in the work shed as an escape from his fatherly responsibilities.

Chapter 29

"...until death do you part..." (cont'd)

After his family's return from Arizona in October, Danos perceived his home, his "castle," had been taken over by a distant wife with unfamiliar children. His environment of solitude and quiet had been seized from him and replaced by inconsiderate noise and continuous commotion. The boy and girl conversed without restraint, as loud sounds and voices echoed throughout the dwelling. The children expressed no excitement about seeing their father after their return. There was little communication between Danos and his son and daughter. He spent countless hours away from the farmhouse each week working for RESC and supplement farming and ranching. His demeanor and habits were closely aligned with Don Pedro Fernandez. Here, in October, 1918, as a twenty-seven-year-old husband and father of two, Danos realized he was not equipped to carry out his roles in these two departments. The responsibilities he assumed working for a railway supplier, planting and harvesting crop each spring and fall, and working for neighbors each day, often well into the night, was difficult even for a strong, twenty-seven-year-old man. To add the responsibility of being a faithful husband and a role model as a father was quite overwhelming. The trip and lengthy stay in Arizona did not help matters. Whatever relationship Danos once had with the children, is not now close. The children are mere occupants in his dwelling. They do not look up to the man as a father, nor do they enjoy being in his presence.

The relationship he once had with the dark-haired, dark-eyed beauty had changed, too. On the few occasions he looked into Helen's eyes, Danos only saw terror projected from within. Helen remained fearful of her husband. The thoughts of Danos assaulting her, demanding she work clearing the field, carrying heavy bags of seed which caused her miscarriage, and his explosive rage were terrifying and would not be forgotten. She did forgive him as the Lord allowed her to do so, but the potential for domestic terror remained. The relationship between husband and wife, a wife Danos could take "just because he could marry," has been effectively destroyed. Danos and Helen infrequently talked to or about each other. They made no plans concerning their future. Child rearing was left to the mother. Helen had the ability to be all things to the children, a competent woman. Danos was relegated to the out of doors from sun up to sun down.

For the longest time, Helen passionately urged Danos to develop and expand his relationship with his son and daughter. He had little desire to do so. His work demanded prime attention and he could not afford to spend any appreciable time with the little ones. As Danos viewed the dynamics, the girl was always crying; she could never be satisfied by either parent. The boy unreasonably clung to Helen, moaning and whining in desperation that he be picked up off the floor. Danos refused to assist or even become involved. Helen often reproached Danos about not being a father to the children he brought into this world. Danos ignored her comments and went about his business. After repeated attempts to mold Danos into a father-type, Helen curtailed her effort, usually saying nothing about the children and crying in despair. Danos refused to assist.

When Helen and the children returned in October from the trip to Arizona, Danos had one month remaining in Texarkana for the completion of the inventory for Railway Equipment Supply, Company. He continued his stay during the work week with James and Irene Stinnett. They became more of a family to Danos than his own. Drinking beer, conversing and socializing as a threesome proved enjoyable and pleasurable for Danos. He even developed parenting skills with their son, helping the boy eat at the table and putting him to sleep on occasion. Why he could do this for a child not his own but refuse to care for his own children was ironic. Danos insisted that Helen assume all the parenting duties for their children, including putting the children to bed until they fell asleep.

After two months of living once again as a family unit, Danos announced to Helen he did not love her. It was as if he struck her with his clenched fist. Helen was crushed; Danos was unsympathetic. He wanted to hurt Helen in a unique way. He seemingly desired to start over without her, without the children. Danos offered her a quiet separation so that no one would know their personal family business. Helen did not buy it. She would not agree for the sake of the children, so she claimed. Danos ridiculed her, laughed at her, demeaned her. When Helen cried with hurtful emotion, Danos laughed even more cruelly and went to bed.

When March came the following year, Helen and the children announced they would leave for another stay in the Prescott, Arizona climate. Danos could not conceal his excitement that they would be gone for eight months.

* * *

He was close to finishing his memorandum recording all the events he wished to include. He continued…

I would have the girl crying.....the boy
clinging to his mother and Helen sad,
Sometimes she would reproach me
other times she would not say a word.

I did not realize Irene was having any
influence over me, I just blamed my wife for it all.
I would often rock Irene's baby to sleep but
I wanted my wife to put ours to bed and make them go to sleep.

I finally tried to get Hellen to agree to a separation
Without any scandal telling her I did not love I wanted to hurt her.
She would not agree to it on account of the children she said.
But I could see she loved me and when she cried I laughed at her and went to bed.
Things went on about the same until time for my wife to take the girl away for the winter.

Chapter 30

"...until death do you part..." (cont'd)

Helen's second eight-month health stay with the children in Prescott's favorable climate was nearing its end in October. Danos looked at his life in retrospect. He was repulsed by the denial of his family when they had returned the prior year. He contemplated he must make amends. As Helen notified Danos of the specifics of her return, he planned to meet them at the rail station on the scheduled arrival date and time. Danos was smartly attired in dress trousers, a long sleeve white shirt, his white Stetson dress hat and a pair of polished, brown boots. He was clean shaven and recently had his hair trimmed. Danos made the effort to make himself presentable to his family for their return.

As they climbed aboard the buggy, Danos kissed Helen on the cheek and hugged son and daughter independently. He brought each child a small stuffed animal as a coming home present as a token of affection.

He was fortunate his bachelor routine at the farmhouse cooking, cleaning and doing his own laundry would be spared by Helen's return. He was most grateful. Helen returned at a normal weight compared to when she left in the spring as a malnourished stick figure. A smile graced her face. Was she content to be back in Little Rock? Danos would find out soon enough. The children were well behaved during the buggy ride back to Creasy Springs

Road. Helen spoke about their time in Prescott in generalities. She appeared to be refreshed and genuinely happy returning from their eight-month hiatus.

As Helen, Danos and the children resumed a normal family life, Danos occupied himself during this month of October harvesting crop, and consequently, adding to their bank savings. He advised Helen of the plans he had been making to continue working for RESC but determined it appropriate to purchase or lease more acreage for growing additional crop. This was the first instance during which they discussed expanding the farm as business partners. Helen was receptive to Danos' suggestion. Perhaps Danos had taken the time over the last eight months to reflect on his future as a husband, a father and considered the four of them a family unit. Danos assisted caring for the children, decluttered the farmhouse, cleaned and cooked, demonstrating his ability to be a model mate.

By the end of three weeks, unfortunately, Danos was unable to maintain his civil mannerism and discourse with Helen. He tried but failed. His attitude and behavior had been contrived since Helen's return. Danos slipped back to his coarse, crude upbringing; he took charge of the house and demanded that Helen contribute by completing her assigned tasks promptly with no back talk. The children were to remain silent when Danos was at home. Loud and boisterous behavior would earn swift castigation. Danos barked orders and found fault with Helen and the children for insignificant infractions. The boy and girl perceived the radical change in their father; they did not wish to be in his presence. The longer he stayed away from the farmhouse, the more peace the children would enjoy. Helen determined she could not live in this negative environment any longer. Danos could not break the habits and attitude he acquired over the past nineteen years, training from the Roberts bunch and experiences as an orphan boy whose parents were taken from him by execution during war times. The tragedy in the short life of Jauan Fernandez, Jim Roberts, and now, as Andrew Danos Knight, was obvious. Helen knew much of Danos' life story, at least as much as he would allow her to know. If she chose to stay, this would be Helen's life with Danos. Such was unacceptable. She had made that decision with the help of her mother, before she returned to Little Rock. She would make her decision known to Danos the following day.

* * *

Early in the morning, while the children slept, Helen awakened from a restful night and made her way to the kitchen. She fired up the wood burner and prepared a hearty breakfast for Danos. Eggs, corn grits, bacon, biscuits and coffee. Danos would be off to the neighbor's ranch to replace a shoe on the neighbor's mare before he left for his job at the Railway Equipment Supply, Company. Danos would be gone working the remainder of the day. When he finished his breakfast, Helen told him she loved him. She hugged him and kissed him on the lips as he headed out the door. When he left the farmhouse, Helen set into action. She packed the hand sewn dresses she had made over the last years, along with her personal items in two cases. Helen had made a mental note of steps she must complete to carry out her plan. Once packed, she woke the children and prepared them for travel. She hitched the single mare to the small wagon. As she lifted each child into the buggy, she also loaded the four suitcases. Helen insisted the children remain in the buggy as she went into the house one last time. The sole purpose for her reentry was to leave a note for her husband on the dining table. The face of the envelope was simply marked, "Danos." The envelope containing her last words to him was conspicuously placed at the center of the solid blue cloth covering the table. He would see the note immediately when he enters his "castle" tonight. Helen extinguished the small oil lantern on the kitchen table. She exited the Creasy Springs Road farmhouse, climbed aboard the buggy and drove to the Little Rock rail station. She would never return.

* * *

The sun was hanging in the western sky illuminating the interior of the farmhouse when Danos returned home late that evening. His morning began with a rambunctious horse that did not care for a new shoe, but Danos accomplished the task with his neighbor's assistance. The office day at RESC was unusually stressful as Malcolm Chancellor was in Little Rock discussing the details of the inventory Danos had completed and submitted. The company was doing well financially but could have been doing much better. As a result of Danos' inventory, together with three subsequent quarterly audits and other damning evidence, Danos' co-worker, James Stinnett, his new friend in the Texarkana office, had been discovered pilfering and selling RESC inventory out the back door to competitors, or to anyone who came with cash in hand. The ongoing theft over the last twenty-four or more months was a personal, ill-gotten gain for James and Irene Stinnett and a significant economic loss to RESC. Chancellor required Danos to accompany him to Texarkana the following day to confront James Stinnett with the details of the inventory, the audits and accountings completed by Danos. James will be made aware of the company's knowledge that his thievery had been discovered and that he had been caught stealing and selling company property. Danos was given the unpleasant task of terminating James Stinnett from his employment with RESC at the conclusion of their confrontation. James would be given five minutes to gather and remove his personal items from his desk and office under strict supervision. This would be the last topic on the agenda of tomorrow's meeting. Chancellor also required Danos to file a criminal complaint seeking prosecution and restitution against James and Irene

Stinnett for theft, larceny and dealing in stolen property with the sheriff in Texarkana before he returned to Little Rock. Today was long, complicated, stressful. Tomorrow would be no better. James and Irene, the couple with whom Danos had lived for nearly six months, his supposed friends, would be unprepared for the events to unfold the following day. Despite his exhaustion from a grueling, eventful day, Danos speculated he would find no rest tonight.

Stressed and totally fatigued, thinking about James and Irene and their boy, Danos entered the farmhouse. No lamps burning. No stove burning. No dinner cooked. No clothes washed. The diminishing rays of the setting sun provided sufficient light in the kitchen area to expose the dining table. The blue cloth was clean and unwrinkled, neatly covering their round wooden table. The envelope centered on the table struck Danos with unease. He noted the envelope simply addressed him by name. This uneasy feeling was compounded by finding the Creasy Springs Road home abandoned. It was quite odd that Helen and the children would not be home at this hour of the evening. Danos sat on one of the three remaining kitchen chairs. The fourth chair, which had been destroyed in his fit of rage about five or six years earlier, had not been replaced. The trauma of those events would not leave his mind. However, Danos did not blame himself for his violent reactions. In fact, he justified his conduct by demanding his wife equitably contribute by working in the field. He offered no remorse. He offered no apology. There was no acceptable justification for Helen's refusal to work the field. Danos was right, Helen was wrong. She deserved everything she received that unforgettable day.

Rather than delay, Danos could not resist the urgency to open the white envelope addressed to him. His name was written in Helen's feminine longhand. Sufficient sunlight continued to stream through the kitchen window. Suspecting unfortunate news, he ripped open the envelope and discovered its contents. He pictured Helen sitting at this dining table, alone, dressed in her favorite yellow patterned dress, as her dark-haired locks fell off her shoulders and draped on the blue tablecloth. He had chosen Helen as his wife affirming so before the Bexar County Justice of the Peace a number of years ago. He pictured her with pen in hand and a piece of blank writing paper ready for her command. She wrote to her husband. With torn envelope hanging loosely in his scarred left hand, Danos read the brief letter from his bride…

My Dearest Husband,
The ending must be started as a beginning. We made our wedding vows "....for richer or poorer, in sickness and in health, until death do you part..." in San Antonio before my mother, my relatives and friends and other witnesses. They all advised me that you would be trouble. I did not listen to them because I loved you. I trusted in you. They all told me I would be welcomed home whenever my reality collapsed. You have given us two lovely children. I am thankful. You offered me a separation sometime back. I could not admit failure, I loved you, and refused. Your personality has not improved since we married; I convinced myself I could change you. I was mistaken. Your attempt to care for me and the children since we most recently returned from Arizona has failed. Your violent ways and temperament demonstrate you are a desperate man looking to blame others for your refusal to come to grips with your deficiencies. By the time you read this note, I will be well on my way to San Antonio with the children heading home to my mother. She loves me and the children. I still say I love you, but there is no hope for us as a family. I will not give you a legal separation. Rather, my lawyer will be filing for a Bill of Divorce for mental and physical cruelty this week. Do not contact me. I want nothing further from you other than to be left alone.
With love,
Helen

Danos read Helen's note three times. He was not offended. He was not shocked. He felt relieved. It was the same feeling he experienced as he woke in the Port of Matanzas with Angelina at his side, dead, having gone to be with the angels. His responsibility for Angelina was taken from him; he would fare better alone. Helen has done Danos the ultimate favor of terminating his responsibility as a husband and a father of two children. Danos was capable and had the power to marry a woman because he could, but he was defective. He knew this. Danos was biologically equipped to bring two children into this world, but he was a poor father, unable to meet his responsibility; he was imperfect. Despite the anticipated stress of tomorrow's dealing with James and Irene Stinnett, Danos slept well this night in Little Rock.

* * *

The visual disturbance which disabled Danos for the past hour and more had not completely resolved. He considered this overwhelming task of organizing, structuring and documenting the past events of his life as mandatory. Not only to verify these events, but necessary to purge himself of the grief accumulated over a lifetime. The picture of his life which he was painting was not as fluid as he had hoped; the trauma he experienced more than two decades ago was just as bitterly recollected as reliving each day in raw emotion. Recollecting and recording the events as accurately as he could was torment. Each scribble, each word he wrote was essential, yet at times, indecipherable and disjointed. His memory had not failed, but his ability to write factually was impeded by this disturbing mental confusion, a "mental fog" as he would later refer to it. He was distressed as he could not precisely describe the events from times past. He recalled that he had become an unsuitable husband to Helen and was never much of a father to his children.

The end of this wretched story is near, he began his conclusion as best he could. He jotted additional nonsensical words…..

I let her live without a word.....
...kind well after they had been...
...is the something...
...as I had to...my
own cooking and see to my laundry....

By the time they were ready to come home
I had made up my mind to tell Hellen I loved
her and try to be kinder to her and the kiddies
I went after them and found Helen
looking fine and almost happy.

More like the girl I married than she had
been for a long time it was easy to say I
loved her and would be kinder.

But soon I let things get into a rut again
after we got settled at home again.
I honestly tried to keep from being grouchy and
fault finding but the habits of a lifetime
were hard to break and my life with the family I grew up with seemed to keep it in my
head I had to growl and fuss to hold my own
with the world.

My wife soon lost weight and lost the happy
smile but seemed to be better contented and
as if it was as good as she could expect.

Chapter 31

Danos toweled the moisture off his brow. He had nearly broken out of his visual disturbance, but he began a fever with beads of sweat forming on his forehead. His effort recording the story was nearly complete. The mental fog was still projected in his writing, but it was not quite as prominent as thirty minutes ago. He organized thoughts of his conclusions, the moral of his story, the lesson to be learned and an ending. It was a success story, as far as Danos was concerned, although he lacked the literacy to suggest his audience provide him with results of their review. Danos was merely an unskilled storyteller. He was not a psychologist or psychiatrist, for he was not educated in the mental disciplines. Danos completed his writing, he believed, but for a line or two more. The lines remaining may be of great import to a family member yet to be born, to a close family member, to an unknown reader seeking advice, to an avid reader seeking to be entertained, perhaps to a class studying the consequences of his life as an orphan. What a shambles he thought!

Danos reflected on the twenty-one written pages he had thus poured onto a blank tablet. His task was cathartic. Demanding. But he felt only modestly improved. The events through which he lived were devastating. He held the hand-written note from Helen which had been stowed away in the black satchel for the last eleven years. He read it again and felt remorse only for his failure as husband and father. There remains no remorse for his conduct. He concluded…

.....changed and.....
....would write...I....our
....have.....
....would help some...
orphan boy to find a home where he
would have the love and guidance of some
a good father mother and father to go with him
through his life.

I would feel as if I had made up in
some other womans life a little of the
....suffering I had caused my family.
Dear readers if you can't give the orphan
a measure of the same love you give your own
children don't take them into your home.

You not only ruin the life of the orphan
but the life of the girl he marries and their
children as well and that is not kindness.

Danos penned his remarks on the last page. He was drained from this exercise. He accomplished his task and kept the promise made to his wife. Danos would reflect on this writing tomorrow, a Friday which he determined to be his off day from work, when he was rested and refreshed. After his final review, Danos will leave his written memoir on the library desk for his wife's review and comments.

Chapter 32

San Antonio March 22, 1929

Martha awakened early this Friday morning. Light rain cascaded down the pitched roof and saturated the grounds in a gentle drizzle revitalizing their lawn and flower garden. The dreary rain clouds settled in the area announcing the mood of this morning. His circulatory system ramped up while getting out of bed after an evening of restless sleep. Danos retired last night reflecting on the hours spent drafting his personal story. His exercise was completed for his wife and daughter, his extended family and friends and acquaintances. It was also meant for those in similar circumstance as seven-year-old Jauan Fernandez found himself twenty-some years earlier, or at any other juncture along an orphan's time-line.

Martha had breakfast waiting. His visual disturbance had resolved, yet Danos was physically and mentally fatigued. The smell of bacon frying in the skillet, freshly baked biscuits coming out of the oven and freshly brewed coffee piqued his senses. A hot breakfast was made to order after completing his mental ordeal yesterday. Danos shaved and dressed after breakfast and prepared to review his memoir. The clouds and drizzle interfered with his day planned for the garden. Danos occupied his seat on the wooden swing fixed under their covered front porch. His black coffee was hot and invigorating as he drank his second cup.

Putting his coffee cup down on the smoke stand next to the swing, Danos picked up the twenty-two pages of his written life. He spent one hour reading the finished product. He marveled at the construct of the document, at the quality of the writer's ability to express himself. Sharp. Concise. Powerful. Purposeful prose. Accurate recollection, he assessed. He was satisfied with his choice of verbiage and organization. Danos closed his eyes and reflected more deeply, more thoroughly. He was lost in thought of a task well done.

While he assessed what was included in his writing, Danos considered and examined events he purposely excluded. Reflecting with inherent bias, Danos concluded the items he had omitted were insignificant and minor. Exclusions from this story will haunt him in years to come. Danos was unaware and unsuspecting. Any reader of his story may include imaginary significance if desired. He so permitted. He never accepted, nor could he justify, the executions of his parents and deaths of other Fernandez family members. Danos was convinced he survived his young life as a Spanish orphan in Cuba. He lived independently on his own accompanied by rats and vermin. He endured his voyage as a stowaway disembarking in Texas. He coped with the disappearance of his mentor, Private John D. Knight. Danos struggled with the Roberts clan which made him only stronger. He did, somehow, accept the disappearance and deaths of several members of the Roberts family. He married because he could. He learned cattle ranching and crop farming. He divorced but was left free and able to run wild again. His life thus far was fulfilled and chronicled at age thirty-eight. He is stable, productive and permanently settled in San Antonio. But did he SURVIVE the orphanage?

* * *

As the skies began to clear on this early Friday afternoon, the dispatch messenger, riding his reliable three-year-old red Schwinn, delivered a telegram to Mr. A.D. Knight. The message was short, as the sun pierced through the gray. It read:

"TO A.D. Knight, formerly known as Jauan Fernandez. STOP Private John D. Knight, now Warrant Officer 1 Knight, will arrive at Port Galveston, Texas. STOP He requests the honor of your presence on the dock Tuesday, 10 April 1929 at 1300 hours. STOP Signed, Reverend Archibald Jennings. STOP, STOP."

Danos handed the telegram to Martha. She quickly scanned the message.

"You will be in Galveston on the tenth of April," she said as matter of fact.

"Yes. This request is not optional. It is mandatory. I'll make arrangements to travel by rail, arriving a day early."

Their home telephone occupied a convenient position affixed to the kitchen wall. The rigid black mouthpiece jutted out from the telephone's base. With a paucity of phone calls coming to the Knight residence, A.D. and Martha were unsure whether their telephone still functioned. Just then the telephone rang announcing an incoming call with a startling ring offensive to any ear. A party call for a different party, Danos surmised.

"Hello," Danos answered.

"Danos, this is Archie Jennings calling. I hope you have already received my telegram. Did you?"

"Yes, hello Reverend Jennings. I just received it."

"Call me Archie, my boy. I managed to discover your whereabouts and phone number. I have many contacts here in Texas."

"By way of explanation, I've known John D. Knight since before he enlisted in the 1st Texas Volunteer Infantry. I met John Knight when I conducted a revival in Corpus Christi some thirty-three years ago. Many souls were saved that weekend. I know John Knight well. I have been his Spiritual advisor since that weekend in Corpus Christi."

"I see," replied Danos. "I've been missing Private Knight since April, 1899. I want to meet him in Galveston on April 10." Danos mused and pondered if there is anyone that Archie Jennings doesn't know.

"That is fantastic. He's been promoted to Warrant Officer 1 and will be separating from the Army when he arrives at Port Galveston. His transport is scheduled to dock at 1:00 p.m. on April 10, 1929, less than three weeks from now. Can you meet him?"

"Yes. Yes. I will," Danos promised.

Their telephone call concluded with no more specifics than this brief one-minute call. Danos marked his calendar. After she read his twenty-two-page memoir, Martha kissed her husband and stated emphatically, "You have not finished your story. You have much more to say." Danos smiled wryly and proceeded to the San Antonio rail station to make travel arrangements.

* * *

Port Galveston April 10, 1929

Danos woke at 6:00 a.m. in the Port Hotel, having spent the prior night. He quickly tended to his personal routine, dressed in a light gray, three-piece suit and a white, long-sleeve shirt with black tie, looking formal for his meeting. His matching leather boots were cleaned and polished. He had black coffee, biscuit and gravy at the dining room conveniently located adjacent to the hotel lobby. The two-story hotel was less than four short blocks from Port Galveston. He returned to his room and made final preparations after breakfast. At 11:00 a.m., Danos walked to the lobby and sat on an overly-stuffed high back, olive-colored chair. He entertained himself scanning the headlines in the morning newspaper. The news was not entertaining. Mostly speculation and opinion of depressed economic times ahead. He folded the paper neatly and placed it on the coffee table, unread.

At 12:00 p.m., Danos left the hotel and began his short walk to the port. The sun was shining, no rain in sight. There were eight or ten ocean-going ships tied down, but they were not military vessels. They appeared to have been docked at least overnight; no visible activity on these ships tethered to the docks. The dockmaster advised there was only one military transport ship scheduled to arrive today, docking at berth #18. Due at 1:00 p.m. It was carrying approximately two hundred U.S. soldiers, equipment and supplies. No livestock. Danos was unconcerned about the ship's arrival. He was sure this was John Knight's transport.

Danos stood on the expansive boardwalk inspecting the berth marked #18. It was approximately one hour before the scheduled arrival time. Danos could see a dot at sea which appeared to be a ship. It continued its straight course toward Port Galveston. The dot in the distance soon became identifiable as a large transport. Within several more minutes, the ship was confirmed as a military vessel bearing American registration and displaying the Stars and Stripes. The ship neared its destination. The captain maneuvered the transport vessel into the port and into the docking area, then effortlessly docked at berth #18. Danos stood nearby on the wooden pier less than fifty feet from the ship's position. Other well-wishers and families joined Danos to welcome the arrival of returning troops. As all tie-downs were secured and the gangways placed into position, a line of indistinguishable uniformed soldiers stood at the forward rail on the top deck, reminiscent of the *MICHIGAN* thirty years ago. One soldier at the rail was most conspicuous as he raised a white sign with a name lettered in black, "JAUAN FERNANDEZ."

He read the sign held by John D. Knight. Danos countered by lifting his own large white placard, dimensioned three feet by four feet, high above his head. His sign's lettering boldly proclaimed "WO1 JOHN D. KNIGHT" on the top line with "Jauan Fernandez" directly below. The two made eye contact with one another. John D. Knight pointed his straightened arm and index finger directly at Danos. Smartly and respectfully, Warrant Officer John D. Knight stood at formal military attention. He crisply snapped his finest military salute to Andrew Danos Knight.

APPENDIX

Appendix – A

Book Club Proposed Discussion Questions

Chapter 1.
Why was A.D. Knight compelled to undertake the telling of his story?
Why was it important that A.D. Knight tell his story?

Chapter 2.
Was Jauan Fernandez aware of the mistreatment of the African slaves and the Chinese laborers?

Chapter 3.
With blood on his face, and shirt flogged, why did Jauan believe his parents died instantly?
What might have happened to Jauan's sister, Maria?

Chapter 4.
Why did Jauan take Angelina with him from Isabella? What caused Angelina's death? Did Jauan fail to protect Angelina?

Chapter 5.
Was Marco unconcerned about the death of his daughter, Angelina? Why? Why not?

Chapter 6.
Why did Jauan find the Catholic orphanage unsatisfactory? Why did he want to escape from food, shelter, clothing and safety back into homelessness?

Chapter 7.
How could Jauan find the drink of slime from the ditch nutritious?

Chapter 8.
What do you believe was the intended purpose of the U.S. Army in Matanzas?

Chapter 9.
Why did Company E accept the homeless orphan, Jauan Fernandez, and permit him to become a mascot?

Chapter 10.
Why did Jauan choose to go to the United States instead of remaining in Cuba, his homeland?

Chapter 11.
What did Jauan envision as his landing in Galveston and his new life in Texas? Why did John Knight decide to go regular Army with Company B, relocating to Austin?

Chapter 12.
What is the significance of the red cloth book mark placed at Psalm 100?

Chapter 13.
Why did the Roberts clan fail to advise Jauan of Ma Roberts' death and burial?

Chapter 14.
Why did Jauan object to the name "Jim Roberts?" Why did he adopt the new name Andrew Danos Knight?

Chapter 15.
What did Ann Meadows' parents find so offensive about Danos? Why did the Roberts brothers hold so much contempt for Danos?

Chapter 16.
Why was Danos so determined to get married? How did Danos select Jane Clark as his choice for a wife? Why was love in a marriage nonessential for Danos? Why was Danos compelled to converse with Reverend Archie Jennings in half-truths?

Chapter 17.
How could Danos be so convinced that Jane Clark would accept his proposal for marriage?

Chapter 18.
Did May Clark intend to marry Danos, or was she merely intent on escaping her sister, Jane?

Chapter 19.
Why did May fabricate storis about Danos and the kidnapping?

Chapter 20.
Why did Maurice T. Clark withdraw his incident report and petition to prosecute? Why was Judge Julius McCrary so interested in the well-being of Danos Knight?

Chapter 21.
Despite Ma Roberts' admonition to Danos that truth was required at all levels, why was Danos compelled to be untruthful in many circumstances? Was Danos' expectation realistic that he would get his herd and equipment back from the Roberts brothers?

Chapter 22.
What did Danos feel when he learned of Pa's death? What did Danos feel when he learned how Pa died?

Chapter 23.
Why did Claire Simmons insist on a civil marriage ceremony in the courthouse rather than a church wedding? Why did Helen and Danos go to Oklahoma City to see the Roberts boys right after getting married?

Chapter 24.

Was Helen unreasonable in her initial refusal to prepare the field for plowing and planting? Was Danos justified in his rage of domestic violence? Or was he being unreasonable?

Chapter 25.

Why did Danos the orphan succeed while others did not? What was Danos measure of success? Why did Danos have no empathy or concern for his sick wife?

Chapter 26.

Why did A.D. Knight refer to his children as daughter and son? Why did he not identify them by name? Why did Helen and Danos go to visit the Roberts brothers after their fourteen days at the West Baden Spa in Indiana?

Chapter 27.

Why was A.D. Knight experiencing visual disturbances near the end of his writing? Why did Danos fail to meet Helen and the children at the Little Rock train station after their first eight-month absence? What prompted Danos to invite James and Irene to spend the weekend at the Creasy Springs Road farmhouse just after Helen returned from Arizona?

Chapter 28.

What exacerbated the visual disturbance experienced by Danos just as he was about to finish his writing? How did clutching the Bible help resolve his tunnel vision?

Chapter 29.
How would you describe the relationship between Danos and Helen when she first returned from Arizona?

Chapter 30.
What caused Danos to abandon his civility merely three weeks after Helen's second trip to Arizona?

Chapter 31.
Why did Danos feel no remorse for his repugnant conduct?

Chapter 32.
Martha told Danos he was not finished with his writing; Danos admitted to some exclusions. What did Danos fail to include in his writing? After holding signs at Berth #18, how will John D. Knight and Andrew Danos Knight (f/k/a Jauan Fernandez) greet each other on the boardwalk at the Port of Galveston?